TRUST

Aphra Wilson

www.aphrawilson.com

Trust

Publisher: Independent Publishing Network.
Publication date: 1st August 2020
ISBN: 978-1-83853-299-4
Author: Aphra Wilson
Website: www.aphrawilson.com
Please direct all enquiries to the author.

ISBN 978-1-83853-299-4

Printed in the United Kingdom

CHAPTER ONE

Sunday

Anna

"Are you seriously going to leave me here?"

Anna watched him flick through two passports, keep one, and toss the other on the bed. Her eyes filled with tears. He looked at his feet. The silence was punctured by a car horn outside.

"Look, the taxi's here, I have to go."

He leaned on the bed, placed his hand on her head, then he ruffled her hair. His eyes met hers briefly before he stood and straightened up his shoulder straps. Then, with a tight-lipped smile, he's gone.

3

Half an hour earlier, this had been the beginning of her new life. In the fuzz between asleep and awake, during the tiny moment where she got her bearings, remembering who she was and what she was doing, a tingle of excitement had pulled her into the morning. She remembered the night before, their going away party, one last big night, to say goodbye and make the money they needed to leave.

As the next layer of consciousness washed over her, the prickle of excitement at what the day had in store took over the ripples of tightness, dull pain, and stomach knots. She opened her eyes, feeling like she'd only been asleep for minutes, her jaw was tight, skin tingling, dirty yellow in her half-sleep state.

They'd set the alarm, the bags lay packed and the taxi ordered for half an hour later, a seamless plan.

They should have made a couple of thousand the night before, enough to buy her ticket and get them a place to rent over there. His mum had bought his, and she'd get hers at the airport. She might have been lucky and got on the same flight, but she was ready to sit in airport limbo for as long

4

as it took.

They searched the depths of her bag, and every one of their pockets. Notes were unrolled, crumpled cash got smoothed into piles. It was soon apparent that they were short of the target. She emptied her jeans pockets again, but there was nothing more to contribute. The total came to less than five hundred pounds, a handful of coins, and a cigarette that had been lit at the wrong end.

"Where's the rest?" Confusion and anger contorted his thin-skinned face. "What did you do?"

"What did I do? It's my fault, is it?" Her voice gained an octave on each word. "People must owe you money for some, who did you give tick to?"

"You know I never do that. You probably gave them away to your stupid wee pals." The blue vein on his temple throbbed.

"Just shut up and check your pockets again, and look down your side of the bed." She wasn't getting into that argument again.

He stood still, watching her searching in the same pockets over and over.

"Look, that's it, there's nothing else here," he said with a new sympathy in his eyes that tamed the vein as he started stuffing the notes into his stonewashed wranglers. "It will be ok. I'll sort it with Archie for you."

"Sort it? Sort what?" She caught a tear on the side of her finger before it made her look silly.

"More pills, just a bit extra to sell to get your ticket, and, well, some money for the last lot."

"I thought they were yours, paid in full? Don't tell me…"

"Look, I'll call the pub when I get there, I'll leave a message when I get a number you can phone. It's not that bad, just a bit extra ok? Like I said, I'll sort it with him."

Any residual joy from their leaving party was squeezed out by a pain in her chest and an ache in her head. Her stomach lurched, and her legs weakened, she knelt on the floor to catch her breath.

"Look again, check your coat," her voice trembled as she reached underneath the bed.

He shook his head while she crawled, head to the floor, hands sweeping into the darkness as if searching for the broken pieces of her life. She kept searching as if everything would be ok if she just kept looking. And that's where he left her.

This was not how it was meant to be. Their new life was scheduled to start that day. It should have been easy - make the money, get the taxi, catch the plane, level up. But she didn't complete, she has to start again, left behind.

She kicked her rucksack off the bottom of the bed and pulled the covers over her goose-bumped body. She took her prescribed deep breaths, reassuring herself that everything would be ok. She wasn't buying it. She stared at the ceiling until the hurt faded a little, she concentrated on her sore dancing feet and her blistered, chewed tongue instead of her breaking heart. Hours passed, or it could have been minutes, but she couldn't lie there any longer.

She swept the change together into a small pile on the empty side of the bed, folded the fiver's together, and sat up. The pillow still held the hollow of Davies's missing head. She thumped her fist into it before turning it over. She ripped the melted end off the curved cigarette and reached over to the bedside table for his silver zippo lighter. An oversight, forgotten in his haste. It shone up well on the pastel striped cotton sheet; she ran the flat of her thumb over the engraving. 'Happy 30th, Love Mum'. He was probably looking for it right now. Patting his pockets down, in his well-rehearsed way, first the front, then the back, then the front again. In the background was her own reflection, she angled it to see her expression. The image was blurred, but the double lines between her brows were visible. Although only 19, her distorted reflection smudged on the chrome was of a woman twice her age.

She thought back to when they got together, late last Autumn. It was cold enough to put rings around the moon, and he had lent her his jumper outside the pub. The same jumper he'd left in that morning, marl grey, the round neck a little too wide. His predictability was endearing. She knew what he'd be wearing, what he'd order to eat, even what he would say at certain times of the day. Not this morning. She could never have imagined his parting gesture would be a hair ruffling.

With the lit cigarette between her lips, she ran her hand through her thick crop. Hair-spray and dried sweat left the shoulder-length ends crispy.

Piecing together faces from the blur of

the night before, her skin crawled with guilt. Her stomach flipped as she remembered snippets of conversations. How many people had she given free pills to? How many 'going away presents' had she gifted. How could those people have meant so much last night, and now she could barely remember their names?

What else couldn't she remember?

She'd ruined everything by getting carried away, and now she had to fix it, or stay there, hopeless.

She lay staring at the empty side of the bed, fantasizing about a giant iced glass of coke. She turned to face the window. She pulled the covers up, then pushed them off. She flipped from back to belly, and over again. There was no comfort to be had. The sour taste and dry crack cutting the middle of her arid tongue finally drove her out of the flat.

The choice of drinks in Roy's Spar was limited, but she still couldn't choose. She stared with glazed eyes from tin to tin, no inspiration came.

"Anna, hey, Anna!" She could hear him but didn't take her eyes out of the fridge.

She hoped his tall, skinny frame would disappear back around the corner it appeared from.

"Hoi, I thought you was meant to be away to Ibiza today. Why you in ere?"

"A few loose ends to tie up first." She needed to change the subject; she hadn't figured out a decent excuse to make yet.

"Anyway, how's your new flat?" She'd last seen him moving house, he'd been dragging a wheelie bin behind him, stuffed with clothes and a cube-shaped TV perched on top like a huge ice-cream cone. The unusual rumbling had drawn her attention, she'd looked over just in time to witness the trailing plug wrap around a wheel. It pulled the TV abruptly, causing the whole set-up to tumble down on to Bazz. He'd lay there, trapped under the bin sprinkled with glass until she ran over and helped him up.

"I love it, me own gaff. No one telling us what to do, and the best part is, no one can chuck me out." He beamed pride and rubbed his hands together. "The dole's giving me a loan, to get stuff, house stuff and that. I'm entitled to a grand because I was homeless! Can you believe that?" Anna noticed the pillow marks on his face.

"That will get you on your feet. You'll get everything you need for your place with that."

"Na, I've got a better idea, and av got a proposition for ya." He raised his eyebrows and flashed his three toothed smile.

"No way, whatever it is, I've got enough on my plate pal."

"Cheers! Na, honest, you've nothing to lose, just get me a hundred E's and I'll give you the money."

"What do you want that many for?" She laughed but felt her ticket out of there suddenly get a lot closer.

"To sell them obviously, to make some money, you should know!"

"Have you got the money now?"

"Not yet, should be in about two weeks the dole woman said, that's next Friday, I think."

"Oh. Right. I'll be away by then." Her ticket turned to dust again, for the second time that day.

"Come on, help a brother out, will ya?"

"I won't be able to. I'll be gone, sorry." He's visibly gutted, she wants to comfort him. "Hey, you know it wouldn't be worth it anyway? You wouldn't make any money."

Her question's answered with a blank stare.

"That's the sale price." Still nothing. "That's how much they cost anyway, a tenner each."

His face sagged with this calculation, and the realisation his plan was faulty.

"Could you not get us a deal? Sort me out with a good price?"

"Look, I'm not in a position to sort anyone out with anything right now. But maybe, if things work out, I could sell you a few a bit cheaper this weekend if you're at the club?"

"Na, am skint till the loan comes through next week." He held a tiny tin of spaghetti hoops in one hand and a packet of cheap pickled onion crisps in the other. He lifted them like dumbbells, complete with straining noises, puffed-out cheeks, and panting breath. Anna couldn't help laughing, her hapless friend with his funny Liverpudlian accent was a welcome distraction.

"Space Invaders. That's the breakfast of champions, how else do ya think I keep on-top of this physique?" He was tall, in a malnourished way. As if his upward growth had robbed the outward growth and the rest of his body had suffered for it. His elbow joints had a wider girth than his biceps.

"Why don't you spend the loan on the things you need, make your flat nice, get a new telly?"

"Things I need?" He shook his head. "You know what ah really need? I need a break."

"Don't we all? I'm supposed to be in Ibiza right now, but here I am, wandering the isles of this dump." She remembered why she was there; her rough tongue ran over her dry lips. She let out a sigh, she knew what was coming next.

"Am fookin sick of being a nobody, everyone always laughin at us." As predicted, all conversations with Bazz eventually went this way.

"Look at me. Scabby clothes, too skinny, nae job, nae lass. Folk thinkin they can push us aside and put us down all the time. All me fookin life."

"You've got it wrong pal, no one sees you like that."

"If people around here knew the real me, the real Barry, not Bazz the loser, they'd give us a bit of respect." His lips tightened, their purple tinge became white as he squeezed his jaws together. Her patience was too thin for this routine today. She shuffled the coins in her hand as he continued.

"One of these days they'll all see. I'll take the respect I deserve."

Dehydration was overwhelming. She nodded vaguely in response to his rant while picking the coldest tin from the fridge. She sighed and offered him an understanding smile; she'd heard this tale a million times before. It flowed out of him like lyrics to an angry song he knew by heart.

"They won't know whats fookin hit..." His flow halts, and his body tightens as a third person joins them in the aisle. Quick sharp movements, like a ferret, the smell of diesel, and a head with corners and edges. Only one family in this town produced skulls like that. The Dougherty's. Ronin elbowed Bazz in the ribs, knocking him into the shelves. The crisp packet burst under his stumbling foot, the tendons of his thin neck strained as he struggled to regain his balance. Anna tried to keep his eye contact, reassuring him without words.

Ronin stepped forward and crushed the crisps into powder. Bazz's fists tightened around the tin. For a moment, it seemed like he might fulfill his own prophecy and swing for him. Instead, he slammed the tin down, turned, and marched out with his arms straight by his sides.

Anna fixed her sights on the darting eyes beneath the gypsy's heavy brow. He was watching Bazz leave the shop, laughing as he shouted after him,

"That boy's a waste of space."

"He's done nothing to you, what's your problem?" Anna scowled.

Ronin tugged on his left earlobe, "What's my problem?" He took a step closer and laughed in her face, and she felt the heat of his breath on her nose.

"You're not funny," she shook her head and studied his features with disdain. She didn't know how many brothers there were, or how to tell them apart, but she did know that somehow, everyone always laughed along. Davie had always humored the Dougherty's, and right now, as this one's lips curled over his teeth into a snarl, she knew why.

"Oh, you don't think I'm funny? Well, let me tell you this; I'm not here to entertain you." More crisps crushed beneath his heavy feet as he stepped closer to Anna. She welcomed the dropping temperature, which dampened her rage as she leaned against the fridge. She should probably agree. Or at least stop talking. But she couldn't.

"He doesn't deserve getting pushed around; he's done nothing to you." She said.

He pointed a ringed finger at his chest. "I'll decide what he deserves. Not you." He grew taller as he bounced on his tiptoes. Anna knew it was breaking point; his animation warned loud and clear. She needed to drink. Her head was getting lighter. She adjusted her weight to steady herself and held one hand up between them.

"It's just after what happened to him...." She hesitates, "What he did - what he tried to do. At the bridge. You should give him a break."

He took a step back.

"Him?" Another step back. "Oh, wait a minute! I heard all about that! He's the idiot that couldn't even jump off a bridge properly?" He roared with fake, embarrassing laughter. He threw his head back so she could see up his nose as he snorted. Under his chin, a silver scar ran through the stubble to the base of his ear.

16

"I knew he was a fool, but that takes the prize!"

Anna wished she hadn't mentioned it, she'd thrown Bazz under the bus, but it had saved her in that moment. She imagined pushing his head into the freezer, watching his skin freeze, frost growing on his eyelashes, slamming the sliding lid into his skull, again and again. But, now he was walking away, as he was served he continued his theatrical display of hilarity. She really could not wait to get out of that town.

Ronin

Ronin turned the keys of the faded blue transit van. It struggled and coughed, but came to nothing. He turned them again, the engine wheezed, but didn't follow through. He pulled at his neckline and blew down into his chest. He bounced on the seat and pulled his earlobe. No way was he walking back to the site and asking for help from any of his family.

He took the keys out, sat back in the seat, and flipped the sun visor down. He still had one garden to do today, and he wasn't going to mess this up. He wiped his brow with the back of his hand and blew inside his shirt again, trying to cool his nerves. He'd wait and think. He checked all the lights and the radio were off; nothing was draining the battery.

He pulled open the bag on the passenger seat and bit into a dry, floury roll. He'd make it look like a piece break, rather than needing help from anyone. As he chewed the dusty, tasteless bread, he's startled by a knock on the window.

"Give us a lift home!" Tina smiles as Maria gets into the passenger side and slides over.

"It's not as simple as that. I've got things to do, jobs to finish." He wiped the flour from the corners of his mouth with his thumb and finger.

"Please, we need to get back before mam checks on us."

Ronin looked at each passenger in turn; they were wearing dresses and high heels on a Sunday afternoon.

"Oh no. No chance am I having anything

to do with this. You girls want to sneak out to parties that's your call, but I'm no accomplice. I'll get shot."

"Just drop us nearby then, anywhere, don't make us walk." Tina pleaded.

"OK, you girls want a lift? You will need to get out and push."

"Push? Are you kidding? Dressed like this?" Maria looked horrified.

"Aye. You two push, and I take you right to your caravan, and I keep your secret. Deal?"

The girls nod, leave their heels in the van and get into position outside.

"Ready? Push!" The transit rocks and he turns the key. It starts instantly, with no momentum required. The battery wasn't flat at all. If he'd tried again, it would have started, and he could have avoided getting in tow with this pair.

As Ronin drives, Maria lights up a cigarette to share with Tina.

"Open your window, that's stinking!" he winds his own down and leans toward the fresh air.

"Where have you two been anyway?"

"At the club then back to a party. You should come one time! You might actually have a laugh."

"Not my scene." He replied.

"You should! It's a right laugh when everyone's high, you'd love it."

"High? On drugs? Are you girls taking drugs?" He breaks and looks at them. Maria looks at Tina with wide eyes and shakes her head.

"Everyone is. It's OK, it's fine; honestly, everyone does it."

"Have you any idea how much bother you'd be in if any of the family finds out?" He asked.

"They're not going to, are they? Unless you want my uncles to know you made us push your van down the main road?" Tina ended the question with a wide smile.

He drove the rest of the way in silence, cursing himself for letting these two get him over a barrel. He knew they'd use this for a long time to come.

On arriving behind their van, they thanked him and promised to 'come round and see him later.' He knew this really meant 'come round and hide while we smoke.' He waved them off and prayed they hadn't been seen. He looked at the clock on the dashboard. He'd left it too late to start the last job; he'd go there first thing in the morning instead. He'd stay low the rest of the day so no one would give him a hard time. He ate another dry roll as he drove around the streets. Bland and boring, like his life. Maybe it was time for a change. He threw the last chunk out of the window and rubbed his hand on his thigh. He'd never been high on the family pecking order. His place was firmly in the bottom few. He tilted the mirror to see that he'd been driving around with a dusty white beard of flour. He sighed at the realisation his 17-year-old cousins were now above him. It was definitely time to make a change.

Jackson

PC Jackson wasn't officially promoted to DI till the next day, but she didn't want to waste the morning setting up her desk. She kept the lights off and quietly closed the door behind her. This was the third biggest office in the building, and Monday at 9 am it was hers. She walked around the desk and tilted the horizontal blind to get the best view of the street. She pulled out the quality spinning chair; it was a serious upgrade from the plastic ones downstairs. The room smelled of polish, and she could feel the residue on the luxury leather. She sat down, maneuvering her bum cheeks into the most comfortable position. She had to do it; she gave it a spin. Round once, then again. Then faster, she used her hand to push off the mahogany desk and propel her.

With a click and a bang, the lights were on, and her predecessor, Andrew Walker, slumped against the door frame. She used her feet to stop her spin and held the table edge with both hands as her insides continued to swirl.

"Would you jump in my grave as quick?" his words slurred as he slammed the door and stepped towards her.

"I am perfectly entitled to be here, but I don't think you should be here in that state." She could smell stale beer and garlic emanating from his unshaven face.

"This was my office for two years, I'm taking what's mine."

Jackson looked around the room and held out a hand.

"Be my guest, help yourself." She watched him sway, losing control of his expression. He was drunker than she first thought.

"You've no idea what you're taking on, do you?" he leaned on the desk with one hand, putting the stapler in his pocket with the other.

His pinstriped shirt had an orange stain. The neck loop of a navy tie was loose, but the knot was too tight to release. Evidence of a struggle. An altercation with himself she deduced, inebriation restricting his ability to undress successfully. The corners of her mouth threatened to curl upward at the sorry state of this man she had once applauded. She didn't want to rile him, so she focused on retaining her steely expression.

"This job. My job. It's a poison chalice." He added the bottle of tipex to his pocket. "And you know what? I'm glad to hand it all over. It's all yours now."

Jackson kept her solid expression, no hint of weakness.

"And, I'll tell you this, you will not do right for doing wrong." He stuffed a handful of pens into his blazer pocket, most of them fell on the floor. "I could have had that David King doing three years for possession and supplying, I could have had Archie inside long ago, and I could have cleared away that repugnant gypsy camp by the river."

His rant was producing white foam at the corners of his mouth, his tirade of bitter words like a nasty waterfall over her new desk. A tiny spit bubble hit the surface beside her hand. Disgust broke her silence, her face cracked with lines of distaste.

"Well, maybe if you hadn't blown the budget on dawn raids every week, with nothing to show for it, your name might still be on the door!"

Walker straightened his stance in response.

"You think this is going to be easy, don't you? Wait and see. You can't please anyone. Your boys underneath you, they want to get out there and get the scum off the streets." He pointed to the floor. "But, you answer to them." He pointed to the ceiling. "And they won't let you take any risks. None. They want certainty." He shook his head. "But, there's no certainty in this job. We act on instinct. Hunches. Intuition. When that gets taken away, you cant do the job." He pointed down to Jackson in the leather chair. Another white spit bubble landed. Closer this time. She used her feet to slide away from him.

"There's a reason I've been promoted." She stood up, circled the desk, and Walker, with his pockets bulging with stationary. She opened the door, stood to the side, and directed him out with a wave of her arm. His droopy features were fluctuating between confusion and anger.

"You couldn't cut it, Walker. That's the bottom line. Now I'm in here to sort your mess out."

His expression now firmly on the rage end of the scale. A twinge of fear stopped her; he was close enough to see the yellowing of his bloodshot eyes. She stepped away and walked behind him. She pushed hard between his shoulder blades. As he stumbled across the threshold, she slammed the door behind him and slipped the bolt across. She held her breath, waiting for his reaction. With her ear to the door, she used the muffled sounds to ascertain his position. After some inaudible shouting, followed by a door slamming down the hall, her pulse slowed. She relished in the post confrontation glow. She was born for this job.

She kept the door locked and sat at the desk once more. Her hands formed a steeple, her lips rested on the extended fingers. She considered her position. Walker's most significant success had been a dopey hash dealer. Too stoned to find a better hiding place for his stash than in the microwave. She would do better than that.

His strategy of steaming in all truncheons blazing had achieved no tangible results. Now, there wasn't enough funding to execute the big operations it would take to clean up this town. Not without clear certainty that there would be bums in jail cells.

Her predecessor's legacy would not stifle her. Out there, kids were risking death every weekend. Cardboard gangsters were making money out of vulnerability. Violence, theft, and debauchery were growing from the streets, her streets, like weeds. She was the one to pull them out. One by one, by the root until her entire town was clean.

She pulled a tissue from the box and spat on it, polishing away the greasy handprints left behind on the mahogany. Sitting back to admire the shine, she went over what she knew. Her sources told her Mr. King would now be out of the picture; he had been the weak link to Archie and further up the chain. Someone new would fill the void, but who? That's all she needed to know, then she'd bring the whole thing down, with a gentle push.

Anna

Back inside, she wriggled out of her grimy party clothes and slid into the empty bed. Savouring the last of the fizzy juice, she lit a cigarette with the silver zippo. With each draw, she relaxed a little more. Resigning to being there a bit longer, accepting things had changed. Just another week, another seven days. It might be better this way; it would give Davie a chance to get a job and somewhere to stay. He had said he knew a few people out there already, so it would be simple for him.

She'd be there soon, bronzed and smiling, sipping cocktails on a balcony, with stars sparkling above. She'd heard about the clubs, people dancing on the beach, the music, the highs, the lifestyle. That was the life for her. It wouldn't matter where anyone was from, what language they spoke, how much money they had. They'd all be on the same wavelength. Her new friends were just waiting. She could almost feel the warmth. Tension released as she imagined dancing in front of a blazing orange sunset. She dropped the burning cigarette end in the coke tin by the bed and dozed off.

She awoke to a knock, the light had changed, it was early evening, and her belly rumbled. The morning replayed in her mind, she rubbed her forehead as she remembered her predicament. A second crack at the worst day of her life. Still here, still skint, still a week to go.

Another knock. She pulled on her clothes and tiptoed to the peephole in the front door. On the other side, a giant blue iris, with a bloodshot surround. She took a step back in fright, the hungry feeling in her gut turned to nausea. When she returned for another look, the eye had receded, and Archie was exposed. As she surveyed him through the tiny round window, he knocked again. He looked down the stairs behind him and knocked louder, the door shook. She took a deep breath and opened it.

"Now, now, now, Davie boy tells me you've made a bit of a mess." He bellowed as his size 10 Adidas Samba stamped over the threshold. He changed the hallway, like he changed every room she'd ever seen him in. His presence fizzed, weighing down the air like a dangerous experiment.

"Well, I don't know what happened…" she began.

"I'll tell you what happened. I'm waiting for Davie to drop off my cash this morning. Instead, I get a phone call from the airport. His last twenty pence, he says. No time to explain, he says. You've made a mistake, he says."

"Me? Well, I wouldn't exactly say…" Anna rubs her forehead, searching for what she would exactly say.

"All I know is, it's down to you." His other foot brings his huge body through the doorway. Anna steps back, shrinking away from the smell of cheap aftershave.

"So, I'll take Davie's word on this, and now you're gonna owe me twice as much."

She wanted to push him out and slam the door on this bullshit, but, getting out to Davie next week relied on managing a meek smile and half a nod. He acknowledged her

submission by stepping in further,
extending an aggressive finger. Aiming it at
her head, he points out each word:

"You. Better. Not. Fuck. Around." He
steps closer, wringing out her personal
space. She forces another weak nod.

"My name doesn't get mentioned. To
anyone. You got that?"

"Yep, sure." She wanted to laugh in his
grizzled face. Did he think he was discreet?
He walks around the town like he's wearing
a crown made of crime, and now he wants
anonymity?

"If Davie told you anything, you'll know
I'm not someone you want to cross."

She steps backward to escape his
overbearing, back and back again, till she
can't go any further. Her hand behind
pushed against the textured foam wallpaper.
She digs her nails into it.

"I don't deal with silly wee girls like you,
you know why?"

She shook her head.

"You can't be trusted, your heads not in
the game."

Her nail had caught an edge, and she
peeled a corner of the foam away from the
wall.

"It's girls like you that bring the heat from the polis."

The little corner of paper was becoming a flap as her fingers continued behind the scenes.

"Davie boy's got the right idea. He's got sense; he got away before he got busted. Ha," he laughed, it turned into a wheeze, "not that much sense though! Leaving a daft wee cow like you here to do his business."

She removed the damaged wallpaper and squeezed it into a ball behind her back.

"I'm doing this as a favour to Davie, not you. You are nothing to me, and I will not hesitate to deal with you the same way I deal with anyone else getting wide."

A little bit more, springy concertinas forming under her nails.

"So, for Davie's sake, I'm going to give you enough pills to sell to pay me back, and if you're careful, you'll make a wee profit."

She squeezed the handful of wallpaper.

"I'll be back here on Sunday, and I'll be taking what's due. Shake on it."

Her knuckles were white from squeezing. She released her fingers, and springy confetti fell to the ground. He shook his head, puffing through widened nostrils, looking at the littered floor.

"What the hell is wrong with you?"

CHAPTER TWO
Monday

Anna

Monday lunchtimes were for Anna and Claire to dissect the weekend, but she wouldn't expect to see her today. It was hot, one of those late May days that gave false promise of a spectacular summer ahead. Outside Miller and Smyth solicitors, a lilac bush draped a branch, heavy with fragrant flowers, from behind the wall where she waited.

At 12.05, two suited men walked out, one tall, one bald. They headed towards the town center, the bald one, two steps in front, their expensive shoes clip-clopping in unison like a pantomime horse. Clip-cop, clip-clop, then stop, the bald head of the horse snorts, and coughs into his crisp white handkerchief. The tail checks the soles of his shoes for shit, flicking his head over each shoulder in turn, raising his feet behind him. Anna recognises the 'Big Bosses', but in all the time spent waiting under that tree, beside that wall, neither had even acknowledged her. Seen her, yes, and seen who she was waiting for, but no nod, not even a grudged smile.

At 12.06, Claire stepped out of the glossy black door; her head was still down as she searched in her bag. With her small frame, the grand sandstone pillars of the building dwarfed her. She looked professional in a white shirt, black shoes, and trousers. Her size gave the privilege of buying work attire from the school uniform section of Woolworth's.

They'd been together when she bought that outfit. Anna, filling her pockets with lip balms and bath pearls and her belly with pick n mix, while Claire carefully weighed up the price, versus stitching quality of garments before making her choice.

Today her hair was in its traditional style; a tight bun with any stray wisps tamed by hair spray and an array of clasps. The contrast between the pair was unmissable. If there was ever an opposite of Claire's white shirt, it was Anna's chosen garment. A black t-shirt, bearing the faded logo of a band she's never heard of, with a burn mark at her navel, that she found in her room after a party. Her jeans were boot-cut, faded at the knees. In her mind wearing multiple denim was a legitimate fashion choice, as her shoes proved. Denim trainers. Two separate tones of indigo wash, stitched with golden-orange thread, for that authentic jeans look. At this point, 80% of the items in her wardrobe were, in fact, denim. Less wardrobe, more bag stuffing, but the contents was the same: shirts, shorts, skirts, dresses, and her ancient Levis jacket. The mini drawstring rucksack hanging from her shoulder was a patchwork creation of denim washes she hadn't known existed. Inside, of course, a denim wallet: empty.

Claire was occupied in the search for her purse, elbow deep in her huge bag, a simple black leather, with a brass clasp. When she became aware of Anna, her entire face smiled, her eyes sparkled, and her nose wrinkled with joy. She stretched both arms out and pulled her in. As Claire squeezed her, she whispered,

"I'm so glad you decided to stay."

Anna pulled out of the embrace, "It's not like that, it's complicated, I am still going, it's just..."

Clarie's eyes narrowed, her arms folded across her chest. Anna hated that look. She looked away to break the stare.

"It's ok, come on, I'll tell you at lunch."

In the old Italian chip shop on the High Street, they took their usual booth. They slid along the benches, taking a position opposite each other across the yellowing marble veneer of the 50's table. So many events of their lives had been figured out there, so many plans made, so many confessions shared. It was there three weeks before that she'd revealed her plans to leave with Davie.

Claire had never been very enthusiastic. She'd asked question upon question. Where would they live? Where would they get money? What if they were ill? Or needed a dentist? She hadn't been satisfied by 'It's all sorted, Davie's got it all under control.' She'd begged her to come too. Tried to tempt her with fantasies of beaches and bars, tan lines and coke lines, sun loungers, and easy jobs. Claire repeated the same thing each time she tried to persuade her - she couldn't do it, she'd worked too hard for everything she had. She just wouldn't do it.

Her objections had eventually turned into acceptance, as Anna promised postcards and holidays. Now she had to do it all again. Sitting in the same place, telling her best friend she was still leaving. Another plan, that's all, merely a setback.

"He left without you, that's the bottom line here, isn't it? And now you are paying off his debt. Are you mental?"

"Things got messed up somehow, I know it sounds bad, but it's going to be fine."

"Not messed up enough for him to stay? You got left behind, and he's off to party his life away." There's no sign of the happy crinkles on Clarie's nose now.

"It's not like that, he had to go, his ticket was bought already. Anyway, it was my fault, I think. Money got lost, or maybe the pills got lost." Anna shrugged her shoulders. "I can't remember the whole night."

"You were in a bit of a state. We all were!" Claire laughed, and the sombre mood dispelled with the force of someone letting go of a balloon. "It was a good night though, apart from us crying till 4 am, trying to say goodbye. I feel daft now you're sitting here in front of me", she giggled some more.

"I meant every word I said. Anyway, I'll say it all again this weekend."

"So, you're really doing it? Taking the responsibility and the risk of jail. That's how much you want to leave this place?"

"Yep, I'll die if I have to stay around here forever!"

"You're so dramatic. It's not that bad, and you could be happy here if you got your life together -"

"It's a stagnant pond, and I'm drowning in it." Anna interrupted,

"But seriously, how are you going to do this?"

"It's already done, Davie sorted it with that Archie guy."

"Oh god, Archie? I should have known it was him that Davie was involved with. Jesus Anna! Don't fuck about with him.

You've got to get him off your back and wash your hands of him."

"He's not that bad, and it's only a week."

"Are you kidding? He's an animal! What are you thinking? You know what he did to Scott, don't you?"

She had heard, everyone had. This was one of the town's biggest legends. Scott was 5.6", with blond hair, broad shoulders, unusually small feet, and a missing left earlobe. Last Hogmanay, Scott had tried to leave a party without paying some money he owed Archie. The version she'd heard ended with Scott curled in a ball at his feet, Archie standing over him, with blood bubbling between his lips and running down his chin. He'd spat the flesh from between his teeth into his palm, and declared to the sickened onlookers that he'd taken what was due. He'd spat a mouthful of blood on the floor and walked out of the party. Everyone knew what he'd done to Scott.

"It's just a wee deal, like a job. It's not like I'm going to start hanging about with the guy. Stop stressing!" Anna tried to shake off the image of Archie's serrated overlapping teeth.

"A job?" Claire snorted, "Maybe you should start looking for an actual job?"

"Aw don't start all that again," Anna sighed and slumped back in the booth.

"You can't live like this forever, relying on crap boyfriends and getting wasted at every opportunity. You need to grow up sometime!"

"Give me a break! Anyway, talking of crap boyfriends, are you meeting Scott later?" Grasping the opportunity to change the subject.

"Nope, he bumped me off last night and was nowhere to be seen at your leaving night. And, there's no way I'm shaving three days in a row, that's self-harm." Anna's lip curled at the thought of a razor rasping over angry stubble. They both laughed, another disaster diverted. "I'm not chasing him; if he wants to see me, he knows where I am."

"Ooh, you're so rigid!" Anna giggled.

"Nope, realistic. I don't wear rose-tinted glasses like you."

The waitress's hair dripped from under her hat as she arrived with the plates and slid them towards their owners. Pink gnawed fingers fumbled around in the front of her apron for cutlery.

"Any sauces?" she mumbled.

Anna looked into Clarie's eyes and broadened her smile as wide as she could. They both knew what it meant. The same as that look always did.

"Aye, four portions of red, please." Claire nodded as the waitress informed her that it was an extra forty pence. She was paying for the meal. Again.

Ideally, Anna would be a vegetarian. For now, she only eats meat if it appears unrelated to its animal counterpart. Sausages are shapes, not body parts. She'd never touch a pork chop, or spare ribs, and definitely not a chicken leg. But, burgers, fish fingers, and today's choice, a king rib, were acceptably unrecognizable. While passing the salt, Claire offered,

"Come round one night, we can rent a video, and I'll cook tea." This was one of Anna's favourite things to do. They never tried new films anymore, always went for the ones they knew. Die Hard, Heathers, or maybe Dirty Dancing if no one else had it already. It didn't matter what they put on, as they talked over it anyway.

41

"I'd love to, and we can decide what to wear on Saturday."

"I'm not coming out again this weekend, I'm staying in to do my ironing."

"Ironing? You're abandoning me for housework? Aw, come on!"

"I don't want to be feeling rough for babysitting for my little cousins on Sunday. It's the only way I'll get a shot of my aunties car."

"Please? Ironing? I can't do this myself."

"I'm sorry, I just don't want to be involved, and I don't want another long night of goodbyes."

"Aw, come on. You don't have to touch any of it, but I need you there."

"I live in the real world, not the party bubble you float around in. And, I can't afford it, I want to see some of my wages not throw them all down my neck."

"But I'll be gone soon, please?" Anna pleads, getting whiny.

"I don't know. Maybe. What about the big club night the week after, won't you stay for that?"

"I can't, this week's too long as it is!"

"Ok, maybe a wee while then." Her mouth turned upwards a little. "But, I'm only having a few drinks. Nothing else."

As their plates were cleared away, Anna inserted the glass coke bottle up her sleeve as they slid out from the booth.

It had rained heavily when they were inside. The sun was burning off the clouds, as the concrete dried, the air filled with the smell of sauteing dog shit that peppered the pavements. As they prepared to go their separate ways, Anna placed an arm around Clarie's shoulders,

"Can I borrow twenty pence for the phone?"

Claire sighed and emptied the contents of her purse into Anna's outstretched hands.

"I'll see you soon, try not to get into any bother!"

She watched Claire disappear down the high street towards her basement office. She leaned against a wall, eyes closed, letting the sun warm her face while pondering the rest of the day and waiting for her turn in the phone box. She had nothing to do, and she was grateful. She wasn't lost or bored, it was exactly how she wanted to be.

She fished a coin from her pocket, sensing her turn was close from the aggravated tone of the woman inside. She watched her slam the handset onto the holder, then kick the metal coin bin below. She pushed the door with her bum and marched out, crossing her arms over her huge breasts.

Anna slipped in before the door rebound. She sat on the little square shelf, pulling her knees up and balancing her feet on the glass wall opposite. A position she'd perfected over years of hanging around the streets. A vacant phone box was a lucky find on a chilly evening when you were in high school. To her left, a primitive monogram scratched into the paint. "A + C". She looked at her finger to see if there was still a trace of the scar. The key had slipped mid gouge, digging into her supporting hand. She still cringed at the layers of skin and flesh she'd seen all those years ago. Faintly, below her knuckle, near the web of her thumb, a permanent reminder. If they ever painted over the initials, it wouldn't be forgotten.

She knew the pub number by heart, she'd

phoned it a million times looking for Davie,
or Claire, or Christine.

"Hello, Nags Head bar, how can I help
you?" the sweet fake phone voice of
Gemma, the barmaid.

"Hiya, it's Anna, have there been any
messages for me?"

"Messages? For you? No. What are you
waiting for like?" her regular sharpness
returned.

"Aw, OK, doesn't matter, I'll pop in and
see you soon anyway." She hung the phone
up before Gemma's interrogation stated.
He'd be finding his feet today, he wouldn't
have time to phone yet. He'd have to settle
in first. She'd check again tomorrow.

As the strolled aimlessly along the High
Street, a hand shot up above the pedestrian's
heads; it was attached to Christine. She
bounced on the balls of her feet like she was
always in the midst of something crucially
important. Everything about her was tight,
too tight. The laces of her white tennis shoes
were pulled so hard the toes bulged, and the
leather cracked. Her eyebrows were drawn

on a little too high. As she bounded towards her, she pulled her already tight jeans up to an improbable height, revealing ankles in white sports socks. Her short grey hair was moulded with wet-look gel. Sharp strands of fringe pointed toward her eyes. The tracks of comb lines ran backward from her temples like a neatly ploughed field.

"What's happening my wee pal? I wasn't expecting to see you for a while. Don't tell me that prick Davie's away without you?"

"Just a slight change of plan, I'm still going, I've just got a couple of things to sort out first," Anna said, as blase as she could make it.

"Ocht hen, come up to mine for your tea. I've got proper teabags. You can tell me all about it."

Christine's house was warm and sterile. The mixture of bleach and clean washing in the air was comforting, almost like simply breathing in there could wash away the weekends tarnish from her soul. She had her own place to sit, she always perched on the footstool under the window with a view of the street, the rest of the room, and into the kitchen. The living room was full of the same stuff every middle-aged woman seemed to have. A framed glittery print of a wolf howling at the moon, a ceramic dolphin ornament on the mantelpiece, and a black glass clock with gold trim and swinging pendulum.

Christine handed the tea over; the cup was clean, the temperature perfect. As it hydrated her lips, she realised how thirsty she'd been. She sunk a little further back on the stool and relaxed her face over the rising steam.

Christine could never stay put for long, so her tea was drunk impossibly hot. The house was always being cleaned, no jobs were left undone, but none were ever finished. She sat on the arm of the chair as if willing the earth to spin faster.

"So, what do you think of the new decor?"

Anna couldn't put her finger on it. She smiled and nodded, scanning for changes. The walls were split halfway up by a vine patterned border. The top was cream with little green Fleur De Li adornments. The lower half papered with vertical green and cream stripes. Christine rubbed her hand along the lumpy paper, trying to smooth out an air bubble.

"The border! It's totally different."

"Oh yeah, that's nice. Much better than the old one." Anna had no idea what had been there before.

"The flowers on the last one, they just wer'nae me. These vines look much more classy, don't you think?"

"Yeah, definitely," Anna replied to the empty room. Christine was buzzing around the house, as she always did. Sweeping the floor, wiping the cooker top, folding washing and checking all the doors and windows were locked. One after another, again and again.

Her cup was cold by the time Christine returned and asked,

"So, why the change of plan?"

Anna relayed her predicament, maintaining the 'no big deal, just an extra week' attitude. Christine looked sad, as if she was reading from a completely different page. One about it being a very big deal indeed.

"Archie? Do you know what your getting involved in?"

"Aye, it's not a big deal. He's not that bad." The wallpaper had an unbearably tempting curled edge where she sat.

"Aye Hen. He is. He's dangerous. Can you not get a loan off someone? Someone that won't bite the face aff you if you can't pay on time?"

"I don't need a loan, it's all under control. It will be all over by Sunday anyway."

"I cannae believe you've got yersel involved with that animal."

Anna looked out under the lace curtain towards nothing in particular. Christine watched, waiting, creating a silent cavern between them. As always, Anna began to throw words into the void.

"Davie had to go. It's actually my fault. We had no other option." Anna continued, still looking out the window. "It's fine." She uncrossed her legs. "It's definitely the best way to do it." She crossed them the other way. "Realistically this is a bonus." She flipped the edge of paper under the windowsill with her thumb. "In fact, it couldn't have worked out better actually." She tugs the corner away from the wall a little. Christine finally gives her a break,

"It's your life hen. You do what you think's best."

Anna sensed sarcasm and mild manipulation, and in a strangely welcome way, it reminded her of her mum.

"Do you think things will be different out there?" Christine asked.

"Yeah, obviously, it will be much better." Anna makes eye contact and smiles.

"I mean you, your life. Will you be happy?"

"Of course, it will be amazing, who wouldn't be happy partying in the sun?"

"Hmm, but even the best of parties end sometime. Then what?"

Anna rolls her eyes and sighs, playing up to the mother/daughter dynamic.

"Give me a break. Has no one got any faith in me at all?"

"Look, I'm just worried. You seen the state of my niece Wendy? You don't want to end up like her, do you? I saw her up the street the other day, clothes pure hanging off her, snottery nose, the lot. That's what happens when you don't know when to stop."

Anna looked back out the window, pretending to examine something in the distance.

"Anna." Christine snipped, "Get your fingers aff my wallpaper."

Ronin

Ronin got up an hour early to do yesterday's missed job in the middle-class part of town. It was the kind of driveway so long that you couldn't see the house from the road. The kind he'd usually be looking for things to come back for after dark. He started work on the hedge that lined the drive; he enjoyed trimming and shaping the privet. He got these jobs as punishment, but he secretly preferred it to mono-blocking with his brothers or roofing with his cousins. He didn't have to be on his guard for a slap from behind, and he could take his time and concentrate.

The dew was drying, and his hands were sticky, but he was making good progress. He was thirsty and regretting leaving too hastily this morning, as he hadn't brought any water with him. He wouldn't usually be so forward, but he was keen to see inside this massive house, so he knocked on the door to ask for a drink.

The woman who opened the door was crying. This was an unusual thing for him to see, it wasn't their way, he stared at her red eyes and dripping nose.

"Oh, don't mind the state of me. What are you after? Are you finished?"

"It's no bother. I just wanted a drink, never mind." He stepped back but couldn't take his eyes from hers. He wanted to know what was wrong. "Are you, are you OK? Can I help you somehow?"

She looked at him like his question broke something inside her. Her face twisted, tears flowed, and a bubble of snot expanded from her left nostril.

"It's all gone. I've nothing left."

He'd never been in a situation like this, he searched his repertoire of responses, none would fit. Not a handshake, not a joke and certainly not violence. Instead opened his arms, moved in slowly, and wrapped them around her trembling frame. She was tense, but she didn't stop him. As he held a little tighter, she relaxed. His nose buried in her curly blond hair. She smelt of vanilla, and her woolly cream jumper was soft to his touch. She was a big, beautiful treat to his senses. He pulled his sleeve over his fist and

used his cuff to dry her eyes and wipe her
nose. She laughed and pulled him inside the
house. She led him through the hallway,
past the scattered muddy riding boots and
horse tackle. She kicked a pair of jodhpurs
to the side to clear a path to the kitchen. This
was the wealthiest house he'd even been in,
and it was messier than the worst caravan he
knew.

They sat at a table that was larger than
his entire home. He listened as she told him
about her husband leaving, how she'd tried
to keep on top of the bills and mortgage
payments, but she couldn't maintain her old
lifestyle. He worked in oil, travelling the
world. The stopovers in Thailand had
become longer and more frequent, till
eventually, he just didn't come back. He
closed all his accounts and left her to pick up
the pieces. Six months had passed, and now
the house, the stables, and her Mercedes
were about to be repossessed.

"Let me help you," Ronin said,
surprising himself.

"You can't help me. I don't even know
you!"

"I've got some savings, I've got a bit of
money. You can have it. I'll bring it tonight."

"That's so sweet. I don't think anyone's ever been so sweet to me. But I couldn't take it. That's not right. We don't even know each other."

"I'm Ronin, and I know you're Mrs Evans. Please, I want you to have it. Let me help you."

"No, this is my problem; you only wanted a glass of water!"

"You can come and stay in my caravan, it's small, but it would be a roof over your head. You could bring the horse too."

She snorted as she laughed.

"Oh, my sweet man! You really are adorable, aren't you?"

He'd never been called such a thing, it felt good.

"I have to give the horse up, I've got to sell him, I can't afford to keep him."

"I can help you look after it. My family knows all about horses."

"This is a pedigree racehorse, not a funfair donkey. He costs an absolute fortune to keep!"

"Racehorse? Do you race him? Are you a jockey?"

"I don't! I'm too big, silly! I've got a jockey, he rides him, and we used to share the winnings. But I can't keep up with the stable fees and vets bills." She stood up and swept the hair from her face,

"Come on, we both better get cracking, eh? It's been ever so nice to meet you, but we've both got things to do". As she pushed her chair in, he took the cue to stand and finish his water, he drank slowly, stretching out the seconds. Then it happened, a light came on inside him;

"I've got a proposition for you. I'll buy the horse. How about that?" This was the boldest moment of his life, and he didn't feel scared. She smiled but shook her head.

"That's a lovely idea, and I'm touched that you'd even offer, but he's worth such an awful lot of money. I couldn't let him go for buttons."

"How much?" he pulled his earlobe as he prayed for a low price. This was it, bringing home his own horse, that would secure his place high in the pecking order. He'd be father's golden boy for a change. Yes, whatever it took. This was it, his ticket out of that tiny tin can.

"He's worth ten thousand, at least."

"But you need a quick sale, eh? With no paper trail. I can give you cash in your hand."

She looked out of the window across the lawn towards the half trimmed hedge that she had no way to pay for.

"Five thousand, and he's yours." She turned her head back to see his outstretched hand waiting to seal the deal. She took his hand and smiled.

He knew he had work to do. She wasn't convinced yet, but what did she have to lose? Maybe she'd never see him again. Maybe he'd be back to rob her house. But, just maybe he'd be back with enough money for her to abandon her sinking ship of a life.

Anna

Without a job, friends left to visit, or money to go to the pub, weekday afternoons could really drag. Anna sat alone in a bus shelter, it was only a few stops from home, but it was all uphill. The fun of seeing Claire and Christine was gone. She was spiraling down into a new phase of comedown, one which veiled everything in doubt. Should she walk for the benefit of her health? Was a bus journey worth waiting in here? Unable to make a decision, she took a bite from the bargain bin sausage roll she had bought for her supper. Staring into the cold, fat-hardened pastry, she ran her tongue over the strange texture coating her teeth. An awful mixture of hunger versus horror bubbled inside. Bringing it closer to her eye to examine the bobbly, grey meat was regrettable. While debating if she could go through with actually eating it, a car pulled into the bus stop—a police car. A disgusting dose of fear and guilt was added into the bubbling cauldron of her stomach.

As the window wound down and the driver became visible, tiny sweat beads formed on her upper lip.

"Surprised to see you here. Should you not be drinking cocktails and nursing sunburn somewhere by now?" DI Jackson tilted her head to the side in what was either sarcasm or genuine sympathy; she couldn't decide. She couldn't answer either. How did she know? Of course, she'd know, the entire North East division probably knew.

"David's away on that lovely long holiday, and you're sitting here yourself. Somethings not right is it?"

Anna used her tongue to scrape off the layer of grease on the roof of her mouth.

Sweat beads prickled her forehead as they pooled together. Anna studied DI Jackson's dark eyes. Somewhere deep inside was a tiny tinkle of a bell of recognition.

"He made a well-timed escape, your David. He was on borrowed time. Dealing drugs round here is a short-lived career. I'm cleaning up this town, you wait and see. I'm going to finish all these plastic gangsters, sooner, rather than later." A crackly fuzz sharpened into a voice, DI Jackson leaned into the radio at her shoulder and revved the engine. She raised her eyebrows, and the excitement was unmissable.

"Duty calls!" Tyres screech as she performed a dramatic u-turn from the bus stop. The smell turns Anna's stomach a notch too far. She wrapped up the cold sausage roll and stuffed it down the back of the bench.

Archie or Jackson? She couldn't decide who was the biggest threat for the next seven days: a flesh-eating drug dealer, or a power-hungry law enforcer.

Claire

Claire shut the heavy door of her

basement office, fully aware that it was, in
reality, just a large cupboard. She watched
the river of feet hurry past the window
above her desk as everyone returned to
work. It slowed to a trickle after 2 pm. She
always worked fast in the morning, getting
as much filing and envelope stuffing out of
the way before lunch. Then she could spend
some of the afternoon dreaming. She would
take a magazine from the waiting room
upstairs, slide it into her big bag, then
devour every page. Drooling over *House and
Country,* studying *Vogue,* and noting the
recipes in *Good Housekeeping.* Somehow,
sometime, this would be her life, she'd have
nice things. She took the little brass nail
scissors from the desk tidy and began to cut
around a picture. A set of red ceramic pans,
with wooden handles. She pulled a green
box file from under her desk and popped it
into the section marked 'kitchen.' She
continued through the pages, but she
couldn't concentrate. Not even an article on
stenciling grapes onto kitchen walls could
keep her attention.

They had become friends on the first day
of high school. Anna had immediately

noticed the girl in the bright orange t-shirt.
Everyone else looked tiny and lost in grey
and white, but she stood out like a rouge
poppy in a cornfield.

The t-shirt had been the only clean thing
she had to wear. Her Mum hadn't put aside
any money, and she'd grown breasts over
the summer and couldn't fit into her primary
shirts. Anna admired her blatant disregard
for the regulations, so she'd carried it, made
it her own. Inside, wishing she could blend
in, merge with the bright white shirts, all a
bit too big, ready to be grown into. Her
Mum was still in bed when she'd left for
school on that first day. She'd got up hoping
that maybe there would be the promised
uniform, laid out on the sofa, ready for this
big step in her life. But, as usual, the
curtains were drawn, and no one was there.
She couldn't remember seeing her Mum in
the morning for a long time. She'd got her
own breakfast for years, usually a slice of
bread and stork margarine. Early in the
week, it was fine enough. By Thursday, blue
dots were appearing, and by Sunday, she
could only pick the white bits left in
between.

They had been in the same home

economics class. No one took this seriously, but Claire looked forward to a Tuesday afternoon and always paid attention to the recipes and the tips. She delighted in adding new meals to her menu. Once she learned how to make a pizza base, her invention and creativity soared. The forgotten contents of her Mum's neglected kitchen could always top a pizza. As long as it was on tomato ketchup, she'd try it. If it was too horrible, like the jar of olives that were three years out of date, she just picked it off and ate the bread.

She was never sure what, where, or even if her Mum ate. So, she always left a bit on a plate for her. Although it was usually found in the bin the following morning, a few times, only the crust remained. She smiled on these mornings as she silently got herself ready for school. She'd never been rebellious at heart, all the bad behavior of the people she ended up hanging around with were at odds with how she felt inside. But, it was easier to say you didn't give a fuck about school, rather than tell the truth. Hiding poverty was a tricky act.

She'd preferred the punishment for forgetting her PE kit, to actually wearing the

ancient t-shirt and shorts. Dealing with the
threat of her toes popping through her
Dunlop trainers was far worse than writing
a million lines. It was always Anna next to
her on the bench, waiting for punishment for
whatever misdemeanor had entertained her
that day. They used to talk for hours about
'when they were grown-ups,' plan the
details, and get excited by the possibilities.
They were sure they were bound for
something more, far better than where they
came. But now she was losing hope; it didn't
matter what Claire did, Anna was still
sliding away. Maybe she couldn't escape her
fate. Maybe she was bound to end up like
her Dad.

She replaced the nail scissors, took out a
compact, and looked at her little circular
reflection. She wondered about her own
Dad, was she like him? The cow's lick of her
hairline, its awkward limitations, and the
impossibility of having a fringe, was that his
fault?
She remembered being small, stood on
the school stage, dressed in a bedsheet, with
a golden halo of tinsel. She'd scanned the
big adult faces for her Mum. The Shepard's

and Wise Men, Mary, Joseph, and the sheep kneeling in front found their waves in the crowd. Mums and Dads. On the slippery walk back to Auntie Jean's that night, she had asked the question.

"Do I have a Dad?"

"No. Not everyone's got a Dad. Some people don't." was her Mum's frosty reply. This was good enough for a few years, until she gained a vague sense of human reproduction mechanics. Of course he was out there somewhere. Lost in the black hole of her mother's past. Somewhere in the missing years between high school and Clarie's first memories.

But, somehow, she knew not to ask again. As the months and years passed, she witnessed the tightening in her mother's body at the mention of the word Dad. She knew it wasn't up for discussion. She would look at the cards on display in the corner shop, wondering if he liked golf, or football or sheds, like other Dads apparently did. All she knew was her Mum had come home from three years at university, with only empty pockets and a swollen belly.

Claire snapped the mirror shut,

dropped it into her bag, and opened the jobs page of the Press and Journal. Using her finger to trace her way through the waitressing and retail work, she thought about Anna. Further down the page, into the framed adverts for the more professional positions, she lingered, imagining what exactly the duties of an 'Account Executive' might involve.

She should have stayed on at school or gone to college, but she had to start making money. She had started at the very bottom, in this basement office. But, she'd get up to the ground floor soon. Reception was the next step. Then administration, and then, if she worked hard for a few years, she could make it to PA for one of the Big Bosses.

She wished Anna would do the same, start somewhere, doing something. Instead of sleeping all day and running after idiot men all night. She slipped the page out, picked out the possibilities with a neon yellow highlighter, and folded it into her notebook.

As she lifted the afternoon's pile of papers to be sorted, the door opened. Sandra from reception hissed,

"Make yourself useful, come up here and

Trust

make a cup of tea for Andrews's client."
Melanie always called Mr. Smyth, Andrew.
Never in front of him, only to the younger
ones.

"Mrs. Evans is in a right state. Posh
cow's crying cos she's going to lose her
horse."

Claire enjoyed these tasks, up on the
office floor for a change. Making tea was a
small job, but it brought a bit of comfort at a
difficult time. Upstairs, Claire walked
slowly with the overfull mug of tea. She
recognised Mrs. Evans as the source of all
the best magazines. She wasn't wearing her
usual flawless skin and perfect blow-dry
though. Her face was blotchy, eyes puffy,
and her hair matted at the back.

"Thank you, dear, sweet girl." She
reached for the tea with a trembling hand.
Claire blushed,

"You're welcome. Is there anything else
you need?"

"Let's see, can you get me, a knight in
shining armour?" she snorted a laugh, snot
gurgling at the back. Claire tried to look
sympathetic, but she felt awkward.

"Or, perhaps a hit-man for my awful
husband?"

"Um, I was thinking more like a biscuit, or maybe some tissues?"

"Of course, I am sorry, I shouldn't say such silly things. But you know what they say? If you don't laugh, you'll..." the sentence turned into a contorted wail.

Anna

She lay in bed at night, listening in to the darkness for Davie coming back.

His unique key jangle. The double shuffle of his feet wiping on the mat outside as he opened the door. That odd fake cough as he hung his jacket on the hook. The feeling was familiar. Staining her ears at the quietest time, holding her breath for a sign. Only now it was a different person she was waiting for. She felt small in her bed again. But this time she wouldn't be left alone.

Just a few more days till she was out of here, and back with him. This was just a pause, not an eject.

She wanted to dream, close her eyes, and be somewhere else. She concentrated on slowing her breath, slower, longer. The edges began softening, the lines between face and pillow, organs, and the universe.

Atoms spreading, merging, changing,
drifting, then falling, faster, too fast. Then
drop. Hard and sharp. Hitting the bed and
back within the boundary of her solidity and
goose-bumped skin. Still here. Listening
into the night.

CHAPTER THREE

Tuesday

Jackson

DI Jackson picked up the brass
nameplate from the front of her desk and
pulled out the yellow duster from her top
drawer. A slow outward breath to steam up
the surface, a hard buff with the cloth,
followed by small circles. She tilted it to
check for smears before adjusting it to
precisely the right angle. She had bought it
herself. The original one was smaller,
brushed steel with thin shallow lettering.
She tutted, seeing her own touch had left a
print. She resumed polishing while recalling
yesterday's meeting with David King's
girlfriend. She was worth keeping an eye on

but useless for any decent information.

As soon as the nameplate was correctly positioned, there was a knock, Desk Sergeant Jamie Baldwin's fingers curled around the door. Then his over-styled hair and pink rosy cheeks appeared—his baby-faced enthusiasm in odd juxtaposition to the police uniform he wore.

"Guess what?"

"This better be worth listening to Jamie. If it's another story from Hello magazine, I'm not interested."

"Nope, much better than that. Wendy Munroe's downstairs again. She got caught in Tesco with six sirloin steaks stuffed in the waistband of her Kappa poppers."

"That's not surprising, or interesting for that matter."

"Oh thanks, I've come up here to help you out, and that's all you can say to me?"

"I'm not interested in shoplifting low lives right now, Jamie. I've got serious issues to be dealing with. In two weeks time, one of the vilest gatherings of reprobates, druggies, and vultures you've ever heard of is happening in this town!"

"I know, but if you'll listen,"

"Listen to you? You listen to me. This

could be the big one. Hundreds of people
will be risking their lives in the guise of
having 'fun.' Our usual tactic around these
events is simply to show face and keep the
risk of violence outside to a minimum. But
I'm in charge now." Jackson rises and glides
to the window. She tilts the blinds a little.
From the doorway, Jamie shakes his head,

"I know, it's…"

"I just need something to go on." She
interrupts, "something solid to base an
operation on. I'll be on the news, the front
pages, I'll be heralded as the only one who
managed to clean up the streets. Parents will
thank me. I'll be a lifesaver."

"I know all this. That's what I'm telling
you. Get this Wendy on side! Let her off
with the meaty theft and see what she can
find out for you."

Jackson runs the yellow duster over the
bookshelves. They filled with legal tombs;
none have as much as a cracked spine.
Junkies, the worst. It made her angry
thinking about how much Police success
owed solely to the absence of loyalty in drug
addicts. They would drop their own
brother's name if it meant getting out of the
cells before the pains kicked in. Her brass

plaque balanced on the corruption she was there to stop.

"Jamie, I've got an idea. I'm coming down to the cells to talk to Wendy. I'll make her useful."

"Seriously? That's YOUR idea?" Jamie swipes the empty mug from her desk and slams the door behind him.

She tilted the blinds to get a different angle. She re-tucked her shirt and straightened her belt—time to make a new friend.

Anna

Anna woke up with the sheet twisted across the middle of the bed, and another useless day of wasting time lay ahead. The weekend felt like a million years away, and Ibiza even further. She pulled the covers up over her head, blocking out the morning light and creating some extra heat. She sank into her favourite fantasy... Aquamarine water lapping at her brown calves, sipping on a flamingo pink cocktail, beneath the dappled light of a giant straw hat. Taught oiled bodies bounce a beach ball across the pool in front of her. As they playfully splash each other, beads of water sparkle on her coconut smelling skin. She'd never actually been anywhere exotic. Her fantasy was built from Thomas Cook adverts and Wham videos.

It didn't last long. The feeling shrivelled away as soon as the mission to get there nudged its way to the front of her brain again. She made a list.

1- Get food

2- Stash the pills properly. Davie would never have allowed them to stay sitting on the bedside table.

3- Wash some clothes

4- Stop drinking

5- Find some way to pass the next few days quickly and quietly.

She kicked the covers to the floor, and added...

6- Tidy this shit hole flat up a bit.

She pulled on the outfit that lay on the floor like a comatose drunk. She splashed water on her face, gave her teeth a quick brush, relegated items 1-6 to tomorrow's tasks, and decided to go out for a walk instead.

Claire

Tuesday lunch was a sandwich in the office for Claire. Chips on a Monday was her main extravagance. She cut back to value bread the rest of the week to balance it out. Staring at the curled crusts and sweating cheese, she heard a knock, above her head. Anna was on all fours on the pavement, looking in. Claire caught her laugh, and skilfully converted it into a complicated cough. Holding two fingers up, she mouthed

"Two minutes!"

Anna jumped to her feet and dusted her knees off, cringing at a sticky patch on her left palm. She'd been warned ages ago not to come to the window, but since it was her last week, she thought it would be tolerable.

They came to rest at their old favourite place. They sat on the wide sandstone steps of the church in the town centre. Almost the entire street could be surveyed from there. Claire offered up the second half of her lunch, Anna accepted.

"I've got something for you." Claire sunk her arm into her bag.

"Ooh, a present?"

"Not really, but it could be a good thing." she handed over the unfolded jobs page, revealing the yellow highlights.

"What do I need that for? I'll be out of here next week." Anna took the paper and refolded it, as small as it would go.

"I hoped you'd change your mind. I thought you might stay." Clarie's sadness was obvious through her heavy lashes.

"Even if I did, no one's giving me a job around here. I've no experience."

"I didn't have any experience when I started there. I just kept applying for things until I got one." This wasn't the first time she'd said this to Anna.

"Davie's got me a job out there anyway, waitressing or something."

"Did you get a message from him?" Clarie's eyebrows tightened in the middle.

"Yeah, today. I'm mean probably today. Later on, maybe." Anna looked ahead, nonchalantly chewing on the crust.

"So, no then. You haven't."

Anna wasn't used to this friction between them. Claire was the one person she could be completely uncensored with. She didn't want to ruin their remaining time together. As she chewed the last hard corner, she made a list of things not to mention to Claire this week.

1- Anything about Davie, rattling that cage provoked questions she couldn't answer.

2- Archie, a definite trigger.

3- Yesterday's conversation with DI Jackson.

She watched the side of Clarie's face as she used a hankie to wipe her lips. Her complexion was grey, the muscles in her face seemed weak.

"So, enough about all that. Tell me, how's your work going?"

"It's OK actually, there's been talk of

some redecorating upstairs, so there will be plenty of files to arrange."

"That's what you look forward to?"

Claire shrugged. "Yeah. It will keep me busy."

"Don't you get bored?"

"Sometimes, I suppose, but that's life."

"Aren't you scared you'll end up bored forever?

"Look, We're poor girls. That's it for us. I'll be bored like my mum was, just like her mum before that. Then one day, I'll pass the tediousness on to whatever unfortunate daughter I might have in the dull future."

Anna laughed and shook her head.

"No, no, no, that's not it! What about the rest? The cities, the adventures, the people you could fall in love with that you can't even imagine from here?"

Claire used the hankie to shine the toes of her shoes.

"You need money for that kind of life. If you take off looking for that with a pocket full of change, you'll be freezing in a doorway by tomorrow night."

"Like that time I hid in the toilets on the train all the way to Dundee?"

Claire put her hand to her mouth to

hold in a laugh,

"Exactly, and you had to hitch home because you had no money. What did you think would happen once you got there?"

"Oh, I don't know, I'd be an artist or something. Sleep, smoke, and paint, maybe."

"Even artists need money, you know, for rent and food."

Bazz

Bazz loved his home. He walked from room to room, surveying his domain. There wasn't much in it yet. The hostel had helped him with essentials; a mattress, a microwave, some plates, cutlery, and a pan. He'd moved up here to stay with his Auntie Kay, for a fresh start, away from the city scheme, and his mother's partner. He soon learned that 'if you ever need somewhere to stay…' was something people said so they felt they were helping. No one really meant it. Turning up on doorsteps with only lip service pity as an invitation, you soon become an inconvenience. But, when all your clothes fit in a couple of Farmfood's bags, it's easy enough to move on.

Auntie Kay was the only one that knew

about his tattoo. He pulled his t-shirt down over his hips as he cringed. It had been a great idea. He'd pictured himself in a hip-hop video, a tight six-pack, a gold chain or two, some quality baggy jeans, and the pinnacle of look, a tattooed torso. 'Gangster' right across the centre of his abs. Irresistible, mysterious. He would look hard, with a history. In reality, the poorly etched bluish letters only read 'gang' and lay too heavily to the left. He just couldn't do it. Lying there on that stranger's kitchen table, he'd wanted to cry. The pain was unbearable. Like he was being carved in half with a burning knife. He couldn't see it through. So there is was, forever, what he expected to be the making of him, in reality, just another thing to laugh at.

After Kay's, then the trouble at Christmas, he got out of the hospital and ended up in the homeless hostel. Now he had a council flat, the first real bit of security he'd known. He'd enjoyed the hostel, the staff were like kind sisters, always helping him out. They'd put on classes in things like 'Interview Skills' and 'Business for Beginners' to help the residents get on their feet. He always went for the juice and biscuits, even if most of the information went over his head.

They had taught him budgeting, planning ahead, and ways to make sure you kept on top of paying things. He'd get a card meter for electric and gas, and write shopping lists for food, so he didn't waste any money.

Those were all great ideas, and once he was set up he would definitely get into budgeting. But first, he had to 'speculate to accumulate' - one of the things he learned from the business classes.

He had never in his life had more than £85 in his hand at one time. His key worker said he would get a thousand pounds from the government in grants, for leaving assisted accommodation. He hadn't believed it. Free money? But he'd seen others go before him and they got the payout, so now he knew it was coming.

He had no qualifications, and he could barely write. His criminal record was a list of the worst attributes in a human. He wasn't strong enough for manual labour, and he couldn't really follow instructions. People got angry with how easily he got confused.

There was only one option for him. He was going to get into selling drugs. Everyone took them. Everyone had the money for them. There was a demand, and he'd be the supply.

He'd be better suited to evening work anyway. He hated doing things in the morning; it always went wrong. He'd slept in for court three times, missed community service twice, and failed to sign on so many times they stopped his payments.

He figured out how to solve it though. These days if he had something to do in the morning, he just stayed up all night. It's easier to go to the job centre for 10.30 am if you haven't been to bed at all. No chance are you going to miss it.

The last time he slept in for community service, they put him in a new van. The first one had been full of young guys paying off football violence. They were always a laugh, and he had enjoyed being part of their squad.

The new van was bittersweet, some of the group were ok. He loved the company of the two shoplifter girls, Wendy and Mags. They always shared their crisps with him. He always wanted to ask Wendy out,

but he never found the courage. He asked
her questions when he could, he tried to find
out all about her, but it was hard with the
others there.

Then there was Jimmy, the old jakey
who battered his dog. This twisted old guy
looked like he had long greasy hair, but the
previous week Mags had ripped his hat off
to reveal the horror underneath. A
granddad hairline, draped in a skirt of hair,
circling a scalp covered in sores, flakes and
pustules. It had haunted them all, they
hated Jimmy, but he was still better
company than the remaining people in the
van. Two Dougherty brothers. Horrible,
hate-filled men that picked on Bazz
mercilessly.

He knelt on the foamy underlay; he had
no carpets yet. He pulled the stopper from
the valve of the bright blue blow-up
armchair. He'd found it deflated in
someone's garden, just lying next to their
bin. He'd been amazed the someone would
be careless enough to leave something like
that outside. Finders keepers. It took about
10 minutes to blow up, and then you had
around half an hour of comfort before you

had to blow it back up again. It was the main feature of his living room at the moment. Sitting on the low seat, his knees were not far off eye level. He thought about how he was going to get into the dealing business. He would try Anna again. He reckoned they were friends. She was leaving soon, so there would be a 'gap in the market' - another lesson that had stuck in his mind.

He rubbed his hands together, imagining the respect. The girls would be mad for him. The boys would invite him to parties, and he'd get to sit on a sofa instead of the floor. He'd smoke Regal king-size, order pizzas for everyone, phone taxis everywhere, and drink doubles at the bar.

His bum made contact with the floor. The chair deflated signalling it was time to get the spaghetti hoops on for tea.

Anna

Anna knocked three times. The door opened on the chain and Christine greeted her with,

"Twice in as many days, what do I owe this pleasure? Skint? Hungry?"

"Oh very funny, I thought it would be

nice to see you, that's all."

"I'm kidding, in you come." Anna relaxed as the clean warmth engulfed her tense senses. Inside, she took her usual seat, and gratefully accepted the cup of tea. She stared out of the window, past Christine's chipped garden to the lush little square next door. The central apple tree still held onto a couple of pink-tinged blossoms.

"Do apples grow on that tree?" she asked.

"Not yet, there's been flowers the last few years, but they've never come to anything. I remember when you and your mum planted it, you know. She had big plans for baking you apple pies and making cider one day."

"It's grown so much. I remember being able to touch the top branch when we lived there."

"You've grown so much! I could see the top of your head when you were my wee neighbour. You were pretty cute back then."

Christine disappeared, and Anna relaxed to the comforting sounds coming from the kitchen. The washing machine, the skoosh of bleach spray, and the odd squeak of cloth on a clean surface. She was still staring at the apple tree next door when Christine pulled the cushion from her side. She dangled it by one corner and slapped it hard. She threw the perfectly puffed square back down and moved onto the next one.

"Drink up. I've got to drop off a bit of hash to a mate."

Anna sighed and made sad eyes; she knew Christine could read her smallest expression.

"You're coming too, obviously." Christine pulled her jeans higher and took a quick look in the mirror. Anna brightened and gulped the last of her tea.

"Cool, who is it? Not that disgusting Jimmy again?"

"Nope, my mate Shaun, I don't think you've met him." Christine pulled her white laces tighter and tied a double knot. Once her purple fleece was zipped up to her chin, she put her hands on her hips.

"Chop, chop, I've got business to attend to, let's go!" She ushered Anna out the door before locking it and checking the handle three times.

Once they got to the iron gate at the bottom of the steps, she turned and bounced back up. She re-checked the door, and then they were on their way.

Christine had got by selling little brown chunks of hash for years. Occasionally some weed, but she reckoned it made her paranoid. More paranoid. She stuck with sprinkling crumbs and burning fingers, medicating herself against the past. And the future.

Anna had to double skip between steps to keep up with Christine's purposeful stride. As they passed Roy's Spar shop, the rain began. Spitting at first, Anna took the warning and pulled her jacket over her head. She watched Christine's unflinching features, even as the drops collected on the tips of her fringe and ran down the sides of her nose, her stride was unbroken. Her sights fixed straight ahead.

They climbed the stairs in the spiralling close. Anna wondered through aching lungs how she could dance for an entire night, but in daylight the slightest exertion nearly killed her. Christine bounded up two at a time and stood pulling her socks up on the landing as she waited for Anna to catch up.

They didn't need to knock; the black door was ajar. Christine gave Anna a nudge and whispered,

"He takes a bit of getting used to, but he's alright. Just don't mention your Davie, I don't want any aggro." She pushed it open and announced her arrival. A greasy slicked-back hairdo emerged from the kitchen.

"Ladies, ladies, who do we have here? The lovely Christine, and who's this? Your sister, maybe?" Christine elbowed her forward to introduce herself.

"Hi, I'm Anna, em, how's it going?" Meeting new people while carrying full inhibitions was hard.

"Come in, come in, have a seat in the kitchen, I'll make coffee." Unmistakably Glaswegian. She was rubbish at guessing ages, but she reckoned late 40s. A definite candidate for heart disease, his blood pressure was pushing his pink rimmed eyes from their sockets.

As his back turned, Anna curled her lip to show Christine her distaste for this man lumbering around like a giant trained pig. Christine returned the look that told her to behave, with only her eyelids.

The uneasy feeling in his presence was soon forgotten when he served fresh coffee and cream, presented on a wooden-handled, oval tray, and accompanied by brown sugar lumps in an orange bowl. Anna used the mini tongs to drop in two. Then four, then a quiet fifth while they were busy exchanging money for Christine's delivery. She observed their small talk, the weather, his gout, something to do with the Labour party, and then she gave up listening to their discussions. Watching them roll and smoke a joint, she drifted off into her thoughts.

On the walls were three black painted pieces of wood. Each had an abstract shape created with little brass pins, each pin linked to another with a copper thread. They reminded her of spirograph drawings she'd spent many hours on as a child. The wide ovals creating tight circles, the thin undulating line was so precise. Great fun, until she got too confident and the biro popped out of the hole, scratching a deep gouge across her artwork. She hated spirograph.

On the counter next to the kettle sat an overflowing fruit bowl. The lustrous apples, firm, dusty grapes, and deep purple plums looked straight out of an oil painting. A string of garlic hung next to the brown enamel cooker, red and green peppers sat on an orange chopping board, a trailing ivy plant hung from a pot on the end of the curtain rail. On the wall next to the fridge hung a shiny pink lobster. As she stared at it, marvelling at the outdated style, she looked back over the kitchen's other items. They were all fake. The fruit, the plants, everything. All the mould lines became visible. The thin see-through leaf fabric, the unrealistic colours she hadn't noticed the first time, all shouting for her attention. She felt a laugh simmering, and her cheeks tingle, so she looked away. She studied her host instead. His accent aroused her suspicion; anything different always did. From her experience, anyone who came from' doon the road' had a story. They were usually running, but sometimes chasing. She watched his waxy complexion as his jowls wobbled. His skin reminded her of the dodgy paint job on the plastic lobster. Again the laughter threatened to leak out. She concentrated on the damp stains under his armpits as they grew larger and darker with his animation.

The tension grew between her eyebrows; then a warning throat-clearing came from Christine. She realised she was staring at

Shaun with a look of disgust.

"Sorry, away in a world of my own there." she offered.

"We were just saying that Archie is bad news, you don't want to be owing to him for long," Shaun said.

"Don't worry about me, it's…" Christine shot her a look that would be undetectable to anyone else. It screamed to Anna to say no more.

"Let's take this through to the living room," Shaun said. Anna looked to Christine for the nod, and he led the way. In the shadow of the hallway, Christine elbowed Anna and whispered, "Follow my lead, I've got it sorted". Anna screwed her face up in confusion but knew compliance was necessary.

The seventies theme carried on through the flat, with cord furniture on varnished floorboards. A record player next to an empty fireplace was flanked on either side by bookcases filled with vinyl. The floor was broken up with two sheepskin rugs, one cream, and one orange. Anna sat on the edge of the cord sofa, next to a three-legged, once modern, side table topped with a heavy crystal ashtray.

Christine remained standing,

"I'm away to the shop for fags. You guys want anything?" Anna pleaded with her eyes to go too, but the message was lost as he handed her another coffee.

The front door shut, and they were alone. The sugary caffeine was fueling her curiosity, and she couldn't hide her interest in these new surroundings. The high tenement ceilings and tall windows created an airy feel. Around the floor, in front of the wide windowsill, sat an array of pot plants, mostly fake as far as she could tell, making a little make-believe jungle surrounding the main event. On the windowsill stood models of Big Ben, the Taj Mahal, and the Eiffel tower. Each two feet high.

"You like my work?" Shaun asked.

"You made these?" resting the cup on the table. Her curiosity was insatiable; she stooped to take in the detail as she drew nearer she asked,

"Matchsticks? I've never seen anything like it, they're incredible."

"I made them in jail. I did a stretch a few years back for eh, some misunderstanding."

"Really, interesting..." she trailed off while imagining punching the clock off Big

Ben.

"Takes patience, you know, collecting the matches, and they aren't easy to get either."

In her mind, she picked up the Eiffel Tower. Smashed it over his Brylcreem cows-lick, while his eyes bulged, fit to burst. A smile began to tickle the corner of her mouth, so she sucked it in and bit hard.

"The screws don't let you use superglue, it's all PVA, nothing you could get a high from, you know? It shows what type of guy I am, patient, creative, good with my hands. If you get me?" He glanced over his shoulder to catch her reaction to this as he flicked through the records.

"Yeah, impressive." But she wasn't looking at him. She was peering down towards the street, hoping Christine was on the way back. She sat on the sofa and prayed for it to be over soon.

"So, you like disco music?" He was kneeling, in pain, on the rug. He put the black vinyl in place and dropped the needle in precisely the right groove. With a light crackle, the first bars of 'Born to be Alive' began. He grimaced, and one knee buckled as he stood up.

"Yeah, I guess. I like most songs I could

dance to."

"Ah, yes, I love a dance, so I do." He began jerking from one foot to the other. She smiled, aiming to deliver a look of appreciation, rather than toe-curling cringe. She lifted the coffee and held it up to her face to hide her smirk. Just when she felt like she would explode with embarrassment, he did the unthinkable. He formed disco gun fingers. He pointed them at her heart, shot one, then the other. Then blew the imaginary smoke from his fingertips. He kept the beat with an awkward shoe shuffle as Anna's guts struggled to wrench the laughter down inside.

"You know what you need? You need a good man to look after you."

The emotion breaks out, holding it in had become painful; she laughed out loud. He finds encouragement in it.

"Why are you single, eh?" He kept dancing, his disco finger gun pointing straight at her, demanding an answer.

"Well, I'm not.."

"Wait, I know, you're waiting for the right guy to whisk you off your feet? A real man to provide what you need?"

He doesn't know about Davie, what has

Christine said?

"Eh, aye, something like that." She was excruciatingly uncomfortable. He was at least twice her age. There was no way.

"You need a man with some experience, show you a bit of life, you know?"

The humour in this situation was dissipating fast. Where the hell was Christine? He took a seat on the other end of the sofa, grunting as he sat.

"Christine tells me you're in a bit of bother? Owe a lot of money to Archie, don't you?"

"Well, it's complicated, but yeah, I suppose so." She leans on the arm of the sofa to create some extra space between them.

"He's bad news, he's no moral compass that man, believe me. Young girl like you shouldn't be dealing with the likes of him." He shook his head in a knowing manner.

"Well, you know what? I'm willing to help you out."

"It's cool, its all under control" she quickly cut him off.

"You're so naive," his nostrils flared, "The way you live now, the drugs, the parties, it doesn't suit you."

"Mate, you don't even know me."

"I know enough, and you're better than that."

"Is that supposed to be a compliment?" Anna felt her temperature rise. He was unreal.

"Yeah, I guess it is." He shuffled a little closer on the sofa. "I don't take any of that shite. I like to stay in control."

"I'm not sure why you're telling me this, I'm fine, really." She hoped her voice was stern enough to finish the subject.

"Why don't you have a little smoke of this?" He pointed towards the ashtray holding the half-smoked joint. "Might loosen you up a bit."

"I don't smoke weed. I don't like it. Anyway, why are you lecturing me about drugs then offering me that?"

"I'm not poisoning my self with chemicals. Neither should you."

"Thanks for the advice, but I'm really OK." Get me out of here.

"Look, I like you. So I'm going to help you. I'll give you the money to get that animal Archie off your back. Then you can get off the drugs."

"I don't need saving. I don't know what Christine's been saying about me."

"She's a good friend to you. She just wants to look out for you."

"I don't need anyone's help or handouts. OK?"

"Look, a couple of grand is nothing to me, and it's a lend. You'd pay me back, no rush." He moved another few inches closer, almost touching. The embarrassment, combined with coffee and his sleaziness is all too much. Her heartbeat inside becomes louder than his disco bass. Just as he moves the last few inches, she leaps to her feet. He's left hanging with his arm outstretched.

"Thanks for the coffee and that, it's been nice to meet you. Tell Christine I had to go, forgot I've got stuff to do." She slides sideways out of the door, he stays sitting, in the centre of the sofa, holding the empty space she left.

Ronin

"For god's sake, can you not wait to cook those? I don't want to smell like burgers!" Maria stuck her nose inside her jacket sleeve.

"This is my caravan, and I'm hungry. And anyway, you pair are stinking it out with your smoke." Ronin turned the gas ring off and opened the little oval window.

"Your Da is going to kill you two when he finds out about you're smoking."

"No one's going to tell him, so stop worrying."

"One of these days, they'll find out you've sneaked out to a party, then there will be big trouble."

"Stop being so serious! You sound like an old man! Listen, why don't you come out with us? There's loads of girls your age. Maybe you could meet someone."

"I'm not interested in any daft lassies. I've met a real woman."

Tina and Maria simultaneously laugh a lot louder than he thought appropriate.

"Are you sure its a real woman?" Maria teases, Ronin remains stony-faced.

"Someone with a bit of class. Something you pair know nothing about."

"Wait till I tell your brothers."

"Don't you dare. It's none of anyone's business. You keep your mouth shut."

"Or... what?" The girls exchange a look that he knows ends in bother.

"So, there's another secret we know about you. And you know ours. It's quite a good deal, really." Tina leans back on the bed. Maria leans back beside her. "How about a little sweetener?"

Ronin rolled his eyes, disappointed at getting himself into this position again.

"Yeah, a little something to make sure we are all on the same page." Tina put her hands behind her head.

"That's a good idea. A little cash upfront, so we know we can trust you." Maria replicated her hands behind the head position.

"Are you kidding? You want me to give you money?"

The girls look at each other, then at him, and they both nod.

"Twenty each should help. I wouldn't want to accidentally tell anyone about your fancy woman."

"Wait, thirty would be better, since what happened with the van," Tina added. He thought about his secret savings; this pair couldn't find out about that, they'd have him milked dry in no time.

"You'll be lucky. I'm the dosser round here. I don't have sixty quid to give anyone."

Maria tutted, "What have you got then?"

"I could give you a tenner each later on

once I get paid, but that's it."

Tina sat upright and smiled.

"That's our weekend sorted then, thank you very much."

"Your secrets safe with us." Maria put her finger to her lips.

"Wait, what will you do with it? I don't want implicated in any of your nonsense."

"Don't worry, none of the family will find out you bought us drugs."

"Wow now, hold on a second!" Ronin bounced on his toes, and the caravan swayed a little. "Don't you say that. I didn't buy you anything!" He pulled his earlobe as his grey face turned pink. Maria laughed. Tina got up and put a hand on his shoulder.

"I'm kidding, don't worry. We will all keep each other's secrets, OK?"

Ronin rubbed his temples and puffed his cheeks out. He shook his head at how easily these girls played him. Tina patted his back. "Come on, sit down, stop stressing."

He squeezed between the girls on the edge of the bed, his elbows on his knees, and his head in his hands. He listened to them talk about boys, and other girls, and what other girls said about boys. He drifted in and out, thinking about Hillary's fluffy hair, and vanilla smell. Then he caught some words that interested him. He tuned into Tina's monologue about "he said, she said, he owed him a tenner for an eccie." He lifted his head and turned to her,

"A tenner? Ten pounds. For one?" he interrupted.

"Yeah, what about it?"

"Wait, so do a lot of people take them?"

"Well, yeah, everyone I know that goes out."

"So, hundreds of people are buying tiny pills for a tenner each."

"Yes. That is correct." Tina spoke painfully slowly and carefully.

"Where do you buy them?"

"It's not where, it's who. Do you know that Davie King? Always hangs about the Nags Head pub?"

"He's about your height, but with lighter hair. Well, you have to ask him, but it's his girlfriend that always carries them."

"Who's she? A friend of yours?"

"Not really, you'll know her when you see her. Shes kind of tall; wears a denim jacket; her hairs kind of…" Maria used her hands to estimate the perimeter of Anna's hair.

"Anna Mcvay? Aye. I know the one. She's a cheeky wee reprobate."

"You going to buy some?" Tina looked hopeful as she swung the gold clown pendant that hung from the chain she was chewing. He winced at the sound of metal crunching between her teeth.

"No, no way. That's not my scene."

From outside came a sharp voice, half singing, half warning,

"Maria Mary, Christina Louise! These potatoes won't peel themselves!" Tina threw the cigarette end in the sink. Then blew the last of the smoke out and wafted her hands around in a useless attempt at hiding the smell as they left.

Claire

Claire battled through the identical 6-year-old cyclone of curly brown hair, arms, legs, and plastic guns, to get into her auntie Jeans kitchen.

"I've had it up to here with that pair today. Little shits." Jean's hand indicated a level a foot above her head. "I don't know why I bother trying to instil any discipline around here. They don't listen to a bloody word I say."

Claire surveyed the hundreds of black footprints marking the path from the back door, up the cream stairs carpet.

"I telt them, take your shoes aff at the door. But no. They cannae be bothered. Noo ma carpets ruined. Again."

The view into the living room beyond was a scrapyard of toy cars, scattered lego and sofa cushions.

"I'll sort it all out when you're at work, on you go. They'll be fine."

"Working at the bingo is the only thing keeping me sane, you ken that? If I wis stuck in the hoose with this pair all day, I'd end up in a bloody straight jacket."

Claire looked at her feet and filled her lungs hard, dragging air inside to stop her reaction coming out.

"I'm sorry hun, I wasnae thinking. It just came oot. These wee shites are doing ma head in. But I didnae mean that."

"It's alright. I cant expect jokes to be off the menu just because my Mum's in the nut hoose."

"Dinnae call it that."

"Why? That's what she is. A nut job."

"Come on now, what's brought this on?

I've ten minutes before I go, come and sit here with me for a bit." Jean took the spare kitchen chair and wedged it under the door handle, locking the twins out. The screams and banging continued in the hall but muffled now.

The back garden used to be a neat lawn, with a border of flowers and a couple of tidy bushes in the corners. Now, the main feature was a dark mud patch in the middle of straw-colored grass. It's strewn with multicoloured buckets and tools for irrigating the boy-made swamp. The broken ends of branches hung splintered from the bushes—their leafy tips protruding as flags from sticky black sandcastles. Jean produced two pre-rolled roll-ups from her green and gold swan tin.

"Look at the state of ma gerden. Ah telt them dinnae pull the branches aff. And whit do they dae?" She held up the lighter as Claire sucked and watched the stray shreds of tobacco turn from red hot, to dust. On the exhale, she asked;

"When was the last time you saw my Mum?"

"I went down before Christmas, remember."

"She didn't ask for me then did she?"

"Well, she didn't ask for anyone. She's not well. She's not herself. Has something happened? Do you want to go and visit her?"

"Nope. I don't want to see her. It was just today, this woman at work. She was about the same age as Mum, something reminded me of her, but she spoke really nicely to me. It just made me think." Claire stared ahead at a little wren splashing around in a yellow plastic dish in the mud.

"Things weren't always bad you know, when you were wee, before she got ill."

Claire dragged in another lungful of air, the words she'd been preparing for years were about to come out. She looked at the family eyes of her auntie, seeing echos of her old Mum. The question finally came.

"Do you know who my Dad is?"

Jean tapped her cigarette on the edge of the step. Claire had never seen a smile so sad. Both comforting and heartbreaking. Jean's hand came to rest heavily on her knee.

"I don't know much. But I do know he's not worth the bother. He hurt your Mum."

"But have you met him? Do I look like

him?" Claire's voice trembled. Jean closed her eyes and shook her head.

"It would break your Mum to hear you talking like this. She did her best for you; you know that?"

Claire leaned away and repositioned to look at her aunt's expression before asking,

"Really? Do you think that was her best? I wonder…"

The lines between Jean's eyebrows deepened.

"Christ girl, you've no idea, have you?"

She didn't like this side of Jean. She looked back at the wren in its plastic bath.

"Look, Jean, all I've got in this world is you and those two wee buggers knocking lumps out of each other in the hall. There's nothing I can do to make Anna stay, and Scott is a useless twat. I just wonder if there's anyone else out there that thinks about me."

"Well stop it, he doesn't care about you. Never did. That's a can of worms you must not open."

They sat in silence as the tempo of the shouting inside quickened and slowed. Claire caught Jean look at her watch and took the chance on one last question.

"Do you even know his name?"

"Jesus, give it up hen." Jean stood up, pinched the bridge of her nose with one hand, and pointed at Claire with the other, still holding the roll-up between her fingers.

"Your Mum's the only one that ever knew him, and if she says he's bad news, then that's all we need to know. Your Mum was never the same again after she came back from Glasgow. He hurt her badly, and he didn't want you. Let that be the end of it."

Claire swallowed back the tears and nodded as she tried to redraw the line under it.

"Please let that be the end of it. He's a bad bastard. That's all I know."

The sounds from the hallway turned into thumps, four small and sturdy feet were kicking the door.

"That's ma queue to go hun, I'm awa to ma work. Good luck with the Kray twins." Jean left via the back gate, leaving Claire to remove the barricade and calm the riot.

"Right, who wants fish fingers for tea?"

Anna

Anna lit the longest cigarette end from the ashtray while leaning on the bedroom wall, surveying the approach through the window. One edge glowed as she puffed, frustrated, she flicked the zippo and sucked again. It burned her lip and fingers. She wiped the hot tarry residue from her tingly lip and squashed it back into the ashtray. She folded her arms, resting her head on the wall. She wondered if the paint colour was, in fact, magnolia, or testimony to someone's bad lifestyle choices; historical fry ups and nicotine.

A cough in the distance.

A scuff from the close.

There he was.

Arms swinging, gut bulging, thinly wrapped in the same blue nylon as usual. She got to the door in time to open it and avoid the jarring knock,

"Archie. In you come, pal."

He forced passed her, the lines of his forehead so deep Anna thought his skull might crack open any second. That chemical reaction his presence caused, the fizzing, popping bubbles, draining the colour from the surroundings.

"Shut the door." He barked.

Anna bit her lip, gaining her composure as she flipped the Yale lock on,

"So, how are…" she started with a sickly smile. This was met with Archie's finger.

"First, am no your pal. Got that? Davie is ma pal. You're just his burd."

Her smile slid down to her feet; something else was formulating to replace it.

"Secondly, how I am, is fuck all to do with you." His finger thrust towards her on all the important words. "Do not ask me how I am. You get to know nothing about me. Got that?"

Anna could feel a vein in her neck throb, and her toes curled inside her shoes, her nails dug into her palms. She nodded.

"For some fucked up reason, I have to trust you with these." He held a plastic bag at eye level between his thumb and forefinger, dangling the white pills before her.

"But first, let's get this straight. I'm only allowing this for Davie. I wouldn't be involving you for any other reason."

She took the bag with her left hand, slowly, revealing neither hesitation nor desperation.

"Understood, loud and clear." She

nodded.

The distaste curled his lip, creating crevasses of the lines that ran from his nose to the corners of his mouth. He took her hand, squeezed hard, and pulled her arm. He stared into her eyes. She felt him searching for a sign of instability. She remained solid.

"I'll be here, Sunday night," she replaced her fallen smile with a new one, more sickly sweet, "looking forward to it."

CHAPTER FOUR

Wednesday

Shaun

He wanted what his Gran and Granddad had. He looked at the gold-framed wedding photo, in black and white, they both looked so smart. He admired his Gran's blond pin-curls, and his Granddads dark cows lick. This ideal had seemed increasingly far fetched. Shaun had no luck with women, but he reckoned that was about to change. The charisma he'd thrown around the clubs in Glasgow had maintained a steady supply of girlfriends over the years. Getting them was easy, but keeping them under control was the hard part. Promises made by candlelight were soon dismissed when they rebelled. However pretty and promising, soon enough, they'd all fall short. He was looking for commitment, the real thing, a wife, forsaking all others. He'd been looking for years.

This young Anna, she was different. She reminded him of a girl he once knew. He'd moved into her tenement up the west end; she had two toddlers already. In the early days, they'd had fun, doing 'family stuff' like walking through the park under fiery Autumn leaves. But, it turned with the season, and he was frozen out on an injunction by Christmas. Anna had bits of her, but with no baggage, that was a bonus. He couldn't be bothered with other people's kids, or any other relatives for that matter. He thought back to Kay more recently, another promising start, but she spent too much time on her lodger, some sneaky lowlife English boy. God knows why. Even after she got rid of him, he couldn't trust her. Anyone willing to let a scumbag like that live in their home had questionable morals.

He limped through to the kitchen. It would be nice to have a meal cooked for him. He doubted if she could cook, and he was certain a proper duster would be alien to her, but she was young enough to learn. Not like the old birds. Like Christine, or that horrible hippie Jenny, who insisted on putting her dirty bare feet on his sofa. He had warned her. Plenty of times. She was thirty-seven, just too old to take a telling. She'd asked for that.

He wondered if she'd be one of these 'career orientated' women. He used to abhor these types. Thinking if they wore some shoulder pads it gave them the right to act like men. No, thank you. But now, with his physical and financial position, maybe it wouldn't be such a bad thing. He remembered his Grace, she was in advertising, with a sleek monochrome flat and matching wardrobe. A very well presented woman, and OK, she had brains, but she took it too far. That one had opinions on everything. She would not back down, ever. Always had to be heard. The last time he saw her she was spitting her teeth out like apple pips onto a white shag pile carpet.

Not Anna, the time he'd spent with her had been pleasant so far, plus, soon, she would owe him big time. He'd only need to make a couple of initial changes. She could do with wearing something more feminine, a blouse perhaps. There were a few hanging in the spare room she could try. He still had a nice one that belonged to that strange woman, Alison. She was unhinged that one. She went to her sisters one day, but never arrived. He had even reported her missing, then eventually the police told him she was alive but living somewhere else. He never could find out where. What kind of woman does that?

Anna certainly had potential, but she would have to kick the chemicals. No girl of his was hanging about the town popping pills with all those sleazy guys on the prowl. She was young enough to be moulded, shaped into an acceptable woman.

He found her vulnerability endearing, quite exciting. She needed help, and a little bit of need stretched a long way with her type. With his help, she'd kick the drugs, then get a nice wee job. Nothing too taxing, she'd need to save some energy for what he had planned. A little bit of extra money around the house would be nice. He hadn't been able to work for a while. He had a medical line for his foot problems. Luckily, because finding employment sympathetic to his violent past was pretty tricky.

As far as anyone knew, he didn't need to work; he was a Weegie. Up this far north in Scotland, anyone from Glasgow was revered as either a retired gangster, or a grass on the run. He used his accent to dramatise second-hand stories and personalising legends from 'doon the road' to make sure it wasn't the latter.

He lived on disability benefits for his feet. Each week cashing his book at the post office, he would always bring a letter to post in case anyone saw him in the queue. He was good with money these days, always put at least a tenner away every week. Ready for when the child he never got to meet finally came knocking on his door looking for their Daddy.

Irene. That stupid cow he'd been with back when Maggie Thatcher got into number 10. When she got pregnant, he'd been delighted initially. She had real potential for a wife, but as always, things turned cold. The rows started with the morning sickness. Maybe he should have let her visit her family, at least he would have known where she came from, and maybe where she went. There wasn't much he'd change about his past. He'd always done the right thing, but Irene was different, it was hard to know what the right thing was. They only knew each other for a few months. She'd danced and drank, and laughed for the first one, then curled up, cried, and shouted for the rest.

So it turned nasty.

She wouldn't listen.

She goaded him.

She overreacted.

Her smarmy solicitor used his previous to make him look bad, and he got two years in Perth prison. He saw her in court as he was led away, she'd stood up in the benches to clap at his sentence. He saw her huge belly and knew she'd kept the baby, but he never knew if it was a little Shaun or Shaunette running around.

But, he took comfort in the money he'd saved for them, for when the time finally came. Junior would know that he was a good guy, he would have been there for his wean, if it wasn't for their stupid cow of a mother. He used to imagine reading fairy tales to a wee girl with ribbons in her hair, or kicking a ball around with a wee boy in a

Celtic top. These days he wondered if he could even be a Granddad.

He sat on the edge of his bed and swept some crumbs off the peach candle-wick bedspread. He opened the centre drawer of the kidney-shaped dressing table and placed the money on the glass top. He counted it often, although it never changed drastically, he liked the feel of. He'd rearrange the bundles, sometimes sets of one hundred, the fifth note folded around the others, as he'd seen in the post office. Sometimes all flat in leafy piles. He'd sniff it, and sometimes even spread a bundle into a fan and look at himself in the mirror. He would only be adding a fiver this Friday, he'd need a bit extra if he was entertaining Anna.

Over two grand there now, his hard saved trust fund for when they come knocking. It was mostly tenners and twenties, with a few blue fivers. That would not do. He went to the kitchen for his wallet and took out brown tenners to swap. No one wants to see blue scabby fiver's in a wad of cash. You could tell it had been scrapped together, and that it's every penny you've got. All signs should read 'plenty more where that came from,' not 'skint and desperate.'

He went for casual rolls, paper barrels, five hundred in each, held tight with elastic bands. The kind of opulent guy who deals in units this size must be worth knowing. He'd only hand them over if he was sure she was good for it, and he was pretty sure she was.

Archie

He aims for silent as he makes his way inside. He knows where to step, which of the stairs to avoid, and the precise thrust to open the door to prevent any creaks, cracks, or squeaks.

There he was, keeping the promise he'd made to his Mum over her last cup of tea a year ago. He'd moved back in then, to the family home. His bedroom had never changed, even his school tie still hung from the end of the curtain rail. A gold cup sat on a red filing cabinet, and two shield-shaped plaques hung from either side of the window. He was thirty-nine now, definitely past ever making it as a footballer. His ambitions were put on hold when, as a healthy teenager with a potential career as a professional, he'd discovered weed and acid. His parents hadn't had the strength to motivate him, so his dreams were kept for later while he dived right in. He'd tell himself,

'I'm just having a break, I'll get back to training next week…'

'I'm young…'

'I've got plenty of time…'

Then, all of a sudden, he was fat and made geriatric sighs while getting out of his chair.

He spent a lot of time with the memory of his Mum's last days, the domino's games, the freesias on the windowsill, the blue tits waiting outside for their daily crumbs. The noise of her china cup delicately rattling off the saucer with her tremors. He was glad she'd died in the summer with the smell of grass and the hum of lawn-mowers drifting in.

The birds soon stopped their fruitless visits; the stone plinth was baron now. Looking out into the garden, he imagined his Mum there, sitting on the step, passing him peeled apple slices. He'd be beside her, with grass stains on his stay-press nylon trousers, dirty fingernails, and a big toothy

smile. Neither Archie nor his father had
even used the back door since she had gone.
A peg bag in the shape of a tiny faded blue
t-shirt hung like a ghost on the washing line.

He coughed into his sleeve, muffling the
sound by pushing so hard his cheeks
expanded. His eyes watered, and he
coughed again, cursing the noise he made.

Hearing the first ring, he flinched but
decided to ignore it, taking the chance that
he might have imagined it. No, the second
two confirmed it. He walked to the only
closed door in the hall, ran his chunky
fingers through his thick hair, before fixing a
rehearsed smile onto his face, and entering.

"Hiya Dad," he whispered through a
beaming smile, "How are you feeling today,
old boy?"

He delicately lifted the head of the thin-
skinned skeleton and plumped up the
pillow. He smoothed the red tartan blanket
across his chest.

"Had a good day? Soon be time for your
supper."

The nurse had been in, and the supplies
replenished, feeding tubes, shit and piss
sacks and medications lay in neat piles by
the window.

He could never look at him for too long; most recently, he could only manage a brief glance. He didn't want to see it. Any of it. Not the sparse white hairs floating on top of his blue scalp, not the vacant glass eyes of an old teddy bear, not the flakes falling from brittle lips, and not the hole.

His voice box was surgically removed a few months before his Mum had died. After the laryngectomy, he was left with a black hole, wrinkled around the edges, like a saggy arsehole. Archie could sometimes hear a little whistle escape, and it made him queasy.

The cancer had never really gone away, and now it was in his spine and bones. The end was soon, any day now. The same any day now, it had been for the last five months. At Christmas, he'd been given days, but here he was. Intaking and excreting every day like clockwork, his flesh made mechanism just wouldn't give up.

His Mum and Dad had planned their funerals together, the special songs, the wood grain for the coffins, the pink-toned flowers. They'd been ill for so long, they seemed to be looking forward to these perfectly executed funerals. Out of everyone

who attended his mother's send-off, only
two people had subsequently visited his
Dad. His aunt Sheena, because she wanted
to claim an emerald brooch, claiming it as
sentimental, but apparently quickly selling it
for £20. Then his Uncle Bobby, who'd
visited often, listening to the robotic sounds
of his father's sorrow, but the visits became
sparse and trailed off long ago.

She would have been happy with the
funeral. It was exactly as she envisioned,
right down to the pink ham in white bread,
cut neatly into triangles. They played The
Lord's My Shepherd as the light beech
wood coffin left the church, to a serenade of
tears, just how she'd planned. It had been
paid for with their savings, and there was
half left for his Dad's, a matching do, with
complementing tunes but a darker
mahogany coffin.

Any day now.

All Archie had to do was get the money
back into his father's funeral tin.

He smoothed the edges of the blanket
down again, looking up at the water-colour
poppies above the bed.

Anna

The bed covers lay mangled, she rolled
over and felt the ends of her hair. The
texture was like the ginger fur on an old 'See
you Jimmy' hat, she thought about buying
some nice conditioner, then remembered she
was skint. She still didn't have any clean
clothes, but lying between the cotton tangles,
she concluded that things were not that bad.
Waking up in a home she couldn't stay in,
with a boyfriend she hadn't heard from, and
a daunting weekend ahead, Anna still found
herself charmed by the sun streaming in her
window, she welcomed the morning song of
birds outside. It wasn't Ibiza, but it would
do for now.

She wasn't sure if she had trained herself
to see the good, or if she was naturally gifted
with a positive outlook. It annoyed others,
Christine thought she was naive, and Claire
thought she had her head in the clouds. She
pictured their faces, imagining expressions
of worry, alarm, disappointment. Then she
stopped. Easy as that. Anna stopped herself
from thinking about it any further, that was
her real gift. She could simply put her
emotions and experiences in little boxes, lock

them up, and shove them in the attic of her mind.

The attic door was bolted shut with drugs, and a thick curtain of alcohol stopped any drafts escaping. It didn't matter how many more boxes of pain and loss got thrown in there, the door stayed firmly shut.

She pulled on a t-shirt from the floor, it had been worn, but not for a while. She sniffed, it didn't smell clean, or dirty. She sat on the toilet without closing the door, making the most of having her own place. As she washed her hands, she hesitated, considered getting in the shower. She weighed up the facts, she was already half-dressed, and there might not be enough gas left. She sniffed her armpit and dismissed any urgency. A cold splash to the face and a good tooth brushing would be fine for today.

As she brushed, watching her face at unusual angles, the day's mental list was compiled.

1- Get proper food

2- Stash the pills

3- Wash some clothes

4- Stop drinking

5- Sort the flat out a bit

Most items were immediately relegated again. DI Jackson shook her up a bit yesterday, so she decided number 2- Stash the drugs properly, would be moved to the top. Davie lived by the rule of leaving them outside, in the coal bunker at the foot of the stairs. Anna had avoided it, mainly to prevent the giant black spiders, which she was certain lived in there, from biting her fingers.

Perhaps jail would be worse than a spider bite, she decided. So, still in her pants and t-shirt, she grabbed the little plastic bag. She unlocked the door, kept her body behind it, and peered her head forward. She surveyed the close, listening hard for footsteps or gate squeaks, or any other indicator of a witness on the way. She bit her bottom lip, then, sure no one would appear in the next few seconds, she stepped lightly in her bare feet to the bottom of the stone stairs.

Trust

The zip-loc seal had been burst open to count them after Archie left the other night. She pondered chucking the unsealed bag into the darkness. What's the worst that could happen? Imagining having to dig through coal and spiders to fish out dirty pills, she tutted at her own laziness.

She bounced back up the stairs to the kitchen and opened each drawer in turn. She'd never looked anywhere other than the cutlery one. She wasn't sure what she was looking for, a small box, cling film, a better plastic bag maybe. There, in the bottom drawer, exactly what she needed. A roll of tinfoil. She ripped off a square, poured the pills like white pearls into the middle, and folded them into an origami treasure chest.

Back down the stairs, she pushed it into the black hole, withdrawing her hand before any spiders fangs could sink into her flesh. She pulled her t-shirt over her bum, holding it down as she ran back up the stairs. She was smiling. Anna loved the sense of achievement when she actually did something she couldn't be bothered to do.

So, with her work done for the day, she could concentrate on passing the time till the weekend.

Trust

Walking along the street in the fresh air,
denim jacket tied around her waist, enough
tobacco to last the day, and no commitments
at all, Anna felt light. She imagined poor
Claire, sat at her desk, in that basement.
Only the occasional glimpse of hairy ankles
indicating it was a lovely day out in the real
world.

 With the liberty of walking around
carefree every day came one major
downside. Besides having no money and
being a little bit hungry most of the time, the
choice of company for entertainment was
slim.

 Anna calculated that she'd exhausted
Christine's hospitality for a day or so, and it
was still hours until Claire finished work.
She had a couple of pounds to go to the pub,
but there would only be the old red-faced
regulars and Gemma, and she wasn't in the
mood for her interrogation. Passing the
hairdresser window, she caught her
reflection. She stopped. She looked at her
full image, and it struck her how much she
had changed while walking these streets
over the years. She'd passed this salon a
million times, always using the last mirrored

window to see how she looked. Not out of vanity, more out of curiosity. She'd never had a full-length mirror, and she liked the different perspective.

She couldn't see anything of the long-haired child from years ago. Nor the hopeful high schooler in short skirts and platform shoes. She was different now, not exactly an adult, but definitely too big for this town.

Nothing around her had changed. The same peace symbol scratched into the window frame, the same faded sticker on the corner of the street sign. The shops and scenery were all stuck in time, but Anna had evolved. She'd already outgrown this place, and now she had to get out of here. This weekend had to work out, her life depended on it.

A minibus door slammed at the other side of the street, muffled laughter and knocking on the windows followed. As the bus full of hilarity drove away, Bazz was left standing on the pavement. His high viz waistcoat hung off one shoulder, and he carried an inside out Farmfood's bag. The sight of him amused her, so she skipped across the road to greet him and seek out some entrainment. As she approached, his expression warned it wouldn't be much fun.

"Alright? What's up?"

"I fookin hate pikeys." His eyes looked a little too full, hovering on the edge of hurt and rage. "Every day since av been in that new van, they make my life a misery. Pushing us, hiding me tools, tripping us up." His bottom lip trembled.

"Can't you get moved to a different van?" Anna asked.

"I'm not a grass. And anyway, Wendy's on that one. It's the only time I get to see her."

"Aw, is she your girlfriend? I didn't know you were seeing anyone." Anna smiled at the thought of there being someone out there for everyone after all.

"Na, not yet anyway. I thought, once I've got something to offer her I'll make a move."

"Ask her now! What are you waiting for?"

"After what she saw today, I'll be lucky if she even looks at us again."

"What happened?" Anna's nose wrinkled in anticipation of something horrible.

"Well, we was working all morning, painting benches in the bowling green, then we went back to the van for piece break, as usual. I was really looking forward to it as well cuz I got bread and corned beef last night and made sandwiches. Right?" Anna nodded, in a tell me more kind of way.

"Me bag was on the floor, all flat, and ripped, someone had stamped on it."

"That's a shame, but it's not that bad is it?"

"That's not it. I took a flat sandwich out, and I took a big bite from the middle, no crusts just the good bit. Every fucker in the van was staring at us. They do that a lot, so I just took another bite. And another. I left the crusts and sunk my gums into the other half. I barely chewed any of it. I was so uncomfortable with them all staring at us. I just gulped it down. I didn't even look up. Then, they all started laughing, so I looked over at Wendy, and she looked like she was gonna throw up."

"I don't understand. What's the big deal?"

"The pikeys put dog shit in my sandwich. And I ate it. I ate dog shit."

Anna bit her bottom lip; she was now

sure she could smell shit.

"Everyone was laughing at us all day. All the way back in the van, calling us a shit muncher. And, they'll still be laughing tomorrow and the next day. My life's fookin ruined."

"They'll soon forget, it'll be yesterday's news." She knew this was totally untrue. If you'd ever done anything shameful, accidental or not, you'd be wearing that badge forever.

"I've still got ages before I'm finished, I've nearly 70 hours still to do. I just wish I could get back at them pikeys, but there's just too many of them."

"That's a fight you definitely don't want to start. Come on, cheer up. I've got enough money for two tins of juice." She took his bony elbow and pointed him in the direction of Roy's spar.

The usual sour smell in the shop seemed amplified today. The culprit was a mop bucket filled with dirty water next to the milk fridge. As they wandered up and down the sparsely stocked isles, Roy followed them. Full of suspicion, and sloshing around

the putrid water as a disguise, he monitored
their every move from sideways eyes.

Anna knew he'd be watching Bazz, but
she didn't know what people thought of her.
She picked up an orange, the bottom of it
was flat, blue, and furry. She placed it back
exactly as it was. Further along, yoghurt
pots stood with lids bulging, daring her to
open them. Dried and tinned goods were
the safest bet there. She brought two tins of
lemon Fanta and two packets of Tangy
Toms up to the till. Roy was there instantly
to take the money for their paltry meal for
two.

He looked them both up and down, then
back and forth between their faces. Thick
wavy wires of grey hair protruded from his
ears. One solitary grey hair jutted out from
his left eyebrow. Anna's gaze fixed on it.
Bazz nudged her to hand over the money.
Roy's eyes narrowed as he counted out the
handful of coins and he asked,

"New boyfriend?"

"Pardon?" Anna replied.

Roy pointed at Bazz, "Him. And you.
That's not the same man you were with last
week."

Anna laughed, Bazz's face was scarlet, he

looked to the ground and shuffled out into the clean air.

"What the hell has it got to do with him who I hang about with?" She was starting to get an inkling of how other people saw her. She really, really needed to get out of this town—this weekend.

They sat on a wall, between the bank and the library. Each building was quite foreign to both, but they sat comfortably in the middle. She spoke till he smiled again, his gummy grin reassuring her that he would get over it. He left for home, full of positive cliches, stronger than he was yesterday. Anna watched him walk away and pull his high viz vest straight.

Shading her eyes from the sun's glare as she checked the time on the church tower. It was still ages until Claire finished. She closed her eyes and let her face soak up the warmth while she considered her next move.

Davie would have left a message by now. She couldn't deal with Gemma face to face, but maybe a quick call from the phone box would answer her question. She sighed, remembering the last pennies she had were in Roy's manky till.

Maybe a stray coin or two lurked in the forgotten pockets of her denim jacket. She unfastened the stiff brass buttons. With two fingers, she fished around in the little breast pockets. No money, but something much more valuable. A lump rose in her throat. She thought this was lost a long time ago. She knew what it was the instant her fingers contacted the delicate metal. She drew it out, carefully, and held it up in the light. A thin gold St Christopher, suspended from a knotted broken chain. It spun before her eyes, its sheen dulled from being forgotten in her unopened pocket.

Her Dad had given it to her on her 10th birthday. The last time she saw him. She thought it was gone, with the fading memory of Andy Mcvay. But there it was, all along, right next to her heart.

She rubbed it with her thumb, bringing back some of its old shine. She squeezed it in her palm, closing her eyes to conjure up a vivid image of him. Running through the usual stock of memories, a flicker of something ancient came into focus.

Her lips were sticky with sweet birthday cake. Her Dad, in a burgundy jumper with a tin of Tennant's lager in one hand, handing her the unwrapped chain, bending down and saying, "Happy birthday my wee darling. Wear this necklace, and where ever you travel, St Christopher will be looking after you."

"Pft, not exactly a substitute for an actual father looking after you," she whispered to herself, then she gasped. Shook her head at the epiphany; the chain wasn't wrapped or in a box, because he'd probably just stolen it off someone.

That was almost a decade ago. She wondered if he'd even recognise his daughter now. Then she wondered if he was even alive. As she was depositing the chain and the memories back in their hiding places, a dusty blue transit van pulled up. Ronin leaned his brick of a head out the window.

"Over here. Now."

In her head, she told him to drive on and gave him the middle finger. In reality, she didn't have the energy for any more drama, so she got up and made her way toward the smell of diesel and dogs.

"I hear your man's left the country. Is that right?" He pulled his earlobe down as he leaned out for her reply.

"Aye, what about it?"

"Who's selling the pills now then?"

"Why? Will you be wanting some?" His eyes were so dark Anna couldn't tell where the pupils ended, this unsettled her. Wariness of people wasn't one of her natural responses, but being close to him, her spine bristled like a cat.

"I'll be wanting them all. And you're gonnae tell me who's got them."

Shit.

"No idea, can't help you I'm afraid." Next week he could take it up with Archie, but not before her weekend payed off.

"Your man got privileges. He was allowed to have the business. Now he's gone, all privileges are revoked. I'm taking over."

"Honestly, it's not me, I've no idea what's happening with all that." This is an enemy she could really do without.

"You?" his theatrical laugh bellowed out of the van and grated against her eardrums. "What idiot would leave a silly wee lassie like you charge?"

"Oh, right, aye. I thought, you thought, I might be trying to sell drugs or something!" she laughed as innocently as she could.

"Your man's an imbecile, right enough, but even he's not that stupid."

"I'll be sure to let you know, if I hear who it is. I'm off all that these days, so I probably won't. Like I don't go out or that. So I won't hear. But if I do, you know, I'll tell you." Shut up.

"You be sure and do that."

She gave him the thumbs up while biting her tongue. It was the only response she could muster with the mixture of fear and rage pulsing through her body.

As the van spluttered into action, she sat back on the wall. Her heart had a little less room to beat, and her legs were a little weaker. She sat heavy, pinned to the spot. Maybe this wasn't going to be as easy as she first thought. She lit a cigarette. She shouldn't worry Claire with this.

Just a couple of obstacles.

Just a couple of days.

Walking the streets and waiting for company was not a strange thing for Anna.

135

As a child, and all through her teens, she'd just walk around the town, investigating places, waiting in parks, sitting on benches, looking in shops, wandering the tennis courts. Always looking for company, someone to have a laugh with. Everyone else was at home, eating their tea, watching *Neighbours* and *Home and Away*. Not Anna, her feet were too itchy, she was too scared of missing out. She'd bite off a chunk of cheese, stick an apple in her pocket and go. She never understood the reverence for tea times and TV habits.

Others had to do homework or chores before they made it out for the night. Her Mum frequently threatened to 'make some changes around here,' but she never followed through. Once, a laminated timetable of household jobs made it onto the fridge, including washing dishes, ironing, and hoovering. It was duly ignored. It slid with its magnetic holder, further down the door, sliding further down every day until it disappeared underneath to join the fluff, peas and soft sugar puffs, never to be seen again.

A few years later, the circumstances different, but she had that same feeling of waiting for the fun to start. It dragged the seconds out. The hours felt like days.

So many times she'd tried to persuade Claire to finish early, "tell them you've got the dentist, let's go to the pub!" or "you're missing the sun, take a sicky." But she never did.

Wandering around the park, waiting for five pm, her situation kept coming to mind. Waves of trepidation threatening to engulf her. She sat down to finish the warm dregs of the flat juice she'd carried along all afternoon. She picked up a triangular stone from the gravel at her feet and started to scratch a smiley face on the brown wooden bench.

As she was engrossed in adding spikey hair to her creation, a car horn blasted from the road behind her. Never sure whether to look, she continued what she was doing. She put people who presumed any horn beeping was for them, in the same box as people who wore sunglasses inside.

Another blast.

Then a third more urgent, so with no one else around, she turned slowly. Pulled up onto the pavement was a silver Ford Capri, window down, with a chubby hand calling her over.

Shaun. Eye contact had been established; there was no way to pretend she didn't see him. She nodded to his enthusiastic waving, accidentally accepting his invitation. As she walked towards him, she imagined a bus driving past. A big, red, double-decker. She'd jump on the platform and swing around the pole and be driven away in the opposite direction of where her feet were headed right now. But instead, she arrived beside his door.

"What are you doing sitting there on your own?"

"Just waiting, killing time till my friend finishes work."

"Hop in, I'll give you a lift." He reached over to open the passenger door with a grunt.

"It's OK, it's only on Spey Court, I don't want to put you out." *And I don't want to get in.*

"Its no bother, hop in."

"I'm halfway there, don't worry about it." She takes a step away, waving him off.

He shoves the door open onto the road, "I insist."

Her toes curl inside her shoes, and her

teeth nip her lip as she tries to combat the discomfort while getting in and pulling on the seat belt. He winds up his window and bumps down from the kerb.

"It's so good to see you again. I've been hoping I'd bump into you soon."

She folded her arms across her chest and gripped onto the seat belt. They drove in silence for a little while. She could feel him building up to something. The full blast heating was drying her eyes out, and she began to struggle for breath. The same vinegary smell was there, made more pungent by the temperature.

"Can I turn the heat down a bit?"

"Sorry, the heaters stuck on. You'll just have to take your jacket off, let some of that heat out." He rubbed his left hand over his chest as he spoke. She reached forward to wind her window down instead and heard a little disappointed sigh.

"You can drop me here, it's quite near, I'll walk the rest."

"Don't be silly, Spey Court you said. I'll take you there." He looked from the road, to her thighs and back again.

Anna looked out the side window, as far away from him and the grotty feeling of his eyes on her. She edged to the door side, still gripping the seat belt, in silence. As he drove, she sensed lots of false starts. The telltale intake of breath, the short pause, then giving up. What the hell is he trying to say?

Anna could feel the silence in the car, her compulsion to fill it kicked in,

"So, what have you been up to?" she asked.

"Ah, you know, a few deals going on, a couple of loose ends down the road to tie up, nothing to concern your pretty wee head with. More importantly, what's been occupying your time?"

"The same kind of thing, I guess, waiting for this weekend to be over so I can get Archie paid off, then get on with my life."

"So, you remember what I was saying the other day? About the money?"

"I remember, yeah, but its OK. I've got it all under control."

"You're out of your depth, you know. You're just a girl, you shouldn't be up to your elbows in that dodgy business."

"Seriously, I'm fine. Anyway, you do know we're going the wrong direction?"

"Do you think I don't know where I'm

going?" he snapped. "You said you had time to kill, and now you don't? What are you all about, I'm not playing your silly wee girl games."

"Sorry, I just…" Anna thought she could hear the blood pumping through his clogged arteries. "It's fine, I just didn't want to waste your time."

"Don't you worry about my time, just relax, sit back. Let me do this for you, it's my pleasure."

These were well-traveled roads for Anna, but this trip had never taken this long, trapped in his tin can bursting with tension. As the car slowed at the bottom of Clarie's street, Anna reached for the door handle before it stopped. Shaun spotted her motion and popped the locks down from his side.

"Woah now. What's the hurry?" The car stopped, and he turned to face her.

"Thanks for the lift, much appreciated. I better go though." She flashed a fake smile to cover the fear taking over her face. He reached over to her knee and squeezed her with his huge hand.

"You could try and show me your appreciation." His hand moved a little further up onto her thigh. Anna's heart rate doubled, a bead of sweat collected on her top lip. How the hell did she end up in this position?

"Sorry, thanks a lot, I mean. I'm just in a hurry now, that's all."

He leaned further over. His mouth was closing in on her face, his hand sliding further up her inner thigh. She pulled back, her face turned away from his. His breath whistled through his nose. A scream was bubbling up inside her, but it couldn't escape. Her breath was held, she closed her eyes tightly as if the darkness could save her. Her jaws clamped shut, and her lips sealed painfully tight. Her fists clenched around the seat belt as if it offered any safety. His hand moved, off her leg, it brushed over her breasts. Anna braced every muscle anticipating his next move.

Then click. He pulled the lock up from the door beside her shoulder. The heat and weight of his presence lifted as she opened her eyes, and he reclined into the driving position.

He was smiling, more than smiling, he was smoldering. He was drunk on her fear, his cheeks were burgundy, and he breathed through open lips. Still tense, she remained in the same position, her eyes wide now, taking in this horrible scene. He dragged his hand across his chest and down over his huge round gut.

"Any time you want a lift, you know where I am."

Anna took a sharp breath to bring herself back into her body, she grabbed the door handle and scrambled out onto the pavement. She slammed the door, swung her bag onto her shoulder and walked away without looking back. The car started, engine revving, calling for attention, but she wouldn't turn around. It was moving slowly, just behind her, then sped up to the corner, he turned at the end of the road, back towards her, she was almost at Clarie's, he slowed to a funeral pace. His window open, his shapeless arm resting on the frame as he passed, shouting;

"Remember, I've enough money to solve all your problems, just waiting for you to say the word."

Anna knocked frantically on the red panelled door. Claire answered with a concerned look.

"What's up? Come in!"

"Nothing, I'm just bursting for a pee!"
Anna barged straight through the open plan
living room towards the bathroom, locking
the door behind her. She knelt for a moment
to catch her breath, resting her face on the
bath's cold surface.

She scrubbed herself with soap, hoping
the bubbles would carry away the shame
along with the vinegary residue. Drying her
face on the soft pink towel, she mentally
packed away the Capri experience and
vowed to never get in that position again.

She edited the list of things not to
mention tonight.

1- Davie.

2- Archie.

3- DI Jackson.

4- The pikey in the van.

5- Getting a lift from Shaun, and whatever
the hell happened in his car.

This would be a nice night, the best of friends, doing what they liked to do. No need to ruin it with any of that stuff.

She came out of the bathroom to the smell of the oven heating up. She wished she could buy the food and rent the video for once, but Claire didn't mind. She was sure. Their friendship was stronger than that.

"Let's watch Countdown before we put the video on." Claire loved the maths problems, and could almost always solve them. Anna tried, but never got them. On the vocabulary round, she would shout out two and three-letter words, while Claire was quietly working on six letter beauties. During the adverts, the signal began to fade. Claire gently tilted the ariel, supported by yellowing crispy sellotape, until a grainy picture came back into focus.

"I've had enough of this. I need a new TV. I spend more time messing about with the aerial than watching anything."

When the last round finished Claire asked,

"Guess what I got today?" She retrieved her bag from its hook and sunk her arm in. "Remember that disposable camera I had for the foam party? I got the photos back today. I haven't looked at them yet. Want to see?"

"Yes! Get them out!" Anna's memory of that night shimmered. Iridescent bubbles, bouncing bass, and pure joy, like floating up to heaven on pastel-coloured clouds. The music had been transcendent, their outfits impeccable, co-ordinated right down to the matching blue nail varnish. She definitely wanted to see that magic immortalised on film.

Claire peeled open the sticker and tapped the pile on the countertop, giving a little cough like a newsreader. She frowned and turned the grey fuzzy rectangle towards Anna. They both shrugged. The next one was similar, but with a pink semi-circle covering half the frame.

"Is that your finger?" Claire agreed that it was quite likely. A pile of useless grey blurs, occasional fingertips, and ghostly orbs followed. Then, two grey faces that they half recognised, with make-up smudged down their cheeks, hair wet with sweat and foam, jaws clenched and huge dark eyes. Their dresses hung limp and dirty in front of a grimy wall.

"Look at the state of us." Anna laughed, "I'm glad the rest didn't turn out."

"What a bloody waste of money, I thought we looked good that night as well."

"Let's not bother with a camera again, I preferred the glittery version I had in my mind."

"I know, that's gross, we look like empty-eyed zombies."

"It was good though, wasn't it?"

"Yeah, it was fucking brilliant." Claire laughed. "But...next time. Well, next time, it won't be the same without you."

"Aw come on. I'm not leaving you completely destitute, what about Scott?"

"Hmm, he's supposed to be coming over tomorrow night. Unless something better comes up, so I'm not counting on it."

"Why do we always end up with shit boyfriends?" Anna asked.

"Maybe because we pick from the bottom of the barrel? Really, if we don't want emotionally bereft alcoholics we shouldn't choose from the drunks holding themselves up on the bar."

"Where should we look? The library?"

"I don't know. Maybe it's a class thing? Can poor guys be good boyfriends? Maybe too much of their energy taken up worrying about money?"

"Of course they can! It's not about money." Anna replied.

"Think about it. If all they can do is scrimp and borrow for enough money to forget that they're poor for one night a week, that doesn't leave much room for romantic gestures or deep conversation, does it?"

Anna would usually step in at this point and defend their bad choices, but she was enjoying it too much.

"Why do we do it to ourselves eh? Why do we live for validation from someone with a fucking penis? I don't know if I even like Scott! For some reason, I keep hanging on for scraps of affection. Hoovering up all those little crumbs and trying to mould them into some sort of self-respect. Here I am, struggling to breathe in a bra like a medieval torture device, to make my tits look more appealing, with constant shaving rash, just in case, you know?" Anna nods, enjoying Clarie's rant, willing her to continue.

"And to be clear, The shaving is far more regular than the sex. And what does he do? Turns up when he has an itch to scratch and moans about how I make coffee."

"Yeah, he's never going to be husband material," Anna adds.

"I'm not looking for that, I just want some kind of spark. I want someone to find me interesting. Imagine being someone's muse? They find you so amazing they have to write a song about you, or a poem. Or paint a picture. I want to be someone's obsession, not just a source of fags and blow-jobs on a Thursday night."

"Why don't you tell him to get lost?"

"Na, I'll still get him round, I've nothing else to do. And, he might get better, you know how boys mature slower than girls. Maybe he'll catch up. Anyway, I'll soon be on my own. You won't be here to smoke my fags, so he will have to do."

"Well, when you come and visit me, you could be a Spanish guy's muse, get serenaded on a balcony or something? You will come won't you?"

"I told you, I will try. It's hard to get time off, plus I have to keep up with my rent, and my auntie needs me to babysit, I'd like to but, you know."

"I know, but I'm getting a job out there, I'll have money, so you won't need any. And I've got a flat, so stay with me, and I'll pay for everything."

"That was quick, so Davie actually came through for you?"

"Well, probably. I mean. He will."

"Wait. You still haven't spoken to him yet?"

"It's only been a few days, and I've not been to the pub to check for a message." Anna curled the edge of the sticker sealing the photo packet, avoiding eye contact. Claire folded her arms, saying nothing.

Anna continued, "Look, I'm not worried, in case you think I am. We've got a plan, he's doing his bit, and I'm doing mine."

"Ah, so, you do have a plan," Claire replied. "It's not as if you're jumping on a plane into the unknown, is it?"

"Oh shut up, it's exciting! At least I'm doing something! What's your plan? Work, sleep, repeat, then die?"

"I want a proper life. With food in the fridge, some nice things, ornaments, clean clothes, and a job that requires a briefcase."

"That's so boring! What happened to all the ideas you had when we were younger?"

"It was different then. When my mum was still around I wanted to get away, anything was better than that. I spent time dreaming of exciting futures to keep me going. But now I've got my peace, this house, with no eggshells to walk on. I can walk in any room and turn the lights on, I can bang cupboard doors, I can have a hot shower any time I like. This is my plan. I'm here now." She stood and picked up the video box, Anna could see her biting her lip, the colour changing in her friends face. She grasped for a way to make it right.

"I know, I'm sorry. I just got excited. I always thought it would be me and you jumping on that plane."

"I'll visit. And you can stay here when you come back for Christmas or whenever. Deal?"

"Deal," Anna smiled, "since that's sorted out, can you make my tea now? I'm starving."

Anna curled up in bed, happy from the time spent with Claire. She pulled her knees up and excavated the fluff from between her toes, promising herself a shower in the morning. As she settled into position, the little tinkle of recognition rung inside again, this time loud and clear. Anna remembered where she'd seen DI Jackson before.

More than a decade earlier, Anna
standing half her height, in a brown cotton
dress, yellow necktie, and bobble hat. Miss
Jackson, then in her early twenties, had been
the second in command at the Brownies:
Tawny Owl. It had been clear then she had
a fascination with crime and punishment.
Her appearance had echoed an owl. Both
sides of her hair were blow-dried out from
her head in large sideways quiffs, her style
fortified with so much hair-spray that white
fibrous dust would appear if the structure
was compromised. Big, brown watery eyes
darted around within the frames of heavy
eye bags. Half angry, half tearful all the
time. Her round head bobbed around on top
of a brown polo-neck, her talons were long
and unpainted. Anna only went for a few
weeks, but Tawny Owl had put her on litter
duty at the end of every meeting.

Her crimes varied, but the punishment
never did. Anything from forgetting to bring
a piece of string in her emergency kit, to
throwing toilet roll bombs on the bathroom
roof. They were all treated with the same

contempt. After singing in a circle, promising to help other people and do their duty to god, an announcement would be made that, once again, Anna had disgraced herself. A black bin bag was ripped from the roll and presented to her.

Occasionally any girls who had laughed or joined in were assigned bags too, but this usually resulted in more hilarity, so the job fell solely on Anna. There wasn't much litter, the odd yellow juicy fruit paper, or the crumbs from a stamped on biscuit. Apart from craft night, the night she remembered, on the run-up to Christmas, after a papermache and glitter detonation. Her crime this time had been crossing her fingers while promising to serve the Queen. This was apparently taken pretty seriously. Long after all the other little brownies and leaders had gone home, Anna was still crawling on her hands and bare knees. Forced to pick sticky newspaper scraps from between the floorboards with her fingernails. A splinter of pine from a rough-edged board lodged under her thumbnail. Her painful protest was ignored, the cleanup had to be completed, the punishment was fitting in Tawny Owl's eyes.

"You need to pull your socks up Missy, or you'll end up like your father if you carry on down this road."

That was the last time she went to Brownies. She'd ripped the pompom off the hat, and pulled every piece of wool out while walking home, leaving a trail of brown fluff along the frosty path.

Anna shivered and pulled the covers up over her nose. She wondered if she'd ever made it up the leader ranks, to the position of Brown Owl. She hoped not, as her last words played over again.

CHAPTER FIVE

Thursday

Anna

Thursday morning. The striped cover had crept off the duvet, engulfing Anna's right foot. The feather stuffing had clumped at the ends, leaving her covered only by empty yellowing cotton.

Today would be a good day to stay inside. To tidy up, sort her clothes out, and generally keep out of everyone's way. But it was sunny. And that was boring. And, there was one thing she really needed to do.

She didn't do it very often, not even Claire knew she did. It was her secret. She wasn't ashamed, she just couldn't say the words out loud. On the way down the stone

155

stairs, she pulled a strand of ivy from the wall; its dry little suckers came away easily. On the corner of the street, she leaned into a garden and snapped off two sprawling stems of sweet-peas, in pastel pinks. Another garden yielded a couple of elegant blue iris. On the next street, she stepped one leg over a wall, to grab a big peony in deep ruby red. She walked around the edge of the park's tidy border. There weren't many roses yet, so she tested those she could find for the best perfume. She settled on a yellow one, turning orange as the petals curled. She snapped the stem and used her thumbnail to coax it from the bush.

Walking under the stone archway, she saw her; the serene expression, outstretched arms, and giant white wings. The marble Angel guided her through the graveyard. Fourth row up, and sixth stone in. She crouched in the shadow of the giant statue, in front of the little granite stone to its right. She'd read the plain gold text plenty of times, each time was as hard as the first.

A rose thorn drew blood from her finger as she arranged the untidy bouquet into a fitting tribute to her Mum. Anna wanted to think about her. Deborah Rose Mcvay. It

156

didn't come easy. She sat cross-legged, ankles exposed to the grass, and she let time pass.

She put her together from the easiest pieces. Big feathery hair. Dark roots, yet so blond, it was white at the tips. A wrist full of bangles. Long strings of tiny glass beads, multicoloured, looping, knotted. Dr Martin boots, scuffed and wrinkled. Opium perfume.

The breeze brushed the green blades against her skin, provoking a shiver, a memory stirred.

She was thirteen, in the bad books, grounded and bored. Her Mum nipped out, to the shop maybe, and she'd run, as fast and as far away as she could. A freedom opportunist in a skirt and vest. Hours passed laying in the long grass, watching a ladybird, with the soft blades ticking her legs. With no demands or curfews on her time, she was free. That freedom she'd longed for forever, and still did. But, night came as it always does. Then she was far too free—bare skin to darkness.

Of course, her perception of reuniting

parents and runaways was based on American TV. She expected tears of joy, she'd be ungrounded, and perhaps even given a gift to prove how much she was missed and valued. She was looking forward to it while shivering and dirty from a night hiding in a barn. The long walk home was illuminated by her rosy vision of a bubble bath, cuddles, apple crumble and her smiling mother who would greet her with open arms and say "I'm just glad you are OK."

She was very disappointed. America. Always giving poor Scottish children unrealistic expectations. The reality was tears of anger, an extension of the original grounding, and a ban on using the phone.

Lesson learned - take many and suitable clothes when you run away. Even the softest of days turns into a sharp night.

Archie

He poured full-fat milk over his four Weetabix. As he sat down, the first ring came. He ignored it. He did not like soggy Weetabix, so he'd eat them first.

Ring ring.

He sprinkled sugar straight from the
bag. Another ring. He gritted his teeth and
tried to enjoy his breakfast.

A quiet spell allowed him to watch the
news, with his feet up on the coffee table.
To the left of the TV sat an abandoned fish
tank. No life apart from algae, the last fish
was flushed at Easter. He tried to
concentrate on the news, but the fish tank
kept drawing him back. He got up, holding
in his grumbling sound, and avoiding the
creaky board. He reached behind it and
retrieved a black tea tin. It was a little rusty,
with a gold and red Chinese garden pattern.
The funeral tin. He gave it a shake. Not the
rattle of change, or a rustle of notes, but the
clatter of something solid.

His father's electrolarynx, the artificial
voice box. He felt a little guilty, but more
reassured, it was still safe in its hiding place.
Around the time his uncle's visits
diminished completely, Archie had insisted
that it needed some essential maintenance.
He couldn't listen anymore. The self-pity of
the broken-hearted, broken-bodied old man
with the robot voice was unbearable. He

was going to send it for some specialist NHS treatment, a service, new batteries and a nice clean. It would be back in no time.

As his Dad's body diminished he'd stopped pointing towards the hole in his throat. All the pens and paper were hidden, and the occasional visiting nurses told that he didn't like using it in front of them. He was self-conscious of them hearing it, so best not to mention it. His only communication was the doorbell Archie had gaffer taped to the side of the bed.

There should have been enough money for his Dad's funeral in there. But it was empty. He'd spent it all on coke and drink. He'd given up his job at the factory to become the registered carer for his parents, so there was no room for luxuries. He was skint and having to sell pills to youngsters to get the money back.

He'd loved those days, dipping into the tin on the way out, snorting lines of coke in pub toilets, with a packed wallet, and a gang of friends hanging on every word. It had been the best remedy for his ailment, the sickness of missing his mother, and having to clean up after his father.

Those glory days were short-lived and

ended badly. He'd always had a reputation
for violence, from way back in school,
maintained only by threatening people
occasionally, a bit of verbal bullying and
intimidation now and again. Until new year.
He'd spent all his carers allowance. He'd
used all the housekeeping money. Then he'd
taken another half ounce of coke on credit
from the Dougherty's. He already owed
them, but he didn't want the party to end.
He wanted to keep it going and never go
home.

As people left, and others slept, with no
drugs or alcohol left, it hit him. There was
nothing left, not even enough to put coal in
his fire.

A young lad was leaving the party, after
making the most of the hospitality. He was
taking liberties. Archie saw the chance to get
some money back. He blanked out, only
remembering a screaming body and blood
on the floor.

On the second of January, while putting
his bloodstained Pepe jeans in for a boil
wash, he'd optimistically checked the
pockets for cash. That's when he found the
boy's earlobe. Between his thumb and
forefinger, he squeezed and rolled it around,

cracking the salty brown crust to reveal the pink jelly tissue inside. He'd popped it in the tin with his Dad's voice and vowed to make all the money back.

He knew dealing couldn't last long, and after the ear incident, he knew he was on the police watch list. He was never arrested, but even the woman in the bakers knew, so the police definitely would.

Davie King had worked the machine next to him. He was younger, bolder, and stupider than Archie. He was delighted to take up the offer of selling the pills for him. It was ideal for both of them. Archie was slowly paying back the Dougherty's, without spending too much time on the front line. There wasn't big money in it, but Davie was making a wage and living the champagne lifestyle he thought he deserved. For a while, it was good. Till Davie got spooked, perhaps he realised he wouldn't cope with the jail. Or maybe his old mother couldn't cope with the rumours around the church coffee morning. So now, he was left with that daft young lassie, with her head in the clouds, forced to trust her doing his business. He would never have got involved with her. She danced too much and didn't pay attention. But, she was out there, taking the risk, and it was short term.

Once he had the funeral money and his Dad in the ground, he would sell up everything else in the house and pay off his debt to the pikeys. The heavy threats had lightened after they heard about the ear episode, so it hadn't been for nothing. They no longer threatened his toes with a claw hammer, and they accepted his payment plan.

He was still in their pocket though, still doing their work. He was looking forward to escaping it. He wasn't top of their grievance hit-list, but his rating could go up at any time, they were an unpredictable lot. He looked forward to the day he'd be free of them.

Then what? He didn't know. He'd never been a planner; the future was intangible to him. His life had always been getting through the days and losing the weekends.

Ring ring.

Archie's nostrils flare. The lines on his head deepen. It really would be any day now. He needed that money. He had to keep his promise to his mother.

He tiptoed to his Dad's bedside, following the worn path on the mustard carpet. He peeled the edge of the tape securing the doorbell.

"Now Dad, I'm going to take these old batteries and get you some fresh new ones for this bell. Don't want them running out now, do we?" From the edge of his vision, he saw a reaction, a gnarly hand jutted towards him, his head was trying to pull off the pillow. This was more movement than he'd seen for weeks.

Archie retracted his hand quickly; there was more life left than he thought. He backed away, dusting the horrible feeling from himself by wiping his hands down his thighs. He didn't look back as he shut the bedroom door.

In the living room, he popped the batteries into the tin, alongside the dried out earlobe and his Dad's voice, and hid it back behind the fish tank.

Jackson

She was offered the unmarked car, but she didn't want it. She wanted to send chills up criminals spines, not sneak about letting them think they were free to break the law.

She'd parked with a view down the High Street to eat her lunch. There was no time to waste in the canteen listening to Jamie's opinions on the latest episode of Eastenders. She picked her way through a bag of peanuts, and then ate two Double Deckers. She didn't like food that took her attention. She wanted an easy hand to mouth action so she could keep her eyes on the streets. She needed to take it all in, learn as much as possible.

As far as she was concerned, there were only three categories of people in this town and she had to figure them all out.

A, those she didn't know, ordinary law-abiding people she had no reason to meet.

B, those she knew well and dealt with often.

C, those she knew of, hadn't met yet, and needed to deal with.

Wendy was a B. Those frequenting the street today were mainly A's, but they could be C's. She still had no evidence of the category C's coming onto the weekend drug scene.

Jackson used the sweet wrapper to dislodge a fragment of nut from between her molars while scanning the pavements. If Wendy didn't come to her soon, she'd go to her, put a bit of pressure on. She unscrewed the flask, placed the cup above the steering wheel, and carefully poured the steaming black coffee. She loved that flask, it was perfect for hiding her sugar consumption. Two was the socially acceptable limit, but she preferred five. In meetings, she'd endure the bitter dose, but out there in her car, with her flask, she was free to enjoy her syrupy fix. The first sip burnt her tongue. She was starting to feel agitated. She took another smaller sip and rested her head back to give herself a little reassurance. This was just her first week. She had time. Maybe this weekend would reveal something. For now, she'd observe it all. Nothing would pass her by.

Anna

Claire was delighted to see Anna waiting

for her.

"Thought I'd walk you home, to see you for a bit before Scott turns up. How work was today."

"Work was alright. I got to sort some files up on the first floor, so that's a step in the right direction. What have you been up to?"

"Erm, not much, killing time. Pretty boring, not seen anyone or anything…" She pulled back and searched for a quick way to change the subject.

"Oh, I like your coat. Is that new, I've not seen it before."

Claire wore a well-fitting beige mac. She looked bashful as her cheeks blushed.

"Thanks. You don't think I look like I'm trying to be someone I'm not?" She tied the little belt around her waist and carefully positioned the ends so they hung just right.

"Nope, you look exactly like the hard-working professional that you are." Anna reached over, rubbing the stitching of the coat collar between her finger and thumb. "Feels expensive." She smiled.

"I got it from my aunties catalogue. I'll be paying it up for a while."

Anna linked arms with her friend, and

they set off in the direction of Clarie's house.

Inside, Claire put her coat on a hanger and stored it inside the cupboard. Anna threw her denim jacket on the sofa and threw herself on top of it.

Claire poured two glasses of lime cordial and placed them on the black ash coffee table, she sipped and wiped the wet ring from the table with a tea towel, while Anna gulped and wiped her mouth with her arm.

"Remember before you got with Davie?" Claire asked.

"Yeah, of course. You were like my wife back then."

"I miss those days, you know. I feel like I hardly saw you for ages."

"Really? Thought you got sick of me hanging around all the time." Anna laughed.

"Well, you are very annoying and expensive to feed, but I did miss us hanging about together."

"Me too, and I'll miss it so much when I'm gone."

"Not reconsidering yet? You could stay here you know."

"Nope, definitely not reconsidered anything. I can't wait to get out of this place, and away from all the small-minded idiots in it."

"Yeah, yeah, so you keep saying. Just remember, this small mindeed idiot will always have a place for you to stay if you need it OK?"

Anna immediately felt guilty. "Thanks, I appreciate it. But hopefully, I won't need it."

"Hopefully? So you haven't heard anything yet?" Clarie's eyes narrowed with suspicion.

"Maybe, well, I might have a message, but I've not asked again."

"Why don't we go to the Nags Head right now, and ask Gemma if there's been any news from Davie? Let's get you something concrete to go on."

"Not tonight. I cant. I'm going to, when I'm ready. I want to give it enough time. I don't want her sneering at me again if he's not managed to." Anna looked down at the table, picked up her empty cigarette packet, and picked its bashed corner.

"Are you scared to ask?"

"No, course not. I trust him, he'll be doing what he can. I just can't be bothered with her judging me. She loves having something over me, ever since I got with Davie, she's been weird." She ripped the box into four pieces.

"You're not starting to doubt him?"

"No, no. It's not even been a week yet. Once all the money's sorted out, I'll get the address before I go." Each quarter was shredded into another four pieces. Claire tapped her fingers on the rim of her glass.

"So, you're not worried he's abandoned you?"

Anna arranged a pile of cardboard and silver paper snowflakes by her glass, and let out the tiniest hint of a shrug.

"He wouldn't do that. He's taking me away from here. I'm just waiting till the time's right."

Ronin

Some people get sentimental over the sound of rain on a caravan roof. Not Ronin. The sound of every drop beats out the soundtrack to his inadequacy. Each rock of the wind reminding him of his position in the family. Right at the bottom, in his tiny tin home, where he can reach the cooker from his bed.

The chemical toilet lies only feet from his head. The cubicle doubles as his wardrobe. His two shirts hang inside, one for work, one for funerals. An odd choice he knew, but he'd rather smell faintly of chemicals masking shit, than heavily of fried burgers.

He looked at the growing damp patch on the ceiling. He wasn't even the youngest brother; he shouldn't be in the worst van. Most rainy afternoons, when gardening work was off, he'd lie alone trying to think of ways to get respect. To somehow climb up the ranks. He'd ensured his place at the bottom years ago and never managed to get as much as a foothold on the first rung of the ladder ever since.

He ran his fingers along the underside of his jaw. Edged by rough stubble, his fingers found the smooth line of the scar.

On the surface, the family business was roofing, tarmac, and gardening. Behind the hard work and sweat-stained vests lay a web of money-making strands. Each branch of the family had their speciality; his father and his oldest brothers made big money with generators and vehicles.

Stolen clothes and fake spirits were the territories of his middle brother and uncle, both called James.

He'd heard word of cousins with drugs and cheap tobacco, but he wasn't trusted to know anything about that.

His mother's brother's side dealt with horses and racing. He was denied involvement in any of it. He felt a wave of sadness, and his stomach knotted at the memory of hanging around the horse boxes.

He'd spent hours stroking their velvety noses, basking in their earthy breath. They'd enjoyed his company more than anyone else.

He'd never meant to kill that foal. He wasn't to know those flowers were poison. For those few glorious summer days, back when he was a boy, he'd made a best friend. He'd found bright yellow ragwort down by the river. He'd brought it back as a secret treat for Abel, he only wanted the horse to like him the best.

First was the punishment, then the shunning. Never far enough for him to go it alone, instead he was kept on the boundary. Never included, but still controlled and desperate for acceptance.

This was his chance. Double his money, get his very own horse, and win the woman.

Tina and Maria hadn't been in for their secret smoke yet. He peeled back the little Velcro strip on the orange curtain and scoped the path as far as he could. He decided rather than have them come in and wind him up, he'd deter them with cooking smells. As the pan heated on the single gas ring, he separated the pink sludge of defrosted meat. It stuck to his fingers as the circles tore into ragged ovals. He did his best to reshape them and chucked them in the pan. They smelt sour, as they always did by the end of the week, but burnt enough, they'd taste fine. The pink turned brown, the pan hissed and spat as he peeled the Velcro back again. The path was clear, and the van was filled with enough burger smoke to put the girls off coming in.

He opened the little door and reached into the chemical toilet. He separated the white seat from the blue base with one hand and released the plastic bag from inside.

He kept out a tenner each for the girls and put the rest of his wages inside. He held it up and calculated there would be over three grand by now. He'd never learned to

read or write, but he could count. He never
spent much money, and he'd been saving
since his first meagre pay. His weekly
budget for burgers and rolls was less than a
fiver. He swapped gas canisters with other
vans while no one was looking. He didn't
eat out, buy clothes, or smoke or drink, he
just put all his money in that sandwich bag
and hid it in there. No one knew he had it,
and they couldn't find out. His brothers
would take it if they knew. That's how his
family worked: take what you want and step
on anyone to get it.

He was over halfway there, and now he
knew exactly how to double it.

He was still on his knees beside the toilet
when the door opened to a chorus of
coughing and swearing. He threw the bag in
the toilet and slammed the lid down.

"What the hell are you doing down
there?" Tina coughed and waved her hand
in front of her face.

"Are you trying to set your van on fire?"
Maria fanned the door open and closed.

"Open the bloody windows it's stinking
in here!" Tina gagged and coughed. Maria
grabbed the handle of the hot spitting
burger pan and threw it outside. The wet

green grass sizzled and singed, as smoke rose from the cremated meat.

"No fucking wonder you get trusted with nothing! You're sat on the floor while your tea's turning black on the stove." Maria's eyes watered as she continued to cough, she stumbled out and pulled Tina's arm, "Come on, he's a bloody idiot, let's go."

Ronin sat on the step of his caravan, elbows on knees, head in hands, watching his aunties lurcher turn its nose up at the burnt meat. He went inside, and psyched himself up to recover the cash from the blue-bleach-shit-soup inside.

CHAPTER SIX
Friday

Anna

As the kettle boiled, she poured the dregs of the last cup down the drain. She optimistically opened the cutlery drawer, tutted at the lack of spoons, and peered into the sink. She didn't fancy putting her hand in there, so she opened the drawer again and selected a rusty whisk from the back. I did a great job of mixing in the milk and scooping out the teabag. Innovative, she smiled.

She sipped the tea sitting on the sofa, with Richard and Judy's comforting presence in the background. She had options and decisions to make. She could go out tonight, a less busy night in the pubs, and make a start, then sell the rest tomorrow. Or, she could do it in style tomorrow, and hopefully, sell the whole lot in a few hours.

Claire wouldn't do both nights, so she'd have to walk into the bar herself, she wasn't keen. There was more chance of getting rid of them all over both nights. But, it was twice the risk.

Twice the risk of bumping into sleazy Shaun.

Twice the chance of the pikey finding out she had lied.

Twice the possibility of getting busted by the police.

She couldn't argue; it had to be a one night only job. She relaxed into the battered chair, comfortable with her decision.

She looked around the room. She was looking for clues to her having lived there. This had been her home for more than half a year, but apart from the stained cup in her hands, she couldn't find even a small indication of her presence. She felt invisible.

She liked bright colours, little boxes, textured fabrics, candles, incense, and hanging strings of bells. There was nothing like that here: just a brown three-piece suite,

177

a pine coffee table and TV unit, and grey nicotine stained curtains. No expression of her personality throughout the entire place she'd called home.

Is this who Davie thought she was? Plain, a bit tatty, and with nothing to say? She couldn't be sure.

She'd liked him because it was easy, he didn't ask any questions. He wasn't interested in her past or her future. Old boyfriends had tried to dig; Are you going to college? What do you want to do with your life? How did you end up here? Where is your dad?

Apart from escaping to Ibiza, they'd never discussed anything further than the weekend. It went both ways though, she had no idea what his dreams were, no hints of his deepest fears. Had he slept with the light on as a boy? Did he dream of speedboats and Ferrari's? Or a country cottage on the banks of a loch and fishing his retirement away? No idea.

He had no idea that she'd spent her life obsessed with running away. He was unaware her excitement about Ibiza was, not the prospect of going with him, but to finally get away from there successfully.

He was the propellant, keeping the momentum going, so she needed him. This was the most tangible plan she'd ever had for getting away, and he was the vehicle.

Bazz

He always walked with his head down. Partly due to lacking confidence, but mostly because he was scanning the path for dropped coins. He had found loads over the years, some silver, lots of lucky pounds, occasionally a miracle fiver, but mostly coppers. They all added up though.

He'd found thirty-two pence this morning. He ran through his brain to think where he could get the most for his money. The Post Office had the cheapest crisps in town, and he could make the change up with flumps. They were pretty filling.

While standing in the queue, he began to dream about Wendy. His eyes glazed as he thought about the way she smoked her roll-ups. She held them between her thumb and forefinger, but inside her hand, like she was sheltering it from the rain. She was so stylish.

He was brutally wrenched from his

heart-shaped, smoke-filled fantasy, by a hard elbow in the ribs and a laugh that filled him with fear.

"Alright wee man, long time no see." Shaun was twice his size, twice his age, and twice as loud. A tiny suggestion of hope rose in Bazz's belly, still wary, he took a step back out of elbows reach.

"Er, I'm OK. Thanks for asking. I'm fine. Quite good even." His throat tightened, and the words crackled and squeaked on the way out.

"Still a scumbag freak, I see." Shaun bellowed with a forced laugh. This drew the attention of the people queuing in front, Bazz was mortified. His face burned, and tears threatened to roll. His teeth ground together. He looked around for back up but saw only disapproving faces. He clenched his fists by his side and marched towards the door.

"See you later freako!" Shaun shouted louder than before. Bazz could hear his horrible laugh all the way down the street.

Anna

The smell of lentil soup drifted from

Christine's open kitchen window, as it did
every Friday. She opened the back door,
and welcomed Anna in,

"Hungry?"

"I didn't come to get fed, you know. I just
wanted to see you before I go."

"You'll have some soup though?"

"OK, if it's going spare, I suppose."
Anna's mouth watered through her
disinterest. They sat on opposite stools, over
a plastic granite breakfast bar. As Anna
watched the soup rise up the soft bread, she
considered telling Christine about her
experience in Shaun's car. She'd test the
water first. Maybe she'd invited it; she had
got in the car after all.

"How long have you been friends with
that Shaun guy?"

"Long enough. Why?"

"I'm just wondering, since you left me in
his house the other night. You must think
he's alright."

"I didn't leave you, I came straight back
up, and he said you'd just left. He's harmless
enough when you know how to take him.
Anyway, I thought he might be able to help
you out of your financial predicament."

"He did offer me a loan, but I don't need

it. I don't want another person on my back."
Anna decided to keep the story to herself.
The only thing to do was stay out of his way
for the next couple of days. She ate the soup
slowly, hoping for the conversation to move
onto anything but her.

"You're awffy quiet today, what's up?"
Christine asked.

"Me? I'm fine. I'm totally fine." Anna
replied.

"You having second thoughts about
Davie?"

"No. Not at all. I cant wait to see him."

Christine put her spoon down, rested her
elbows, and laced her fingers together
beneath her chin. Anna prepared for a
grilling; there would be some price to pay
for this hot meal.

"I know what it's like you know, how you
feel right now. Everything you thought you
could count on, all gone. I've been there."

"It's not gone, it's just been delayed, that's
all."

"When you've been with someone, you've
got shared plans, ideas, and visions of your
glorious future together. Then it all falls
apart. The pain's not only from missing
them. Its grief. Grief for the life yet to unfold

that's already been lost."

Anna struggled to swallow the last soggy carrot, a lump of sadness was blocking her throat. She left the spoon in the bowl and wiped her mouth with her cuff.

"He's stolen your plans. He's crumpled up your future, not giving a single fuck." Christine used two hands to squash and roll up some air into an invisible ball.

"Everything you were counting on, working towards, it's gone. It's like part of you's dead."

"Don't be so dramatic. Nothing's dead, it's going to be fine. You don't know Davie at all. You don't know he's like when it's just us."

"I don't need to. I can see exactly what kind of man he is."

"I'm not listening to this. You're so bloody cynical."

"I'm realistic, not cynical. You've got your head in the clouds as usual! By the time you're my age, you'll be the same."

"Not all men are bad. There are plenty of good guys out there. Maybe you were just unlucky."

"You'll see. You'll wake up to Davie King's bullshit and move on sooner or later."

Anna took a cigarette from Christine's packet to see her through to the end of the lecture.

"Sure, you will meet someone else, make new plans, even shinier ones than these. But soon enough, they'll get crushed and kicked to the side too. Again and again, man after man, till all your possible futures are in the stinking gutter. And you're alone. That's me. I made plans, with men. But none of them happened, they were all cut short before I could get a foothold. I never made it out of this place. I always got dragged back here when the shit hit the fan."

"But you're OK, aren't you? Your life's not that bad." Anna's trademark rosy tint was doing nothing here. Christine ignored her sentiment.

"Every time you put yourself back together, there's a wee bit missing." Christine held up another invisible idea, between her thumb and forefinger, as if she was examining it.

"The part of you that was imagining hold hands sixty years down the road, it's gone, left behind." She blew into the space, dispersing the magic particle into oblivion. "You know what I mean? Those situations you create, with whoever you're writing your future with, once you're finished, you don't get those bits back. They're gone. Another chip off your heart until eventually, you don't bother, because you don't have it in you."

In the time it took Christine to get it all out, Anna had swallowed her sadness back down and resolved to lift the mood.

"I'm going to miss this. Your delicious soup and salty lectures are my favourite."

Christine laughed, breaking her bitter trance.

"You're still going to do it then. Trust a man that's already left you, and run away on a promise?"

"Yep. Its all I've got." Anna smiled from her eyes, beaming sincerity.

"You're off your head. Your entire life, it's like you're having a fucking picnic on the train tracks!"

Tina and Maria

On the wall next to Roy's Spar, Maria lined up the coins in her hand in order of size. Tina's were sorted into ascending value, a task that wasted some of the time it took waiting for a bite.

They were fishing for a favour, someone to buy them alcohol. On a weekday, with no makeup or padded bra, there was no way they'd get served. They always started early as competition would be too fierce on Saturday to find someone stupid enough to help a couple of under-agers get drunk.

They knew what they were looking for — target: Male, alone, and a little bit sad looking, preferably chubby. Women, mothers, grannies; never.

"What about him?" Maria nodded towards a grey-haired man shuffling towards them.

"Too old, he's probably got granddaughters." They smiled, and he gave a little gentlemanly nod as he passed.

Then they spotted him simultaneously, the perfect catch. Agreeing with only their eyes, Maria cast their line out.

"Hey, pal!"

"Do I know you?" Archie sucked in his gut, puffing his chest up under his blue football top. The pair got up and stood close together in his path.

"Oh, sorry! I'm so embarrassed! I

thought you were someone else." Maria put her hand over her mouth. Archie deflated.

"He might still be able to help us," Tina added.

"Oh, he looks too busy to bother with us. Sorry pal, on you go." Maria broke away, clearing his route, both girls smiling and fighting for his eye contact. He looked from girl to girl, his spine straightening.

"I've got five minutes, what is it you ladies need?"

The girls closed the gap. Maria took his hand and opened it, palm to the sky. Archie warmed at the physical touch, his mind raced. He had no idea what these girls were going to do, but he was happy in this rare moment between two sets of sparkling eyes. They were both touching him now. Something stirred in his stomach, a smile electrified his face. Tina and Maria filled his hand with their coins, keeping unbroken smiles and holding his gaze.

"Get us a bottle of vodka from the shop pal," Maria said, in a husky voice.

Archie caught the overspill of coins with the other hand, like he was winning at the slot machine. He poured them all into his front pockets. With one girl's hand on each

shoulder, he nodded. They sat back on the
wall, watching their defenceless prey doing
exactly what they wanted. He returned
minutes later, handing over a carrier bag.

"Where are you girls going with this?
Having a celebration?"

A car pulled up behind Archie. Maria
quickly lowered the bag down behind the
wall; her expression changed. Archie turned
to see who had ruined his party. James
Dougherty slammed the car door behind
him, waking up the sleeping dog on the
back seat, sending it into a snarling frenzy
against the glass. He slapped a hard hand
down on Archie, asserting the pecking order
instantly.

"Why would you be sniffing about my
wee cousins here? I hope they aren't asking
you to buy them alcohol?"

"Don't be daft uncle James." Tina looked
nervous.

"That kind of disrespect is not tolerated.
You wouldn't do that now, would you
Archie?" Another giant slap stung that point
home. "You two girls get in the car. I'll take
you up the road." They didn't argue. They
knew there was too much at risk for all
concerned for Archie to grass on them. They

got in and calmed the dog down.

"You don't mess about with those lassies, you understand?" James' brick-like forehead loomed over Archie's red face.

"Of course not, you have my word."

"Your word's not worth much, is it now? You still owe me. And I'll tell you what; I'm getting mighty bored waiting."

"I've been keeping up the payments. I've never missed one." Archie wished he'd never left the house today.

"Next week, make it double. You sniff about Tina and Maria; you pay the price."

"I wasn't. I was just…" Archie stopped, he knew that look. The darkness below the ledge of his forehead, the curl of his top lip. He'd made this mistake before, he recalled as he ran his tongue over his broken front tooth.

"Double it is then."

The men shook hands on their new deal. James gave one last shoulder slap to seal the contract, then swaggered into the shop with that odd dip in the hip that the entire family had.

As Archie walked away, he felt the girl's eyes on him again. So self-conscious and full to the brim with shame and rage, he forbid himself from looking back at them. Each step on the pavement felt like a mile in the desert, dragging himself through hot sand towards the corner, desperately seeking shade from their burning eyes.

All Tina and Maria could think about was how they'd get that bottle of vodka back.

Anna

Claire arrived home to find Anna scratching a smiley face on her path with a stone.

"Thought I'd come and see you for a bit. Get the kettle on." Anna put out a hand, and Claire pulled her up. Inside Claire regaled some office dramas, while Anna watched her own words carefully, avoiding everything on the list. They laughed and chatted and sat in comfortable silences.

"So, you're definitely coming out tomorrow?" Anna asked.

"Yeah, I suppose so, but I'm not taking anything."

"I've heard that one before."

"I'm serious, you know why? Because I've had enough of the fear." Claire said.

"The fear of what?" Anna tilted her head, confused.

"You know, waking up, stomach in knots, wondering if you've done something terrible. Or worse, remembering that you definitely did."

"Ah, the guilty sweats." Anna laughed.

"I can't figure out if it's worth it. Trying to crawl out of my own skin the day after. Is that a reasonable price for an easily forgotten laugh? Sometimes at work, I get a horrible twinge of shame from the weekend. When I remember something I was talking about, some mundane shit that I thought was the best thing ever." Claire wrinkled her nose up, like a piglet, shaking her head. "Honestly, it puts me off my work, thinking of the fuss I made about how much I love, love, love The Beetles, or people who wear odd socks, or nineteen fifties hairdos."

Anna laughs; she knows the feeling well. Claire sits forward, and she places both hands on the table. "And you know what? I don't give a single shit about any of it. It means nothing to me. I just say whatever resonates at the time."

Anna shrugs. "We all do, it's just the chat. Getting on the same wavelength, human connection, that's the best bit."

"No, not for me. It feels so fake. It is all fake. It doesn't feel it at the time, but after." Claire shudders.

"That's why we do it, to escape the crappy truth for a bit."

"It's like there's another person in me, dormant. More interesting. With quirks to suit whoever shes talking shit to at the time."

"Well, I love it. I love being interested, and interesting. I love the conversations with your next soul mate about the random thing you've got in common."

"And you don't cringe, remembering the nonsense you said?"

"Na, its all fun." Anna shrugged.

"I heard you talking to a coke-head last week about considering Buddhism as a new life-path."

"Yeah. Well, maybe I am." Anna felt her neck getting hot.

"See, you're cringing." Claire laughed.

"Look, all I'm saying is don't let it stress you out. Everyone gets wrecked to feel different, get out of our boring lives, who cares if we talk shit?"

Jackson

This time she took the unmarked car. She also took the risk of assigning Jamie as her partner.

"Can I put the radio on? This is boring." He asked.

"No. I need to concentrate, and I don't want to draw any attention to us."

Jamie laughed, "Wait, do you think you're undercover?"

Jackson was wearing a plain white shirt and navy blazer. She looked down and realised she didn't look quite as casual as she had imagined.

"Just shut up, and cover your side of the street." She snapped.

Jamie sighed. "So, any idea who exactly we are looking for?"

"Shh, concentrate." Jackson regretted taking him away from his desk. "We are gathering information right now. This is the start of a bigger operation. We watch. We take it all in."

"Should we be taking notes?" Jamie stared glassy-eyed at the empty High Street.

"Very funny. Look, our aim here is to observe, see who's talking to who, watch for anyone that's getting unusual attention.

That's how we narrow it down." Jackson explained slowly. Jamie sighed, a long, dramatic sigh. He pulled down the sun visor and checked his spiky fringe.

"I hope nothing kicks off tonight. I don't want to put my hat on."

Jackson adjusted the rear-view to make sure she could see the bridge near the post office.

"Tell me something," he continued, "did you always want to be a police officer?"

Jackson was warmed at his interest, "Yes. As long as I can remember, I think when I was around…"

Jamie interrupts, "Did you think it would be as boring as this?" he punctuated with another sigh.

"For the love of God, will you please stop asking ridiculous questions!" she snapped. He folded his arms and looked out of the side window, as the tension grew, she vowed never to take him out again.

They had been there for two hours, and only the post-work drinkers were moving between the pubs. A couple emerged from the Italian restaurant, arm in arm, giggling as they passed the silver Vauxhall.

They observed in silence as a hen party of

10 women, decorated with feather boas, made a fuss around the central brunette with an 'L' plate pinned to her dress.

All type A's in Jackson's book, not out to cause any bother, and she had no reason to cross paths with them. Once they disappeared into the next pub, Jamie announced;

"You do know that no one goes out at this time? It's silly sitting here."

She didn't reply, but she conceded he was correct.

"So, Could we go and get chips instead? I'm starving." Jamie asked.

"Give me strength!" She hissed as she started the car and pulled out in the direction of Cadoras. "Anything to shut you up."

CHAPTER SEVEN

Saturday

Anna

Before she opened her eyes, or her body stirred, Anna's mind jump-started. It was Saturday. She'd stayed under the radar last night, leaving Claire's early and making no detours. She'd saved it all for tonight.

She had never been a particularly nervous person, but she recognised these feelings in her stomach and tried to convince them away.

She'd soon be sitting at the airport, with enough money to finally get out of this place. Finally, she'd get away from the small town mentality and constant reminders of her losses. She was going somewhere no one knew her, and no one wanted anything from her. Best of all, no one telling her what to do.

She rolled onto her back, kicked the covers off, and let the morning light illuminate her naked body. With her arms behind her head, she stretched out as long as she could, imagining herself on a hammock strung between palm trees.

Her nerves transformed into excitement. Tomorrow morning she'd go see Gemma at the pub and pick up Davie's message. The address would be waiting there by now. It was almost a week. She had been avoiding Gemma's interrogation, just in case he hadn't called. He would definitely have left the message, so she would get in the morning.

It was only hours away now, so she made a new list;

1- Pack bag

2- Tidy flat a bit

3- Decide what to wear tonight

4- Stop drinking

5- Sell all the pills

6- Pay Archie

7- Figure out getting to the airport

She had never had this much to do. So many things needed put in place before leaving. She had to get on it straight away, there would be plenty of time to lie around when she got there.

After emptying the rucksack in search of clean pants, the floor was strewn with crumpled clothes. She decided to relegate number 1 on the list to later on.

She would tidy up later as well, so number 2 could wait.

Maybe Claire would lend her a top for tonight. That was a good idea, saved washing anything. She crossed 3 off the list.

She reconsidered number 4. She wasn't taking any drugs tonight, but she would need something to get her through. 'Stop drinking' was once again relegated to some time in the future.

The rest were out of reach right now, so she crossed them off.

She smiled at her efficiency at getting through the list, pulled on the same jeans, chucked a bit of minty chewing gum in her mouth, and headed for the door.

Standing quietly, she listened for anyone approaching. She peeled back the gum and peered down the stairs, all clear.

A few hours later, while flapping away a cloud of extra firm hair spray, Claire poured another lukewarm vodka into a chipped mug. She topped it up with cola.

"We should have got ready at mine, I've got ice." She said, leaning over the edge of the bed. She ejected and turned the mix-tape in one well-rehearsed action. "And a CD player."

The tapes title read Take That, but Radio 1 Dance Anthems were recorded over it repeatedly. The little square holes were stuffed with cotton wool and taped over. The tunes were sometimes fuzzy, stretched in parts, deformed through religious use.

"You can keep that tape, you can listen to it while imagining me by the pool getting a tan," Anna said.

"Wow, thanks, your prize possession. So, what about this place, the furniture and stuff?" Claire asked.

"The notice was handed in when his Mum bought his ticket. It's all in Davie's name. We were supposed to post the keys back through when we left."

"So, you shouldn't even be in here now?"

"Suppose not," Anna shrugged, "I was kinda hoping the landlord wouldn't turn up yet."

"This just gets worse." Claire lit a cigarette and spoke with it between her lips.

"I'm not bothered, it's nothing to do with me. The place came furnished, all I've got is that pile of clothes, and I'm leaving tomorrow, so I'll go if he appears."

Claire raised both eyebrows and gestured the vodka in her direction.

"Just a small one for me, I've got to keep it together. I'm a businesswoman tonight." Anna held an orange plastic beaker with a sophisticated outstretched pinky. Right now, I owe Archie seventeen hundred quid. There's enough here to sort him out, and get the cheapest flight to Ibiza. I'll just go to the airport and wait. I don't care if I end up sleeping there for days till a cheap seat comes up, I'm out of here!"

Anna could see anger simmering as Claire

rubbed her eyeliner off for the third time.

"Why can I never get it right the first time? This is just getting worse the harder I try."

"That's why I go for a smoky eye," Anna laughed, using her finger to smudge the Kohl pencil. "I know it looks like I haven't taken yesterdays off, but I can't be bothered with all that."

Once they were both happy with their makeup, the need for precision blurred by three house measures of vodka, they got changed. Anna wore a top she borrowed. She pulled up the belt loops on her low rise jeans and wished high waists would make a comeback. She looked in awe at Clarie's perfectly ironed black trousers, pretty purple lace top, and matching eye shadow.

Claire poured another drink and asked,

"What kind of friends are we?"

"Eh? Best, obviously."

"I mean, is it by choice? Do we compliment each other? Or is it more like the last two losers on the gym bench, kind of thing?"

"It's a choice. I chose you years ago. And well, you kind of let me keep you." Anna replied.

Claire tapped her cigarette on the edge of the ashtray and used the burning point to build a tiny bonfire of ash in the centre.

"So, why is it so easy to leave me?"

"It's not. You are the best thing in my life. Leaving you is the hardest part. That's why I've asked you a million times to come with me."

"Is this it then? Our last night."

"For now, for this chapter. There will be loads more. We still have years worth of peeing in the same cubicle, eating squashed chips in taxi ranks, and mine-sweeping drinks at the end of the night."

"I guess so, just not for a while. Maybe I'll have totally grown out of this phase by then."

"We'll just be another phase, that's all. Maybe we'll be into fancy wine instead of vodka. Remember that time we spent seven pounds on a posh bottle of wine."

"That's never going to happen again; it was disgusting. Give me Lambrini any day."

Their exit routine was always the same.

First, the front inspection, followed by a twist to view the back. An all-encompassing swirl of hair spray, enough to create a mini-ecosystem of safety from frizz for a few hours. Then finally, a couple of sprays of CKone to the wrists and neck. Ready.

The only thing left to do was pick up the pills from their outdoor storage. At the bottom of the stone staircase, Anna crouched next to the coal bunker. She peered past the pieces of black rubble lying around the sliding hatch. She tentatively probed her hand into the damp darkness, hesitating as she pictured the giant spider's fangs. She held her breath and braved going deeper. After fumbling around in the black hole, she finally presented the silver treasure box.

"Why are they wrapped in tinfoil?" Claire looked scared.

"I didn't have any cling-film, I ripped the wee bag at the top, it didn't seal properly, so I just... what?" She couldn't comprehend Clarie's expression, so she started unwrapping the foil. She wiped the black dust from her fingers onto her thighs and opened the parcel between them. With foreheads almost touching, they looked at the contents. The short white cylinders stored there in good faith yesterday had morphed into a soggy, lumpy, damp paste.

"Fuck." A fizz of realisation sunk through Anna's legs. She sat on the second step putting her head between her knees. Claire took the third step, lit two cigarettes, and handed one down to Anna's shaking hand.

"Condensation," she offered.

"Fuck. I can't believe this. What am I going to do?" Anna's face was white, her body trembled as she tried to put the cigarette to her mouth.

"Tell Archie what happened, that you've mucked up, and you want out."

"No way." Anna took two hard sucks on her cigarette.

"Tell him to take it up with Davie."

"I cant. I'm not…"

"Get a loan then, borrow some money to pay him off, and keep away from the whole thing."

"I'm not spending my life here. I have to… wait! Maybe..." she squashed the burning end underfoot. "Can you please lend me forty quid?" Her hands met under her nose in prayer.

"Forty, that's not going to put much of a

dent in it, is it?"

"Come on. I've got it! Come and help me."
She placed the foil like a precious relic
inside her bag and offered a hand out to
Claire. She shook her head but accepted her
hand, and was pulled up from the step and
into the plan.

A walk across town and fourteen boxes of
cheap painkillers later, they stood admiring
their criminal genius.

Rows and rows of double-ended,
coloured capsules. Red, yellow, green, blue,
and white, in every combination. The mush
of 200 had somehow thinned out to fill even
more. In the centre of the table, a snowy
heap of discarded powder, surrounded by
empty boxes. Popped strips of paracetamol
and cold and flu tablets littered the floor.
The air tasted of chemicals. Anna licked her
lips and remembered being forced to
swallow yellow medicine as a child. The
front of Clarie's trousers had a dusty white
line where the table met her thighs.

Split into piles of fifty, plus a bonus

twenty-four, Anna wrapped them in the newly bought cling-film. Much bulkier than their original format, but far more interesting. As Anna tucked the parcels away in pockets and bra cups, Claire swept the debris into a carrier bag.

Buying the materials had been easier than Anna had anticipated. She'd got a little worried when restricted to two boxes each in the supermarket, but the other ten boxes came easily from Roy's Spar. He was the kind of retailer who turned the fridges off overnight to save electricity. It was a gamble buying milk from there; it was a 60/40 chance your semi-skimmed would come out in lumps. The shelves were full of things that were 'part of a multi-pack' and 'not to be sold separately,' so it wasn't too surprising that he was happy to help what looked like a teenager's suicide pact, if it made him a small profit.

It was nearly 10 pm, the atmosphere in the club would be warming up, everyone would be looking for Davie, and she'd be there to help them out.

"Well done Anna. I can't believe you saved this."

"You saved me more like. It was your

money that bought them." She stood still, looking at her friend's face, for longer than usual, past the glittery violet makeup, deep into her eyes. "I really appreciate it. Every single time you help me out."

Claire looked away first as her eyes welled up,

"It took me four attempts to get this eyeliner even, please don't make me smudge it now! Come on, let's do this! Get rid of them all, and get rid of that bloody Archie, before he does something you regret," she fanned her eyes with both hands.

As Anna surveyed the crowd on her way to the bar, a few people were waiting to catch her eye, eager for her nod. They were Davie's regulars, and they were looking for him, but tonight she had something better in store.

Claire ordered them both a long vodka. An elbow came in from the side as she sucked the first bubbly mouthful. Next to her stood a tall blond woman, with short hair and big gold earing's, she spoke from the corner of her mouth.

"Is your Davie about tonight?" She looked like a ventriloquist who'd lost their dummy.

"He's not, but I might be able to help you."

"Any eccies like?" She sounded like the tin man before he got his mouth oiled. Her theatrical discretion made Anna giggle, she nodded and pointed towards the toilet door.

Walking past everyone, letting them know that she was in business, felt good. Everyone was happy, they'd get an escape from reality for the night, and together they'd help her escape reality for good.

She smiled to herself as she shut the cubicle door, the kind of smile that makes your cheeks fizzy. She pulled one of the parcels out of her bra, as she peeled back the clingfilm the heat drained from her face. This was not what she expected to see. The damp salvaged contents had started to dissolve the plastic capsules. The sticky heat from their intimate storage place had melted them together. Locking the door, she wobbled on jelly legs, her heart cracking on her ribs.

"What the fuck?" She whispered to herself.

What now? They were ruined. She prodded her finger into the coloured goo.

Should she chuck them down the toilet and admit defeat? Or she could bite a chunk off and chew her way to oblivion? She was in real trouble now. She slid down to crouch as the blood whooshing through her ears distorted her hearing. The chatter at the sink faded as the acid in her stomach rose. Her mouth watered a sharp warning, she leaned over the toilet and threw up everything she had.

Staying there in debt to Archie was not an option. Neither was running away with no money. She used the inside of her denim jacket to dab away the water from her eyes. She spat hard into the bowl to get rid of the remnants of sick. Her stomach was empty, and she was very, very sober.

She stood up. She dragged air into the bottom of her lungs and remembered a name she'd been called, plenty of times, by lots of people. 'Hard-necked.'

She'd never been sure exactly what it meant, but she knew what she was about to do would absolutely be in 'hard-necked' territory.

She felt around in her bag and pulled out a packet of green Rizzla rolling papers. Pinching a bit out of the strange abstract blob, she wrapped it in a skin. With a handful made, she was ready to go and meet them at the edge of the dance floor.

The ventriloquist and her friends were waiting outside the toilet door. They gathered round, creating a tight circle. Inside it, Anna presented the sticky paper balls on her palm.

"You are in luck tonight. This is the strongest stuff that's ever been made, totally pure."

"What the fuck is this?" A sharp-faced woman with fake dreadlocks squeezed the rubbery little parcel and gave it a sniff. Her eyebrows raised as the chemical whiff entered her nostrils.

"Honestly, ladies, if you're not up there dancing all night on this, I'll give you the money back." Anna played sincere and experienced without wavering. The circle conferred through expressions and whispers, culminating in subtle nods all around.

Most people were easy to convince. Some were suspicious, but the idea of something more exotic than the usual tempted them in the end. As the evening progressed, Anna elaborated her story.

Adding that they came from Liverpool, and the chemical formula was unique. She enjoyed adding the extra details to make it more realistic.

Claire nudged Anna, pointing out one of Davie's old friends had spotted her across the dance floor. Instead of circumnavigating the crowd, he tried to dodge dancers while heading straight for her. What started off as cool and unshakable, ended up with sore, stamped on toes, and him apologising to four people on the way. He was flustered and obviously regretful about the route he chose when he got to her.

"Alright doll, how's the big man getting on in Ibiza?"

"Aye, good, spoke to him today, he says it's great." This lie was rolling off her tongue now.

"I'm looking for some pills, I hear you're the person to ask."

Anna cupped his ear, explained that he was about to try something quite different. She took his money and watched his face as he examined the little parcel with a squeeze and a sniff.

"I used to take these years ago, long before your time, doll." He said.

"Really? That's so cool." Anna smiled as sweetly as she could while depositing his notes with the rest in her bag.

She had never stayed sober inside a club, and she'd certainly never stayed straight with drugs in her pocket. This was a new experience. The idea of being left out of the fun had always scared her. She'd imagined standing cold, with crossed arms, under a grey cloud in the corner, while everyone else bathed in rosy laughter, music, and rainbows.

She was enjoying this against her judgment. She was acutely aware of everything. Making her way between the bar stool and toilet door, she could see everyone. She recognised clues in body language across the room. She knew who would be approaching for more and who was approaching their limit.

As people came up, Anna and Claire studied their faces. The way their breathing changed, the extension of their jaws, the glimpses of more white around their rolling eyes.

Anna nodded towards the ventriloquist and her pals; they looked like entirely different people now,

"What a state to get in!"

"Take a look around," Claire said, "what's everyone got in common?"

"They're all having fun?"

"Yeah, but why? Why do we spend all our money on drink and drugs?"

"Because it is fun?" Anna replied.

"Look closer, during the week, not one person here is happy with their lives. We are all fucked up, lonely and poor. Getting wrecked at the weekend is all we've got."

"Claire, this is supposed to be a happy night, get another drink ordered."

"I used to think all the people clubbing and hanging out in bars were really living, but they're not. They're hiding from life."

"I'll order you one then. In fact, I'll get you a double."

"It's why my mum drank herself into oblivion, it's why your dad fucked off. We are all fucked."

"Jesus Christ Claire, you're so pessimistic. I was kind of looking forward to the rest of my life, but you're really putting a dampener on it," Anna laughed.

"Sorry, I'm just starting to see this all differently now. I'm probably just down because you're going."

"There's still time for you to come with me."

Claire shook her head and ordered another drink.

The club was thinning out, but Anna wasn't finished, she still had too many left. They needed to find a party. She asked a skinny guy at the bar.

"Any parties happening tonight?"

"A house party?" he was high, confused.

"Yeah, I've got some pills left to get rid of."

"Right, sound, I'm going back tae the Viper Room, if you want to come?"

The Viper Room. That name had been around as long as she'd been on the scene, but she'd never had the chance to go. This was exciting. She'd imagined it often. It sounded so exotic, like they'd be sprawled out on big floor cushions. The walls softened by drapes, candles, with nice trance music, not too loud. Clean ashtrays, paracetamol, and chilled drinks would be flowing in the Viper Room.

"Yeah, can bring my pal?"

Trust

"You can bring all your pal's doll."

Their taxi drew up at the address he gave. Every light on the ground floor was on. No curtains hung in the windows, the stark white interior was illuminated by bare lightbulbs.

A window opened, signalled by the volume increase from within. A body tumbled out from the window, rolled across the garden, stumbled to its feet, and limped away in one seamless movement.

"This place is a shit hole. Let's go back to mine instead?" Claire suggested.

"I've got to get rid of these last 25 bombs, every penny's accounted for, and I'm not hanging around another week to make it up. Please, come in with me? Just for a wee while?" Anna pushed her bottom lip out and fluttered her eyelashes in an animated plea.

"This is our last night, our last party?" Claire replicated the sad-looking pout. "And you want to spend it there?" She unbuckled her seat belt, shaking her head. "The first sign of trouble, and I'm out of there. Come on then."

They stood under a street light, and Claire lit them both cigarettes as Anna counted her takings so far.

"I've got nearly two grand in here, once I get rid of these last ones that's me. I can't believe I've pulled this off, at six o'clock tonight I was ready to give up, I thought I'd ruined everything. And when I saw the melted blob, I'd made, Jesus, what a comeback!"

Claire stared into the middle ground, unblinking. She took a last draw on the cigarette, rolled her fingers into position, the end poised for take-off,

"Well, let's go and sell the rest of that dodgy shit to these dodgy fuckers." She pinged the glowing fag end through the darkness like a shooting star.

Anna's anticipation of an invitation to the Viper Room had been unwarranted. They walked in the wide-open door, into the ugly light. They stepped over a recognised face, but neither could place him. Two am party people don't look much like their

Wednesday afternoon counterparts.

The door to the living room lay on the floor. Splinters of wood angled out from the door frame, where hinges were once inlaid. It served as a makeshift rug, protecting guest's feet from the sticky floorboards. The cardboard lattice inside the door was visible where the heaviest footfall had pulverized the wooden veneer.

The walls of the living room were lined with three sofas in varying degrees of decomposition. They created a horseshoe shape, opening towards a Calor gas heater, burning the colour of molten lava.

No soft furnishings, no atmosphere, only the big light glaring, not even a lamp. But, the place was full. Full of desperate people clinging onto the weekend. Desperate to squeeze every drop out, dragging Saturday into Sunday. They were happy to pay, with money they couldn't spare, to put off real life for a few more hours.

The sofa's occupants were also in varying degrees of decomposition. Anna perched on the armrest nearest the heater, with Claire tucked in the cosy corner beside her. Anna watched with interest as her wares kicked in around the congregation.

217

Under the bright light they watched the effects in technicolour on each face around the horseshoe.

Next to her, sharing a cigarette, sat two younger looking girls.

"You got any pills left?" The first girl with four gold chains around her neck asked Anna.

"I've got a few, but cash only, no tick," she replied.

"Wait. Do you know any of our brothers?" The smaller one in a pink vest joined in.

"James. Or Stephen?" Goldie asked.

"Robert. Or big Stuart?" Pinkie added.

"Dougherty's." Goldie clarified.

"Coz you can't tell any of them," Pinkie ordered.

"As long as you've got the money, my lips are sealed," Anna nodded.

Pinkie and Goldie smiled while pulling cash from their bras. Warm damp tenners could always buy secrets.

Wedged between unconscious bookends, a guy who looked older than the average, sat with a tray on his lap. He had all the kit, a grinder, long skins, and a pile of skinned filters with the curled white tails. He was demonstrating the merits of different types of roach. A younger guy appeared to be hanging on his every word.

"Oh aye, makes sense like. Cheers for showing us, appreciate the time……" he trails off, becoming aware he sounds like he's taking the piss when all he really wants is the joint passed his way.

In the far corner, Anna spots Wendy, eyes closed, riding the wave of the last pill hitting her system. Jaw muscles visible from the other side of the room, her face angled upwards, towards some invisible source, as she nods to the beat. Someone leans on her foot and breaks the spell. Still engulfed in the beat, but eyes open now, she takes a swig from her can of lager. Her face changes, she sprays a toxic soup of flat beer and sodden tobacco strands, over herself and the floor.

"What fuckin idiots puttin fags ends in beers? Use a fuckin ashtray!" Laughter erupts, and the word junkie pings around the room, but she's oblivious, back under the music's spell.

Anna looks at the next sofa, a boy with shiny chestnut curtains flicks his hair out of his eyes. She tuned into his conversation.

"The millennium, the year two thousand, the start of a new century. What do you 'hink's going to happen?" he moved to the edge of the seat.

"Same as this year probably, and the last." Replied the man in the bucket hat next to him.

"Na, 'hings are going to change. We are the children of the future. The world is ours man." Curtains spread his hands in wonder, moving them slowly, conveying the breadth of possibility.

"Nut, nothings going to change, we've nae future, the only social mobility we've got is the number 7 bus, and we cannae afford a ticket because all our money goes on getting ourselves in this state."

Curtains deflates back into the depths of the battered brown sofa, then nudges the girl next to him.

"Here Emma, what do you 'hink's going to happen in the new millennium?"

Looking at him from under heavy eyelashes, she wiped the foamy corners of her mouth,

"We'll probably have robots and that eh?"

This is clearly the kind of response he

was looking for. Anna smiled as he angled his body towards the sparkly dressed girl, interested in her opinion.

They had managed to stay straight, only drinking a few vodkas all night. Now, with two pills left, a bag full of money and mission accomplished, it was time for Anna and Claire to join in.

Claire found the splinter cell of the party, in the darker bedroom. The bed's occupants all moved up, happy to let them on. Now five people lay along the length of the double bed. This kind of tight proximity would be heavily avoided in daily life. But here, uninhibited, leaning your head on the shoulder of someone you just met wasn't only fine, it was welcomed.

Anna held Claire in the crook of her arm. They lay, absorbed in the music, feeling absolute security. There on a dirty bed, in a dismal house with people they vaguely knew. It felt like the only place to be.

They talked and laughed, confided and conferred, expressed and agreed. They slipped in and out, between this world and that.

"What will you do when I'm gone?" Anna asked.

"I'll do the same things, with a bit more money and a lot less drama."

"Won't you miss me?" Anna sounded sad.

"What do you think?"

"Well, I'll miss you. I already miss you every day, when I'm bored, and you're at work.

"You know you can come back if it doesn't work out?" Claire said. Anna pulled her in closer,

"I'll miss you when I see funny things and you're not there to laugh." Anna said, "and, I'll miss your cooking."

"I'll miss you waiting for me after work." Claire replied.

"I'll miss using your hair spray."

"I'll miss you laughing at my jokes."

They stayed there, happily drifting in and out. The washes of love and connection, decreasing in frequency as the hours passed. As it became harder to sink back in and recover from a lapse into reality, Anna opened an eye. Dust in the air looked like glitter in a thin beam of morning light injecting the room.

Clarie's side was cold; she was already gone. At the head of the bed, someone was smoking, wearing his coat backward to soothe his shivering body.

CHAPTER EIGHT
Sunday

Anna

"Your wee pal said she's away to look after her aunties kids. She says you've to go and see her before you leave."

Without a full dose of chemicals, and the company of Claire, Anna's vulnerability was overwhelming. Dragging herself to the edge of the bed, she recoiled as her feet touched something soft. A person, sleeping soundly on the floor, about to wake up from the euphoria of yesterday and find himself drooling on dirty floorboards.

The smoker in the corner held out the remainder of the cigarette, she accepted. It wasn't a gesture made in generosity, but a means of getting rid of the burning ember without moving. Last night she'd have thought he was kind and appreciated his sharing. Now though, she was disgusted and deposited it in a beer can next to the bed. He pulled his jacket collar up over his mouth and closed his eyes.

She saw the arm of her denim jacket under the two sleepers in the centre of the bed. She leaned in and gently pulled, nothing budged. She pulled a little harder. The two young men were entwined, one of their legs flagging the others, a caring arm resting on the opposite chest. She pulled again, harder, the jolt woke them. As they became aware of themselves, they turned away to face different directions.

Her jacket and shoes were located, but the bag,

The bag.

It had all the money in it. Over two grand. Everything she had.

Why did she leave it?

Where was it?

No one would have taken it.

Would they?

Should have stayed straight.

Who was here?

Should have gone back to Claire's.

Her stomach dropped past her knees.
She tiptoed around the room, lifting jackets,
peering into the darkness under the bed.
What had she done? Her flat key. Her fags.
All the money.

She made her way into the living room.
Bodies were strewn around the sofas and
floor, some holding onto a sliver of
consciousness, some more like corpses. A
couple of eyes met hers as she scanned for
the patchwork denim bag through the battle
scene. One of them? Someone else? Who
had come in when they were hidden away
in the dark?

Onto the kitchen. She surveyed from the
hall; there was only a cooker and dirty
cavities where a white fridge and washing

machine should be. A dishcloth with a black burn mark sagged from a curtain rail covering part of the small window. The surfaces were covered with empty tins, of beer and cheap cat food. The sink was full, and the tap dripped, the overflow was blocked with cigarette ends like a beavers dam. The floorboards were saturated as the drips made their way down the side of the unit. She thought about pulling the plug and took a step in, but immediately retreated when she saw the contents of the basin. On top of plates, mugs and cat food encrusted forks, lay chunks of orange, red and brown, in a yellow liquid. Someone had vomited in the sink. She raised her jacket to her face, hoping for lingering remnants of her perfume to give some protection from the smell.

No bag in there.

Wiping the sweat from her palms, she pushed the last door open, the bathroom. The sun was beating through the patterned glass, heating up the urine-soaked floor, the smell was too much, but she had to look. Behind the door, there it was, her bag. Sitting like a cherry on top of a pile of fossilised washing. Thank fuck. Blowing a stream of air from her relieved chest, she picked it up and shut the door behind her. Resting the bag in the sink, and leaning her weight on the cold ceramic edge, she met herself in the mirror. She blew again, from puffed cheeks, exhaling the fear.

Every pore on her nose was visible. Her nuclear-toned skin seemed to blur at the edges. Last night's 'volumised noir' eyelashes worn to stumps. She turned her head from side to side and noted her well-toned jaw muscles. She swung the bag over her shoulder and ran the tap. She let it run, longer than usual. She wanted the water she washed with to be virgin to this place, not stagnating in the pipes for god knows how long. As it flowed, her mind took her to the edge of a crystal blue swimming pool. A fluffy white towel and cold pina colada waiting. She'd dive in and rinse off all the grime of last night, then emerge refreshed — water droplets glittering in the morning sunlight.

Back in the viper room toilet, she splashed her face and dried off with the inside of her own musty smelling top.

Wait.

She hadn't even checked. Pulling the drawstring open, exposing the dark interior, she gasped. She pulled the lining out, the inner edges coated in grey fluff and tobacco strands. Three brown coins fell, then rolled to a sticky halt below.

The zipped compartment and the side pocket produced a coffee shimmer lipstick, a brass Yale key, and a rolled-up KitKat wrapper. No money. No piles of twenties, no tenners. The entire sum of last night's mission to save her own life, gone.

Bazz

He lay on the mattress on the floor, fingers entwined across his chest. Once he was in business, he'd buy a double bed. No, make that a king-sized one.

Soon, he'd make a move on Wendy. He'd see her walking down the road, and offer to take her out for a drink and a meal. He'd buy her a new tracksuit. And, once things were going well, he'd let her choose a gold chain from the Argos catalogue. Maybe for their one month anniversary, he'd get her a nice big pair of gold hoop earrings. He liked girls who wore those, they looked classy, but obviously up for a carry-on. You'd always get a laugh with a girl in big gold hoops.

He made a list of the things he knew about her.

Her favourite band was the Beegees, unusual choice, he thought, for someone her age, but he could get used to that.

Her favourite food was a cheese and onion crisp sandwich. His was salt and vinegar, which would work well in the future when they'd buy multipacks.

Her favourite film was Ghost. He'd never seen it to the end as it was a bit too sad for him, but maybe she'd appreciate his emotional side and hold him in her arms when he cried.

Also, She was a compulsive liar addicted to heroin. Well, everyone's got some issues, haven't they?

He'd have a car soon enough, something white, convertible perhaps, but definitely with a spoiler. Of course, one day they'd have kids. Those little guys, they'd want for nothing. Tiny Nike trainers, little wardrobes filled with designed gear, fresh haircuts, and brand name play pieces. No kid of his was hitting the playground with value crisps. They'd go on all the school trips and have money for the gift shop. They'd have cool wallpaper to cover their school jotters too.

He wiggled his fingers and curled his toes to bring him back down to earth. He was dreaming too big now. There was work to do first before any of that could happen.

He thought back to the business class, as he tried to recall lessons, he wondered if it had even been real. He thought hard. He'd never been one for a formal setting, he couldn't listen for long, the big words confused him, and he lost track easily. As the words came in fuzzy parts, he pieced them together.

He'd sussed out the supply and demand bit.

Advertising. Was that something drug dealers did? Somehow people just knew who had what they needed. Word of mouth. That was it. People told people, and customers came from that.

Investment. Well, that was in the post. That big crispy giro was on the way. Money had always been the impossible hurdle for him, but not this time, he had the letter to confirm it. 'Your application has been successful and payment is being processed.'

Competitors, who would they be? Archie was old, Davie was gone, no junkies were into uppers and clubs, the pikeys had their hands full with the fags and horses. Nope. This was his for the taking.

He was pleasantly surprised with the amount he remembered, maybe he wasn't so daft after all. It was all in order, and he had the perfect business plan. All he needed now was the goods. He needed some way to convince Anna to hand it all over to him. He'd never been very good at knowing what people were thinking, but she did seem to like him. She always asked what he'd been up to and seemed interested in the answer.

Last Christmas, she'd been the only person who wanted to know why he'd jumped from the bridge. Everyone else had just laughed. 'Cannae even kill himself properly' was all most people had to say. He didn't like thinking about that time, but so many things reminded him of what he did. It made him miss his auntie Kay. She wasn't his real auntie. She was just one of those, friends of your mum, kind of aunties. Turned out it was a 'I'm here if you need me

- but please don't take me up on that' kind of offer. He'd been in and out of his Mum's home plenty of times through his teens, he knew the script, but he'd thought she was different.

She'd moved up here years before but still visited every summer. They'd have barbecues and drink coke-floats in the garden. Every year she saw his relationship with his step-dad getting worse. She was there to see the repercussions of putting too much tomato sauce on a burger roll. He'd done it to make his cousins laugh. The farting noises of the bottle, followed by the red drips down his chin. Six Stella down Bruce was not amused.

Bazz rubbed the thick white scars on the back of his hand. He remembered the smell of his own skin sizzling on the grill, and the pain of the slap to his face for daring to scream. It was in the wake of that painful episode that Kay told him he had a home with her. She'd said, 'whenever it gets too much, you know where I am'. He realised now, she'd been full of alcohol too. He'd taken so much comfort from the offer, never realising it wasn't really on the table.

The final time he'd got the belt, the

buckle side drew blood from his bony ribcage. He'd hidden under the corrugated iron archway in the corner of the bowling green, wedging himself between the blades of a lawn-mower and a pile of shovels and spades. Under there, with rusty water dripping on his head and the scuttles of rats around him, he felt safer than he had for a long time. He slept, cold, wet and bleeding, but out of danger. When morning came, he knew Bruce would be sleeping off his hangover till ten, at least. He crept in early and ripped the page with Kay's details from his Mum's address book. Bruce's wallet was in the side pocket of his ski jacket. He took the lot, even the coppers. Enough for a one-way ticket, and that one action was enough to ensure he could never, ever go back.

Kay's had been alright for a while. Obligation and pity had kept the roof over his head, but then Kay got a new boyfriend. A horrible old Weegie gangster with greasy hair.

Bazz and Kay would sit together on Fridays and watch Top of the Pops, but not once he was on the scene. The two of them would share a Battenburg cake and a pot of tea on a Thursday, but never the three of them. Kay used to laugh when he got things wrong, but not once Shaun got involved. She'd barely talk anymore. She'd snap for things that didn't matter before.

Shaun said he was freeloading. A scrounger. Good for nothing. Taking her for a mug.

She'd told him to leave as the snow began to fall. It was lying that night. He remembered the huge flakes glowing amber in the street lights, the kind of night that made dreams of hot-chocolate, fluffy pyjamas, and bedtime stories. But for him, it was the end of the line. Nowhere else to go, just the hoodie on his back. No family, no friends, and no hope. Just a pain in his chest and an empty feeling that was impossible to fill. He carried on walking as he had nowhere to stop, right to the end of town.

He came to the edge of the gorge, the river flowed far below, bridged with concrete and iron. He sat on the metal crash barrier. The snow filled his hood and blurred his sight as the flakes settled on his eyelashes. A car passed slowly, but it didn't stop.

That would be his sign. He gave himself three more cars to pass. If anyone cared enough to stop and ask if he was OK, then maybe he could be OK. If three cars passed and no one cared, that was the confirmation he needed.

It took nearly an hour. As soon as the third car's lights were out of sight, he positioned his toes at the edge of the pitch-black gorge and jumped.

He tensed for impact, held his breath, expecting the pain and freezing water to take the air from his lungs. Instead, a hard jolt under his arms. A tightening under his chin. The backs of his ankles scraped at the rock face till they found a small ledge. His hood caught on a broken branch of a hardy old oak tree that clung to the cliff face. There he stayed for the next eight hours. Alternating between gently swaying, and frantically scraping for a foothold when he slipped.

The gritter had raised the alarm at first light. After a chaotic morning of blue flashing lights and tinfoil blankets, he was admitted to the psychiatric ward. Then began his journey through supported accommodation, towards the security of this flat. Now for the next part of his journey; the shiny future almost within reach.

So Anna knew all this, knew how far he had come, that this was his chance to really make it. He just had to ask in a way that she couldn't resist.

Anna

The walk of shame. This was not her run-of-the-mill going home in party clothes walk of shame. Nor the embarrassing kind, where she didn't know the person she'd woken up beside. This was a deeper kind of shame. A gigantic mistake. Not one that could be forgotten about as the red face subsided, but one so huge it was a life-changer.

She felt grubby and strange, like she was dragging someone else's shadow down the road. She needed to get out of sight. As her feet tapped out an increasingly urgent rhythm on the concrete, she wanted to slap her own face. Hard and sharp. The faster she walked, the faster the thoughts came.

Archie's warning. That poolside, the vision of it less tangible with every step. Staying here alone. Always being skint. Second-hand denim for the rest of her life. Half the week in mental torture. Three-quarters of the year freezing. All her money spent on escaping her life, but never getting anywhere further than this.

Anxiety was knocking on her chest, her heartbeat cracking her ribs. The attic door holding everything in was rattling. The magnitude of the situation about to burst open the lock and drown her.

Scanning through the faces in her mind of everyone she'd seen in the Viper Room made her feel sick. Just hours ago, she'd have vouched for any of them, in the middle hours between coming-up, and arriving here. But now, she knew that one of them had stolen not only all her money, but any credibility she might have been clinging on to, and her entire future.

She walked faster and faster, till she was running, trying to create some distance between her stupidity and herself. The empty bag bounced off her back. She couldn't look too far ahead. She couldn't look up at the people going about their lives. Normal people, who'd woken up in normal beds, going out to buy normal bread and milk. She didn't want anyone to see her face, to see that she wasn't like them. She was something different; half running, sweating, her soul shaking inside, threatening to pour out of her mouth onto the pavement. The bile was rising, acidic, warning. She needed to stop, get out of the light. The Nags Head was closer than home, and she needed Davie's message.

The smell of putrid beer and heavy old smoke was masked with polish. All the wood shone, and the beer taps were clean. In this state of care, with fresh mats and laundered drip cloths, you could forget that the place was cluttered with secrets and regrets.

Gemma put a halting hand up,

"No drink till twelve, you know the rules. I'm just setting up."

"I know, but I need to ask you about something." Anna panted as she fanned her face. Gemma's interest piqued. This was a woman with eyes that saw everything, from beneath a pristine fringe of mousy brown. No revelation could ever shock Gemma. Her habitually held cloth was her ticket to listen to every conversation that interested her. As she slinked between people with the guise of mopping up spills and wiping

239

down sticky table legs, she missed nothing.

"Aye? What is it?"

"Wait till I get my breath back, it's roasting out there. In fact, can I just get a blackcurrant and lemonade first?" Anna wiped the sweat from the bridge of her nose.

"Aye, alright," Gemma replied in her usual clipped tone.

Anna took a stool at the bar while Gemma filled a glass.

"So... don't leave me hanging. What were you gonna ask?"

"Has there been any messages for me? Phone calls? Answering machine or anything?"

"Hold on! Is Davie supposed to be phoning here for you? Coz he hasn't, no way. I'd know."

"Aw, no, he mentioned yesterday, I think it was, that he might call here sometime, that's all."

"Have you spoke to him since he left? Is he even alive?" Gemma asked.

"Aye, of course I have. He's just getting a place ready for me coming over."

"Well, I'll be sure to let you know when he phones here." The sentence was delivered so slowly the bare bones of the truth shone through. She felt her face reddening; this was not the news she had anticipated. A week had passed, and he hadn't tried to contact her. He was out there enjoying himself, and she was here. Alone and in trouble.

Anna forced a fake cough, Gemma placed the sparkling juice on a mat. Anna patted her pockets, and sucked some air between her teeth,

"Ah, Gemma I've no change right now, can I give it to you later?"

"No, no, it's on me." Gemma offered a sarcastic smile. Anna took four long, welcome gulps, and wiped her mouth.

"Hey, you've not got a spare fag as well?"

"Christ sake Anna, you're bloody useless."

Shaun

Lonely Sundays would soon be a thing of the past; he was sure. He hadn't stopped thinking about Anna since she was in his car. He had to see her again.

He probably wasn't her usual type, but those kind of girls usually lacked in father figures, so in some messed up Freudian loophole, he'd find a way in. The money was a safe bet, he'd planted the seed, now he just needed the patience to watch it bloom, right into his hands. His stomach gurgled as the smell of melting cheese filled the kitchen. He wondered if she knew how to wash dishes properly, or she was one of those slobs that left bubbles on things.

His brunch was burning, he grabbed a damp dishtowel and reached for the grill pan. Searing heat pained his fingers. After juggling the blackened slices onto a plate, he sat at the table, furious with his stupid mistake. He blew on his fingers, then sunk his teeth into the toast, as he pulled away, a string of molten cheese stuck to his chin. He ripped it off and spat the hot mouthful on to a plastic bunch of grapes. He growled and threw the plate at the wall. It smashed, a greasy stain grew on the matt paint as the toast slid towards the ground. He was down to two plates now.

After sweeping away the debris, he washed the grapes and cooled his injuries with a cold compress. He needed something to cheer him up.

Standing in front of the open wardrobe

in the spare room, he took in the scent. Old perfumes, mothballs, and shoe polish. Using his left, unburnt, hand he fingered between each coat hanger. He examined the texture of each garment. Women's clothes felt so much nicer than men's. Soft silk, smooth cool satin, even the strange acrylic crimploine was more interesting than the plain old cotton his shirts were made of.

What size was she? He positioned his hands as if around her waist, moving them in and out as he tried to gauge.

Smaller than Kay? Yes.

Bigger than Jenny? Slightly perhaps.

He'd go for a 10. Druggies were always a bit too skinny. He picked out a cream polyester blouse. The neck was high, with little pearly buttons, and a lovely thin scarf attached to the back. He would suggest tying a nice bow at the side.

He flicked the hangers between a navy pencil skirt, and a burgundy pleated one. He tutted at his daftness and pulled out the navy one. Young ones didn't wear pleated skirts these days.

There were a few nice looking pairs of shoes at the bottom of the wardrobe. Anna was tall, so, unfortunately, she probably had big feet. Not ideal, but he could overlook that. Taking on a diamond this rough, there had to be a few snags along the way. He chose his favourite pair, black patent kitten heels. He didn't remember who's they had been, but none of that mattered now. He shone up the toes and positioned them on the end of the bed.

The outfit lay perfectly in the centre, as if his dream woman had lain down and evaporated, leaving only her clothes. He sat on the edge, then shuffled on a little further, swinging his legs up. He leaned back while stretching an arm behind her invisible head. Turning on his side to face his creation, he stroked the delicate pearl buttons. He started at the neck of the blouse, then slowly down, one by one.

"You be good to me, and I'll be good to you."

Anna

By now, this kind of Sunday should be a thing of the past. She shouldn't still be there, penniless with only a dried-up bit of emergency tobacco.

Locking the door, she removed the key.

Then she put it back in. Then she pulled it back out. She'd heard of burglars being able to turn keys from the outside. These paranoid thoughts never lingered, except on Sundays, and today she was particularly conflicted as the key had to stay in, in case the landlord came.

The tasteless gum she'd chewed for the last few hours became a new cover for the spy-hole on the door, although she knew no one could see in, it comforted her to blank it out. She rubbed her thumb and sticky fingers on her jeans. She pulled all the curtains closed and prayed there would be enough gas for a shower.

In the bathroom, she kicked off her denim shoes and peeled the socks away. Her feet were white, saturated with sweat, blue veins visible through fragile skin. Sitting on the closed toilet seat, she inspected the hairs on her legs. Dark spikes protruded from skin the same colour as the old chewing gum. She stood and faced the mirror, now in just her pants. The fabric was faded, with a tiny floral design and obligatory bow on the front, the elastic of one leg was tight, pinching into her bum cheek. The other cheek was free, framed by a fringe of dangling elastics from the burst edge.

She was thinner than she'd ever been. Her ribs cast shadows of their own under the harsh light bulb, but her little potbelly still remained. Dusty white tide marks left by her deodorant circled her armpits.

She looked closely at her nails, all different sizes, some rough-edged, some black underneath. The first two fingers of her right hand were stained yellow with nicotine. Disgusted, she reached for the shower control in hope.

As the steam began to rise, she stepped in. Water ran down her body, waking up dormant nerves. She couldn't resist anymore. Tears began to flow. Sobs wrenched her torso, her arms wrapped around, and her hands gripped any flesh they could find. The clean water and salty tears and engulfed her. She let out cries of pain, hurt, and frustration. She cried loud and unashamed, for the first time she could remember, maybe even forever. She cried for loss, for grief, for all the times she didn't cry. The attic door of her mind was kicked apart, and all the lead boxes sprung open, their contents demanding attention. Anna came down to a crouch, in the square base of the shower. She knelt, the sobs kept coming, she held herself tighter than anyone else ever had. The muscles in her face had never been used like this, it felt alien, but free.

Then the water went cold. No more gas. No more tears.

Wrapped in a crispy blue hand towel, folded over her chest and too short at the back, she filled the kettle. She put two value tea bags in her Garfield mug. The milk wasn't off, so things weren't that bad. She added a third tea bag and poured in some sugar.

It was now mid-afternoon, on a warm Sunday, everyone would be back in the pubs. All the Sunday Dads would be at the park with their little ones. Claire would be taking her nephews for a burger in her aunties car. If Davie was here he'd be at the pub, like every Sunday. And Saturday, and most weekdays. What was he doing right now?

The outside world was thriving in the bright light of early summer. Anna was shrinking in the darkness of a huge mistake.

She filed her nails on the side of a

matchbox, they smelled of sulfur, but the smooth edges felt good against her cheek. Claire would be expecting her, as they'd planned to meet before Anna headed to the airport. She couldn't bring herself to get dressed. She was safe in there, with the curtains shut, key in the lock and peephole blocked. She wasn't ready to go out. She wasn't ready to admit how stupid she'd been.

As the day passed, with bad tea and harsh, dry rolls ups, she found the time to ask herself questions she'd previously avoided. She could let the thoughts come. Usually, they'd be swiftly halted, replaced by imagining faraway places and fantasy lives. But today she reckoned she couldn't get any lower, so why not, maybe she would just let them all out to do their worst. Kick herself while she was down.

A feeling creeps into Anna's stomach. Something more than the usual come-down unease, and more urgent than the murmur of hangover palpitations.

She's hungry, for food. Usually, she'd pop an extra sugar in her tea, smoke an extra roll up, or stave it off with a packet of Bacon Fries at the bar, but she needed more than that. It took a massive effort to roll off the sofa and head into the neglected kitchen.

Opening each cupboard in turn revealed nothing but a scattering of rice, a cheap tin of peaches, and a half-used stock cube. All these things had lived in this flat longer than she had, and probably longer than Davie. She was certain he'd never had use for a stock cube.

Their eating habits had been sporadic, delivered hot to the door, or from the microwave. She wondered if they even had the means to cook a meal. She moved her attention to the lower cupboards near the sink. In it, she found a surprising collection of cookware. They must belong to the landlord, she thought. Claire would love these, she'd actually try and cook something in them too. Stacks of casserole dishes, saucepans, plastic tubs and, something else. In the dark corner, a familiar shape.

She reached in a pulled out a bottle of Macallan whiskey, tipping a pile of baking trays to the floor with a metallic clatter. Wincing at the noise, she unscrewed the top and took a cross-legged position on the floor. She wafted the bottle under nose and baulked at the smell. She'd grown up with that scent, but never got used to it. On adults breath, those whiskey drenched kisses at Hogmanay. In strange prescriptions for hot Toddies, or on cotton wool for toothache, although she'd always suspected, it was more of a deterrent from moaning than a certified cure-all.

She put the bottle to her lips. A vivid memory of a cocktail from someone's parent's drinks cabinet came flooding back, along with a surge of bile in her throat. Her body and brain were both screaming to stop, but she knew after a few swift swigs, the hunger would be gone, and the palpitations would ease off.

Whiskey was never her drink of choice. But, right now, cursed with a clear head and time to think, getting as much of this down her neck as she could stomach was the only choice. Her tongue burned and eyes streamed as she forced her throat to swallow against all her natural instincts.

Her face screwed up so tight it hurt. The warmth travelled down, deeper than her stomach, right into her core. She took another, then a third. A wave of relief spread down her legs. As the fourth swig settled in, the edges of the world began to soften. On the fifth, she relaxed her back onto the wall, her shoulders dropped, and her thoughts slowed.

She'd come this far, she'd saved last night from two disasters. Leaving the cash in her bag was a silly mistake, but she'd learned a lesson. She'd never make that mistake again, and she'd never go to the fucking Viper Room again. She pictured the faces in that house, trying to remember any comments, or any clues, proved totally useless.

The TV in the corner had been on low all day. She'd melted into the sofa, so getting up to change the channel was out of the question. There was no remote control, only five buttons and a volume dial. She was trapped there, in the grip of a tiny towel, exhaustion and utter laziness. She sipped on whiskey, with half-hour programs marking the passing of time.

Songs of Praise. Its host was her ideal Granada. She'd always wished for one exactly like him. One who wore those kind of v-neck jumpers, with diamond patterns, and blazers, and fresh white shirts. He had a silver side parting and wore gold-framed spectacles perched on a friendly nose. *Songs of Praise* Granada could sing too; she watched him belting out his glorious devotion around a beautiful church. Maybe she should go to church? As she warmed up to contemplate Jesus as her possible Saviour, it was time for the next half-hour segment of the evening.

The Antiques Road Show, something was enthralling about watching those normal people with their treasure. Teddy bears, teapots and trinkets all paraded, and their stories told. Pretty boring on the surface, but sometimes it was worth it when a shock valuation came. Many Sunday nights had gone this way; the tail end of a come-down, overlapping with the onset of sleep, to the soundtrack of pensioners TV. She drifted off before the expert revealed the Tudor desk was a fake.

The sky took on a purple tone through the window as the hours passed, remaining lighter near the rooftops. As the temperature dropped, she stirred. Only half awake, she staggered from the sofa to the TV's off button and headed towards the bedroom. The darkness and heavy covering of the duvet became a comforting cocoon.

She wanted to stay in the half-sleep, where things didn't matter, no plans were needed, or explanations demanded. Only softness and safety in darkness existed.

A hard knock on the front door ruined it, and the world came into focus. Another three hard thumps, not another knock, but a hefty kick. The door handle rattled up and down. She pulled the cover, up over her mouth.

"Are you in there?" Archie shouted. Three more kicks. She shrank further below the duvet, pulling her knees up towards her chest.

"You were supposed to pay me tonight." He tried the handle again, with more force. Imagining his cheeks blowing as he shouted at the door, she had to hold in a little giggle.

"Don't you take me for a mug!" He shouted loud enough for the surrounding houses to be alarmed.

"Remember who you are fucking dealing with." He gave one final kick to the door before his steps faded into the night.

She waited for her pulse to subside. The flat's familiar nighttime serenade of ticks, creaks, and hums played in the background. Alone in bed, the sharp edges of her predicament kept her awake. However hard she tried, the safe fuzz of sleep was unreachable. She needed a plan.

CHAPTER NINE

Monday

Anna

Anna's body lay still, her muscles and bones slept on while her mind raced. In the distance, she could hear the rumble of lorries making their deliveries, and the far off screams of kids waiting for the school bell.

She denied her body's instinct to move, convincing herself she could go back to sleep and escape reality. The tension grew in her chest. Her calves tingled, she flipped onto her other side with a loud sigh. Her eyes open now, watching the light change as the wind blew clouds across the sun's path. She looked over the wrinkled sheet on the empty side of the bed.

Davie's leaving gesture of ruffling her hair replayed. She had avoided thinking about the exact moment her life was ruined, but now with the clarity of daylight and sobriety, the unedited version was coming into focus.

At that moment, his true personality had outshone all the plans and promises he'd made in the weeks leading up. He was ten years her senior, but just a scared wee boy inside. He was running away from his fate, doing what his Mummy told him, and he'd left her behind to deal with his mess.

He was going whether Anna had existed or not. She was merely a side note. An optional extra, like a baggage increase. And he had opted out.

A pain in her hand brought her back into her fragile body. She became aware of her nails digging into her palms, and the dull ache of her clenched jaw. She loosened her grip and took a deep breath. She stretched her mouth and rubbed her temples as yesterday's events began to solidify in her consciousness.

The money.

Archie.

Life in this town stretching out before her for eternity.

She groaned in agony, and then she remembered what was in the living room. She got up and dragged various denim garments out of her rucksack, for the second Monday in a row. She got dressed, pulled her hair into a messy bun, and retrieved the Macallan bottle from beside the sofa. In the kitchen, she picked up a glass that was clean enough and slumped down onto the floor. She sat cross-legged again, rolled a cigarette of dry tobacco, and poured herself a large firewater measure.

The smoke hit her throat hard, and the whiskey burned on its way down. A truly disgusting breakfast, but a fitting start to the week ahead.

Ronin

Ronin pulled into the hedged drive he'd passed hundreds of times that week. He wanted to see her, hold her again and tell her he had the money for the horse. He still didn't have anything concrete, but he had to see her.

The front lawn was strewn with black bin bags, like monstrous molehills on the green grass. Some were burst, with fabric spilling from them. He slowed his van, noticed her car was missing, and a horrible feeling pulled at his stomach. Was she gone already? Was he too late?

Then, something landed on the grass—a heavy bird with white wings.

And another, and two more thudded to the ground.

He squinted, opened the door, and approached them.

Three more landed before he realised they were books. He hurried to the corner, looked around and up, to see the source. In the upstairs bay window, he could see Hillary, throwing books out one at a time, from an armful. He watched her, fascinated. She disappeared from the window, then returned with another armful and resumed launching.

He waited for a gap, then stepped out where she could see him.

"Erm, hello, Hillary."

"Oh, goodness! Hello. What are you doing here?" she leaned and shouted out of the window.

"I came to, em, check the hedge." He shuffled from one foot to the other and pulled his earlobe. Hillary leaned her elbows on the sill, smiling.

"I do apologise. You must think I'm nuts."

He didn't answer, just shook his head and returned her smile.

"Hang on, I'll come down!"

He waited by the door, rehearsing his speech, but as soon as she was in front of him, he forgot every word. She invited him in, with her open arm and guided him through the devastated hallway, into the kitchen. Half packed cardboard boxes covered surfaces, and bin bags filled the floor.

"That's his stuff out there. And those were all his favourite books." She leaned by the piled-up dishes in the sink, looking out to the garden and laughing.

He began to bounce on his toes as he prepared to talk. He bit his lip, took a breath, then hesitated. He looked at her curved back, the nip of her waist, and her peach-shaped cheeks in tight jodhpurs. He stepped a little closer.

"I'm... eh... I'm going to help you. I've almost got all the money." He moved closer; he wanted to touch her. He cautiously reached for her shoulder, but she stood up, and he retracted his hand. She remained facing the window, not laughing now.

"Look, darling, there's nothing you can do. There's nothing I can do. No one can help me now."

"But I'm going to buy the horse."

"The horse is going imminently, and short of that bastard paying the last nine months of mortgage and clearing my credit card bills, I'm finished."

Ronin's helplessness transformed into determination. He pulls her arm, and she spins towards his touch.

"Come and stay with me. I'll look after you, and I'll sort that man of yours out!"

"Don't be silly." She leans away and lets out a little nervous laugh. "I'll have to stay with my sister. But let me tell you, going crawling to her after all these years is probably worse than having the Merc repossessed." Her bottom lip trembles, her eyes fill up.

He's overwhelmed with the need to hold her. He takes her in both arms. He buries his nose in her fluffy hair. He bathes in the vanilla smell and takes her weight as she relaxes in his embrace. He talks gently, rubbing her back.

"You can stay with me. I can take care of you."

"Sweet boy, if only it were as easy as that." She sniffs into his shoulder. He feels her limp arms move and lightly circle his waist. He draws back and gently tilts her chin towards him. Her face is blotchy; her eyelashes are wet and stuck together. Damp curls cling to her cheek. He's never seen anyone so beautiful.

"I'll do whatever it takes to look after you." He pulls her hips closer with his other arm. She lowers her eyes and shakes her head.

"I've never met anyone like you. I want to help. I can get the… money." His voice cracks as he feels her hands spread across his lower back. She pulls him in and presses her hips into his. He takes a handful of hair from the nape of her neck and draws her head back. Her lips part, and she draws a sharp breath. With his lower arm, he slides her up onto the worktop, she spreads her legs and pulls him in further. His lips connect with her neck, a soft, delicate kiss. She touches his skin, her hand drawing his shirt up over his taught back. He kisses her neck, harder this time, his tongue trails towards her jaw.

"I can't do this." She pushes him away and jumps down. "I'm sorry, I shouldn't even be…" She straightens her jumper and adjusts the waist of her jeans.

He stood, wide-eyed, with his shirttail tucked under one armpit, torso revealed, and a bulge in his jeans.

"You should go, you know where the door is." She turned back to face the window. He placed his hand on her shoulder once more.

"I'll be back with the money to buy your horse, trust me."

Jackson

No matter how hard she rubbed, a little tarnish remained on the corner of her name plaque. Her ritual is interrupted by Jamie's cheerful face appearing at the door.

"You are going to love this!"

The last time he got excited like this, he had spent all the coffee kitty on a watermelon.

"Jamie, I don't have time for…"

"Come on, come on! I promise this is what you've been waiting for!" He doesn't wait for a reaction. He's halfway down the corridor before she can moan. Today she finds his enthusiasm equally intriguing as it is annoying. She replaces the plaque, at just the right angle, and skips after Jamie.

"Come on now, catch up Mrs!" The annoyance starts to outweigh the intrigue as she follows his smugness through the swinging doors and downstairs. They stop outside the observation room. As Jackson reaches for the handle, Jamie stops her.

"Wait! Guess first. Who do you think it is?" Jackson gives her sternest look, and Jamie shrinks away, holding both hands up to let her past.

Inside, they stand shoulder to shoulder in the dark, looking through the glass into the interview room beyond. It's painted white, housing a single table, three chairs, and two bored-looking officers. On the table sit seven packets of Gillette razors and two big bottles of Joop. Opposite, with her head in her hands, sits Wendy Monroe.

"Yes! Just as I thought. She can't help herself that one."

"Yup, but wait till you hear what she's got to say! Just as I thought, well YOU thought, she's had her ear to the ground and there's something big going on. Something you definitely want to know about." He pointed a finger at her shoulder.

"For Christ's sake, Jamie, just tell me." He looks offended at her impatient tone.

"OK, OK, she's been mumbling about us wasting time with her when there are bigger problems. The usual junkie drivel, but...the word is, there's a new supply coming here. New drugs, strong stuff, and Scouse gangsters!" He finger quotes around 'Scouse' for some reason, and she hates him a little bit more.

"From 'down the road'. You know, England." He does it again.

"OK, Jamie, get PC Smith out of there, I'll take it from here."

He pokes her shoulder again, "See, I knew you'd like it!"

She takes the vacant chair, slides the contraband to the side, and presses stop on the interview tape. The snap drags Wendy back into the room. She pulls her hair back from her skeletal face.

"So, Wendy, here you are again. This will definitely get you a little holiday in Cortonvale this time." Jackson began. Wendy shrugged, the movement of her shoulders created dark caverns under her collar bones. She was so thin and her face so drawn in, Jackson wondered if her cheeks might touch inside her mouth.

"Do you understand, Wendy? You are going to jail this time."

She shrugged again; she was well versed in the Scottish legal system and knew nothing was going to happen very quickly. Jackson could see her words had little effect. Wendy was used to getting home the same day, so she moved up a gear.

"You'll not get police bail this time. You're getting kept in till court tomorrow morning."

Wendy sat up straighter, and scraped her hair back from her face again. Jackson knew she'd caught her attention.

"Unless, of course, you remember our little chat last week?"

The hollow of her mouth widens, the black hole of a missing front tooth looks like the entrance to a cave.

"Aye, but, I've already said it all. I need to get hame. I told them all I know." She nods towards the other officer. "Ask him. But I've got to go. I need the chemist."

Jackson lets out a fake laugh.

"You don't get to decide when you go, Wendy. You've been arrested. It's not up to you. It will be up to the judge tomorrow. And with your persistent offending, it's extremely likely you'll be going straight to jail. Do not pass go; do not collect any opiates."

Wendy's restless feet swipe the floor under the table.

"But I need my methadone. I'll get sick." There's desperation in her voice that Jackson's been waiting for.

"Ah, that's unfortunate, you'll have a rough night in store for you then."

Wendy looks down to her knees, still pulling her greasy hair back from her face. Jackson nudges her quiet uniformed companion,

"Get the girl a glass of water." The disinterested constable nods, relieved, then pushes his chair in under the table. As the door shuts behind him, Jackson stands up.

"I think we both know how this works by now? Yes?"

Wendy looks up as Jackson sweeps the razors and aftershave into the waste paper bin. Wendy licks her dry lips and nods. Jackson sits back down, turns to a fresh page in her notebook, and taps her pen on the table.

"You'll be out of here before the chemist closes this afternoon, just tell me everything you know about these new drugs and where they came from."

Anna

For the second unplanned Monday, Anna set off to meet Claire. She took the back pathways, scanning for Archie, and hoping to avoid anyone from the Viper Room. Yesterday she couldn't picture any of them being capable of ruining her life. Today's clarity of vision provided her with endless possibilities. She didn't know any of them properly, they were all as capable, and likely, as the next person.

As she kept to the park's leafy edge, prepared to dive in a bush at any moment, she replayed the scene and listed the suspects. Today everyone was guilty. Even the curtain-haired space-cadet. All the unnamed casualties left on the floor. The pink and gold gypsy girls, and of course, Wendy.

Her list of motives included jealousy of something or other. Revenge for something she'd done in the past, but seemingly forgotten all about. But, most likely, a simple opportunist strike.

She walked and replayed the night.

This time, in a better version, she pulled the bag straps tightly over both shoulders, leaning her back against the wall all night to protect her profits.

She played it again. This time, forcing everyone to stand in line, and pull their pockets inside out, till the money flutters to the ground, and she picks it all up.

She played it again, in the best version, she left with Claire in a taxi, bag full of money, wiping their feet on the way out.

As she passed Roy's Spar, the crosshatched billboards read bold reminders that the real world was rumbling on around her. Back inside her bubble, she rehearsed announcing this new predicament to Claire.

The bald one and the tall one marched out of Miller and Smyth's in their expensive tailored suits. She was still invisible to them, but today found comfort in remaining unseen. She pulled up the collar of her denim jacket. The clouds had collected and reclaimed the blue sky. She leaned against the wall. The lilac flowers scent had blown away in the wind, and the edges of the delicate purple blooms had curled and browned.

When Claire stepped out from the giant stone columns, she saw Anna immediately. Her relieved expression soon turned to worry as she examined the previously unseen expression on Anna's face. She wrapped her arms around her friend's tense body.

"I was so worried when you didn't come last night. I thought you'd left without saying bye."

"I wouldn't do that. I just couldn't face seeing anyone. I really fucked up this time. Worse than ever."

Claire looked hard at her downturned mouth.

"What do you mean? Did you not make enough money?"

"It's worse than that. I've got nothing. I've lost it all." Anna looks to the side to avoid Claire's eyes.

"How could you lose thousands of pounds since Saturday?"

"At the Viper Room, I think someone emptied my bag when I was wrecked. I found my bag when I woke up, and it was totally empty." Her eyes darted to the other side, avoiding the gaze waiting for her in the middle.

"So, let me get this straight. You put all the money in your handbag? Not in your pockets? And then you left your bag lying around for anyone to find?" Claire stepped into Anna's line of sight.

"I didn't think, I was having a good time." Anna pinched the bridge of her nose hard. Claire linked arms at the elbow, and in a much sweeter tone said,

"Let's get food, then figure out what we

are going to do." She pulled her close and coaxed her along the street.

She didn't let go till they separated at their usual booth in Cadoras chippy. They ordered some battered sausages, chips and coke. Claire asked for extra red sauce before Anna even hinted.

"So," Claire began, softly, but a little sarcastically. "Let's see what we are dealing with this week."

Anna groaned.

"You left your bag, full of cash, unattended in that shit hole? At a party full of pikeys and neds. And Wendy fucking Munroe!"

"I know, give me a break, it was a mistake."

"You'll never get that back, you know."

Anna shrugged, "Maybe not, but..."

"But nothing!" the softness turned stern. "That's it. You have to stay here, give all that up. You have to admit defeat. Send Archie to Davie. This is all his doing."

"I can't do that, look, I've got an idea that might work."

"No, please! No more! I can't listen to this!"

"Look, it's just another setback, that's all."

The raw fingered waitress delivered the drinks, distracting them from the tense exchange. Anna took her bottle and concentrated on the bubbles forming from nothing inside the brown liquid. She followed them up to the surface and watched as they popped with a tiny spray. An eternity passed, and the bubbles slowed.

"So you'll tell Archie, right? Its all over, it's time for Davie to sort out his own mess?" Claire's eyes were wide with hope. Anna ran her thumb over the condensation, collecting the drips.

"I've got an idea though, if I take that loan off Shaun…"

Claire's body language radiated what she thought of that. Her eyebrows hit a new height of shock, and her nostrils flared.

"You're already in twice as much trouble as you were last week! That old creep Christine hangs about with? You better not be getting involved with him? Have you got a death wish? Scott told me about him, you know he's been in jail?"

"Yeah, but that was ages ago, I think he's chilled out a bit now. Anyway, I'm extremely short on options right now."

"You are so naive! Why do you get involved with idiots like that?"

The plates arrived, the greasy suppers lay ready to coat their arteries and shorten their life expectancy. Claire first passed the salt, then offered the vinegar. Anna declined the second. The hot vapour from the freshly seasoned chips carried the memory of those horrible minutes in Shaun's car. She pushed the bottle to the far side of the table.

"I've gone right off vinegar these days."

The argument continued in silence. Anna became highly aware of every movement, awkwardly manoeuvring chips into her mouth, the tension putting every move under scrutiny. The gap between them was agonising for Anna. She wanted Claire to laugh, or tell her about work, or show her something she'd cut out of a magazine. She wanted to say sorry. She wanted to reassure her that it would all be OK, and that Claire's cold shoulder was the worst thing of all. But all that came out -

"Can I borrow £20?"

Claire placed her fork and knife side by

side.

"I've no gas, but I've got it sorted, I'll pay you back everything on Friday night."

She didn't answer at first, only slid out from the table, opened her purse, and pulled out two brown notes. In this position, her small frame towered above Anna.

"How? How is it all sorted? This entire situation is a disaster! You are in so much trouble." She held the cash like a conductor, adding flair to her sentiment. "You could have said you weren't going and forgot about bloody Ibiza and Davie fucking King." Claire's lips were tight with anger. Anna looked behind to check who was listening, then put her finger to her mouth,

"Shhh, Calm down, it's going to work out."

"No! I will not! You're mad. It's going to go wrong. You're relying on all these idiot men to save you, and you're just dragging yourself further and further down." The money swayed from side to side, her hand moved like she was manipulating an orchestra of rage, her volume rose and pitch increased.

"Do you want to end up like Christine? Still hanging around the same pubs, adding

arms and legs onto every story to make
yourself sound interesting? Pouring alcohol
over all your issues? You always talk about
getting away from here, wanting to really
live. That's not going to happen if you carry
on down this road. You'll be stuck here
handing over your giro to whoever you've
let down next!" Her hand swept upward
with the crescendo of her row.

"I'm done with this!" and down, striking
the table at the finale,

"And I'm done with you!"

Anna sat alone in the post-argument
electricity. She couldn't look around in case
anyone had witnessed her berating. Instead,
she pulled over Clarie's almost full plate,
picked out the best crispy chips, and peeled
the batter from the end of the sausage. She
sat for a while, picking the label off the
bottle, running through the list of suspects
again. It was a waste of time. It wasn't her
usual crowd. She didn't even know half
their names, let alone where to ever see
them again.

The waitress passed, looking for empty

plates to remove and hurry diners along. Anna needed to go before her next round. She never paid in there so they wouldn't be expecting her at the till. Those two notes were the only security she had for the foreseeable future. She definitely wasn't handing over the best part of a tenner already. She poured the rest of her coke into Clarie's bottle, slung her bag over her shoulder, then, keeping her eyes on the door, walked straight out.

Once on the street, her pace quickened, like an eight-year-old running up the dark stairs to bed. She leapt in the first corner available. She leaned against the beige mosaic tiles in the shade of Woolworth's doorway, waiting for the chase. It didn't come.

As her breathing returned to normal, she felt jarred at how angry Claire was. Them falling out was the last thing she wanted, but she had a full belly, and twenty quid so not a total disaster.

Anna headed for the graveyard's leafy safety and positioned herself with a view of all the paths. She leaned against a beech tree and began picking the bark of a fallen twig while looking for a good thing about her situation.

It would make this week easier, not having to hide things from Claire. She would stay out of the way for a few days, do what was necessary to get back on her feet, then see Claire once it was all sorted out.

Yeah, this was for the best. She closed her eyes and tuned into the birds. Little tweets and big squawks surrounded her. Wings flapped above her, and a branch rustled nearby. All these animals were going about their lives oblivious to the madness of human behaviour. Anna imagined herself as a raven, taking off, leaving this place, flying far, far away.

Gravely footsteps approached. She opened her eyes to see another person well used to travelling the back paths. Bazz. He approached with his shoulders low, weighed down by carrier bags on both sides. She was genuinely pleased to see his gormless face.

"Ere, I've been looking for you." He said.

"Been shopping?"

He drops the bags at his feet, "Nope, its just a few Argos catalogues I picked up today."

"What do you need all them for?"

"Ah ha, that's what the security guard asked too. I told him they were for me Mam and me aunties." His face tells her he has the best idea in the world.

"Who are they for?"

"Me! The new me. Watch this." He takes a huge breath in, with a bag in each hand, starts lifting them up and down, slowly, tensing his biceps. He trembles and puffs out like a circus strong-man.

"I'm getting myself in shape. I'm getting my life in order. No more dossing around."

"That's great, well done."

"Well, that's why I've been wanting to see you." He dropped the heavy bags at his feet and bent over to rest his hands on his thighs while regaining his composure. He straightened up and took a folded brown envelope from his pocket.

"Told you, see, a grand. Coming this week." He held the letter up, pointing out the payment date. "So, I was gonna ask ya again, to have a think about setting me up with your dealer, I need a break…"

She cut him off. She didn't need to hear any more.

"Ok, you're on. You give me the cash when you get it, and we can figure out the details then."

His mouth dropped open. She could see black holes in his gums, memorials of the teeth long gone, as he processed the information. He leaned against a marble cross, stumbling over a dried-up wreath at its base.

"So, you'll sort me out? Put me in business? And then I'll be the main guy in town?" The skin around his eyes puckered, he started rubbing his hands together in delight.

"Yeah, whatever you want to do. It will be really cool." He rose to his tiptoes, bouncing from side to side. "As long as you think you can handle it all?"

"Aye, of course I can. I can handle anything. Wait, are you for real? Honestly, you'll really give them to me."

"Yeah. I'm done with it all. I'm out of here as soon as possible, and I need a hand from someone I can trust."

"I guarantee you can trust me." Bazz rubs his hands together, "This is it now, this is what I've been waiting for, finally getting my life on track."

His enthusiasm creeps over Anna, she smiles wide, for the first time in ages. She laughs as he continues with joy.

"Time for this town to know who they are dealing with. The real Barry, coming right at ya."

"Aye, they won't know what's hit them, I'm sure." She offers him a cigarette from her seat by the tree, he declines but reaches down for the other hand to shake on it. Anna obliges.

"Meet me back here on Friday, at 6 pm. Just bring the money, and I'll sort the rest out."

He shakes her hand, rocking her entire body. When he eventually releases her, she watches him go, content she witnessed a celebration skip in his step.

CHAPTER TEN
Tuesday

Anna

Boredom drove Anna out of the flat earlier than usual, and she'd rather a lecture from Christine than absorb any more daytime TV. Deciding to skip the bus and save the pound, she took the back roads to avoid bumping into, well, anyone. As she crossed the churchyard, the sound of a car slowing down behind her stirred a strange paranoia.

Her instinct was rewarded when the car stopped inches from her leg. DI Jackson again, goosebumps covered her body, was this it, was she busted? A quick mental inventory of her bag and pockets reminded her she was innocent today. She swivelled her head, scanning the paths and park beyond. She did not want to be seen entertaining the police. Selling dodgy pills was one thing, but any suggestion that she was an informer, and she'd be right down the social ladder.

"Still here then? I take it you're going down to the big night at the club on Friday?" Jackson asked.

"Na, I'm done with partying, I want a quiet life."

"Mm hmm, I've heard that one before. Well, let's just say, we know what's going down this weekend."

"I wouldn't know, like I say, done with all that." Shit. What does she know?

"My sources tell me things are changing around here, guys from England, thinking they can muscle in up here."

"I haven't heard."

"Well, you watch yourself. We've heard about the new stuff coming up, dangerous stuff."

Anna threw a little extra on the fire -

"From Liverpool? The plasticy, coloured ones?"

Jackson bites her entire bottom lip, and

hit the wheel with her left hand. She looked like a mad scientist who's new theory's proved correct. She pushed her head out of the window, looked left, then right before whispering;

"These Scousers are planning to take over up here. You wouldn't be involved in that, would you?"

"I'm not that daft. Those guys are bad news."

Jackson nods.

"And the drugs they've got are well dodgy." Is she actually believing this?

"You'd do well to stay clear. Your David might have been a big fish in this little pond, but compared to him, these guys are sharks."

Anna nodded sincerely like she was soaking up great advice. A crackly radio and a couple of beeps called Jackson to action. She dismissed Anna by simply rolling the window up and driving off. She left her on the low wall in the shade of a lime tree, puzzling over how quickly lies became facts around there.

Bazz

This was the longest week of his life so far, and it was only Tuesday. Bazz picked the ears from his last potato and put it in the microwave. He'd wanted to eat it last night, but he knew a thing or two about budgeting, so he decided to stretch it out to today's meal instead. It was 11 am, so this was realistically brunch, not breakfast, and Americans ate hash browns, which are made of potato, so this was practically the same. He was going to buy Coco-pops next week, once the cash was rolling in. Maybe Frosties too. He would have a choice. He'd be able to open the cupboard and take his pick. What a life.

As he stared through the brown drips of the door into his spinning meal, he listened to the whistles of steam escaping. He wondered what kind of cereal Wendy liked. She seemed like a Rice Crispies kind of girl.

The snap of the letterbox burst his cereal dream bubble. His eyes widened in excitement as he concluded the big cheque had come early. He rubbed his hands together and ran to the front door.

The envelope was face down, it was white, not the colour he'd grown to expect from a giro. He stood motionless, with an odd feeling, deep in his stomach that he couldn't place. Crouching down, he picked it up with his starchy fingers and turned it over.

The bold black stamp of 'Her Majesties Court Services'.

That niggling feeling, that he hadn't allowed to interfere with his dreams, was starting to punch its way to the surface. He ripped it open, taking the top corner of the letter with it. He read it quickly, then again, very slowly, hoping he'd read it wrong.

'A warrant has been issued for your arrest.'

Community service! How could he have forgotten? He should have been there on Friday. He was already on his last chance. Now there was a warrant for his arrest. The judge made it clear the last time that his lives were up. He'd been promised nine months in jail if he breached his conditions again. He balled up the paper and punched his leg, he collapsed onto the floor in front of him and began hitting his forehead off the ground.

Trust

Why did he always fuck everything up?

Why was he so fucking stupid?

His life was about to change, but he ruined it again. He was so close this time. He had almost had everything he dreamed of.

Now he was going to jail. He'd lose his house and have to fight his way through every day.

He was no one, the kind of guy that gets used and abused by the real criminals.

He was going to get it tight in there.

He started to cry, like a little boy.

So close.

He was finally getting one foot out of the gutter, but he'd tripped himself up and slid right back down. He lay there, tears streaming off the end of his crooked nose. He knew they were all right. Everyone who'd said he'd never amount to anything.

Everyone who called him an idiot. Everyone who'd bullied him. No wonder his mum's boyfriend had hated him. The only person who had any faith in him was Anna. And now he'd let her down too. He couldn't take over from her; he'd be in jail by Monday.

Monday…

If he kept his head down for the next few days, he could make it to the weekend. He could still get the money, still get the drugs. Still be the main guy this weekend!

Could he?

Could he prove himself and everyone wrong? A few days. That's all. He could stay out of the way till the big night. He just wouldn't answer the door, wouldn't let anyone see him. He got to his knees, wiped his face, and clapped his wet hands together.

Anna believed in him, and he wasn't going to let her down.

Anna

It took a bit of persuasion, but she finally got Christine down to the pub. Anna asked Gemma for the remote control as she served their drinks.

"What do you want that for?"

"Ceefax, I'm looking for flights, the cheapest ones are on there."

Gemma tutted and handed it over. They settle into the leather sofa, Anna saw a cheap one come up, but before she could write the phone number, it was gone. Another 29 pages before it would come up again.

"Did you get me down here so you could look for flights? You could have done that at mine."

"No, I thought it would do you good to get out of the house." Anna glanced between the TV and the door.

"Are you up to something?" Christine asked with narrow eyes.

"Like what?" Anna picked up Christine's cigarette packet and looked inside to avoid eye contact.

"You're acting strange hen. Stranger than usual."

Anna felt her skin prickle, warning a red face was coming,

"Hey, what's this?" she rattled the open cigarette packet. "Why do you turn some of them upside down?" Anna knew the story, but it guaranteed Christine's attention. She took the box, and lit one, holding it like a dart, between thumb and forefinger. She took a long draw and started the performance by blowing out smoke rings.

"It's respect. You turn one over for each friend you've lost. They aren't here anymore, but you have to remember them. Ken what I mean?"

Anna glanced at the door as Christine continued;

"That one there is for your Mum. I've never forgotten her, you know. My best pal Debbie Mac. I've turned a fag for her every day for five years."

This was both heartwarming and bizarre. A brief sense of guilt crept up Anna's spine as she questioned why she didn't have a daily memorial to her mother. Her cheeks began to burn again. Heat spread around her neck, threatening to suffocate her. She swallowed a ball of sadness, and opened her eyes wide, hoping the tears would be reabsorbed.

"Who are the rest for then?" a quick distraction, and a story that could take hours as she kept one eye on the door. The afternoon stretched out, games of pool were won and lost, stories told and elaborated, drinks emptied and filled. Christine became more philosophical with every passing minute. Anna kept her eye on the entrance while picking the corner of a Tennent's beer mat with its familiar red and yellow logo of beer bellies and shit jokes.

As the afternoon wore on, she felt more like a paid extra for Christine's rants than a real human companion.

Finally, that familiar lump in the door frame. Archie filled the width. He didn't look her way as he sauntered towards the bar. Anna kept him in her peripheral vision. He ordered a double Southern Comfort and coke, as he got the small talk underway, without taking his eyes from the barmaid, he raised his right hand and pointed straight at Anna. Christine nudged her with a sharp elbow.

Of course he'd seen her. She would have been the first thing he saw as he entered. And, of course, he was looking for her.

Beside the jukebox, a spiky-haired man began to raise his voice at his partner; this caught Gemma's eye. She picked up her polish and yellow duster and slid towards the source.

Anna's toes curled inside her shoes. She

wiped her palms on her thighs and walked straight towards Archie. He swivelled his entire body on the wooden bar stool, standing up as she met his side. His face was angry, and his usual alcoholic redness had a darker undertone. His fist clenched on the bar, so tight his big flat thumb was white.

"I've been looking for you," he growled from between clenched teeth. She was a little taller than him, so she sat on the adjacent stool and gifted his pride the extra inches above her.

"Did you get the message?" she asked with a smile, as casual as she could, faced with this rage.

"I've had no message and no money." His teeth still clenched, but the lines around his eyes seemed to soften.

"About the money? The bank transfer? From Davie?"

"What are you talking about, you stupid wee cow?"

"Aw, come on now! I just did what Davie told me. He said I had to prove myself. He needed proof I was paying up. He told me to put the money in his bank, and he'll transfer it to you."

"Are you kidding me? What sort of simpleton is he? A fucking bank transfer for a drug deal?" he shook his head and let out a wheezy laugh. "I don't want a bank transfer. I'm not a fucking building society. I could understand you coming up with a stupid idea like that, but no Davie."

Anna shrugs, crafting a look which she hopes says she's been swept along in someone else's madness.

"I wish I'd known, I wouldn't have put in into his account, I'd have just given you the cash."

"Fucking idiots, this is unbelievable. Give me his phone number right now!" Archie thumps his fist on the bar.

"He doesn't have one, he just used a payphone. He said he'd call you. Hasn't he been in touch?"

"Has he fuck."

"Look, I can sort this out, I could sell more this weekend. It's a big night on Friday. I could get rid of as many as you want. I'll give all the money to you, I won't keep any of it, and we will be square?"

"I do not trust you." His teeth clench, the words distort past them.

"You don't really need to. You'll be there,

won't you? I can just hand the cash straight to you."

His Southern Comfort was hitting the spot, diffusing the mood. Anna saw his fist relax.

"And, I know you won't want them on your hands with the police getting so heavy."

He drained his glass, leaving only ice.

"Davie's got my seventeen hundred quid, so you make it nineteen for the inconvenience. I'll give you two hundred pills tonight. You pay me first, and you can keep the rest."

"Sure, that seems reasonable." She smiled, nodded, and took the hand he offered. He squeezed it tight. Then tighter. She smiled sweeter. He stared into her eyes, knowing he was causing pain. Anna locked his gaze and continued shaking his hand. He cranked up the tension another notch, watching for cracks, but she just kept smiling.

The argument at the jukebox hadn't amounted to much, and there was nothing left to polish, so Gemma returned to the bar and let the gate down. She was in time to see Archie drop Anna's hand and quickly pick up his glass. He nodded and crunched the ice in his teeth. A drip rolled down his stubble. He wiped his mouth and turned from the bar, pointing at Anna's chest, he whispered, "Nine pm. Be in this time," before heading toward the door.

"Away already Archie?" Gemma called after him, "Where you off to?"

He drew a finger up and tapped his nose, "Nosy bitch," and walked out. Gemma tutted and polished the ale tap. When he was out of sight, Anna flexed her fingers in and out. It burned from the inside; she blew on the palm. She checked that all the bones were in place, and there was no broken skin. She shook it as she walked back to the sofa.

Christine took a long drag on her cigarette,

"You know, if you dance with the devil, you have to wait for the song to stop?" She blew the smoke out as if she had just summed up the whole world.

Anna laughed, "Yeah, yeah, it's all fine. You saw us shake hands, didn't you?"

Christine's suspicious eyes narrowed.

"I've got to go anyway, cheers for the drinks, I'll see you soon yeah?" She was

going to get Gemma's attention to say bye,
but she was already looking their way,
straining to hear the conversation, so Anna
gave her a little wave like the queen.
Gemma's embarrassment at being caught
was obvious.

"Oh, I was in a wee world of my own
there!" She moved onto the next brass tap.
Christine shook her head as Anna swerved
the pool table and disappeared out of the
door.

Ronin

He'd thought of little else but Hillary for
days. Her voice, her smell, her shape. He
knew what he needed to do. He'd driven the
streets for hours looking for Anna Mcvay.
He wasn't giving her a choice now. The time
for niceties was long gone. His priority was
doubling his money this week, buying the
horse, and getting Hillary to take him
seriously.

The diesel warning light had gone on
long ago, so he would have to go back to the
site for money from his stash. That was the
last place he wanted to be. He was avoiding
his brothers and uncles, as always, but he

also had to stay away from Tina and Maria at all costs. They brought nothing but trouble.

He promised himself one last circuit of the town centre before heading back and thinking of another plan to find her.

No. That wouldn't be necessary. There she was, half running up South Street, denim jacket tied around her waist, smoking a cigarette. He braked hard, sounded the horn, and reversed till he was level with her. He beckoned her over and leaned through the window.

"You lied to me."

"Me? What do you mean?" Anna replied.

"I heard about the new stuff you were selling there at the weekend. You told me you didn't know anything about that. So now you owe me a favour."

"How do you figure that out? I don't owe anyone a favour."

"You don't seem to understand me," he pulled his left earlobe, "you lied, now you owe me a favour."

"What's the favour?"

"I know you deal for your man Davie, and I've heard the new stuff is NOT his gear." He unbuckled the seat belt. She dug her nails into her palms and kept her mouth shut.

"Well? Cat got your tongue there, girl?" The door swung open, a black brogue with a shiny buckle swung out and hit the ground. The sun glinted off the sharp edge of an axe on the front seat.

She took a step back, grip tightening on the strap of her bag, and still said nothing. His forehead became a ledge, from the darkness beneath, his eyes darted around her face. He stood on the road, and she was on the pavement. He pushed her back and stepped up. She kept her stance. She didn't sway or stumble, just took two steps back, and remained there, firm. Now his eyes were level.

"I'm going to do you a favour instead." He pointed the black tarred edge of a nail at the end of her nose. She swallowed hard. He saw this gulp as a sign of weakness, a crack in her solid facade, he smiled.

"I'm going to let you carry on dealing here. How about that?"

She looked like she might cry, or maybe slap him. Then her face changed, and she gave him a nod.

"Ah, so you can hear me in there? I'm going to let you carry on. You'll still be allowed to deal to your daft wee pals. That sound good?"

Another nod,

"That's a deal then." He lowered his hand, and his chest expanded.

"Deal? I didn't make a deal," her voice cracked.

"We made a deal right there, you are allowed to sell a few pills, and you give me your contact. Otherwise, all deals are off. Terminated." He pulled his earlobe three times, longer each time. He watched her take a lungful of air, and her jaw tighten. Then she smiled, an odd, one-sided twisted smile.

"How much are you looking for?" she asked.

"I need three grands worth."

"Oh. Right. You're serious then."

"Yes. I'm very serious, and you better start talking," he replied, getting impatient.

"I can sort that out for you. But only if I can trust you?" Anna said.

"Trust me? I'll be the one judging that." He moved a little closer.

"The thing is," she shrugged, "these guys

don't do tick, it's only cash upfront."

"Cash it is, that's no problem for me."
The money was ready to go.

"My order comes up on Friday night. I can get them to add yours on."

"You have misunderstood me. It's not your order now. It's mine. And now you order from me. You understand now?"

"Sure," she shrugged again, "it's a deal then. But what about Davie?"

"You leave him to me. You're in my pocket now. I'll take care of him. Just you worry about getting what you promised."

"I'll sort you out on Friday, and then I'll introduce you, yeah? I think they'll like you. But, cash first though, I need something to bring to the table before I introduce you. You know how it is, you're much more experienced in this kind of thing than me."

"Of course, that's how the big boys do it, cash first little lady, I've been doing business since you were in long socks. I'll meet you inside there. You can carry the pills in; girls are less likely to get searched."

"It might be better to meet somewhere before? Get the deal done first?" She suggested.

"Do you think I'm a mug? I told you,

inside. You take the risk. Then I'll take over in there, got it?"

"OK, whatever you think, you know better than me. Wait for me at the last table on the left."

He got back in his van, started the engine, and watched her skip up the road again. She wasn't right that one, he'd get her out of the picture as soon as possible.

CHAPTER ELEVEN
Wednesday

Anna

On Wednesday morning, Anna made an extra thick roll-up and put an extra tea bag in her mug. She tried to figure out the exact moment Ronin had made himself part of her plans. Every word from his thin-lipped mouth was a step deeper into trouble. His hand felt like a splintered dry log for the fire, his callouses sharp against her damp ivory palms.

She laughed, a little surprised recalling her quick thinking while standing on the pavement, in the firing line of his particular brand of intimidation. She could have told him there was no contact, and there was no new supply. She could have confessed that all she had was a big debt, looming homelessness, and a missing boyfriend. But, this 'silly wee girl' had too much to play for. He had seemed happy with the outcome, she'd successfully convinced him he had the upper hand.

Things had certainly gotten a lot more complicated, and there were still a couple of elements to sort out. It was overwhelming, but it would all be worth it, to be free of this place.

How many times had she tried to escape?

The first time she was just eight. She'd emptied her school satchel into the bottom of the wardrobe. Packed a pastel yellow nightie, some pink nail varnish, a napkin full of pickled onions, cubes of cheese, and mini sausages that she had stolen from a birthday party buffet. She left with a Scrabble box under one arm and walked as far as she could through the nettles and brambles. She'd sat in a little clearing, nails freshly painted, with nothing left but a soggy napkin, until the realisation that Scrabble needed another player drove her home.

No one noticed she had left. Everything at home was the same, but it felt different. She knew then it was easy to leave, staying gone was the tricky bit.

Claire

She drew back the heavy old curtains as far as they would go and arranged the folds under the tie-backs until they were perfect. The room was small, her single bed, sat to the left, her dressing table in the middle and wardrobe to the right. She began by pulling the bed out as far as it would go, jumping over the headboard and pushing it with her knees.

She opened the top drawer of her dressing table and swept her collection of bottles in with clink and a clatter. The wobbly-legged table was dragged to the left side, and then the bed shoved back into its old resting place in the middle of the room.

Claire sat on the same single mattress she'd slept on as long as she could remember. It had moved from house to house, first with her Mum, then her auntie, then here. To her very own home. Soon she'd get a nice new one, but not yet.

Last week she'd rearranged it all to make space for Anna, figuring that she'd need somewhere to stay. She hadn't found the right time to tell her, and now it was too late.

She worked on her toiletry display, arranging bottles from tall to small around the mirror's edges. She consoled herself by remembering that living with Anna would have been a nightmare. She would have used any of these willy-nilly. Never even considering if they were for regular use, special occasions, or aesthetic purposes. She just didn't get that kind of thing. She'd grab the pink display towel in the bathroom and waste it, leaving black eye smudges like a skanky Turin shroud.

She was also oblivious to the use of tie-backs. Claire had once seen her open just one curtain in her living room, for the sole reason that she couldn't be bothered to do both. Ridiculous.

She laughed at her reflection as she remembered watching Anna, a week earlier, flick cigarette ash in her own shoe because the ashtray was at the other end of the sofa. It would have been terrible putting up with her.

Claire rubbed the faint trace of dust from her treasured collection of empty perfume bottles. Before placing them in a prime position on the middle shelf, she opened each one in turn. She took off the tops, waved them under her nose, took a deep sniff, and waited for the memories.

Closing her eyes, she was taken back to the thrill of fancying boys at school discos, the anticipation of new years eve parties, and carefree summer days by the river. And, of course, Anna was there, swimming around in each of the bottled memories.

She missed her.

Bazz

Twenty-four hours had passed since he'd eaten the last potato. He wasn't going to cross that threshold unless he was going to the post office with a giro in hand. He felt light-headed as he blew up the armchair. He got comfortable, making the most of it before it went flat again. He reclined and folded his hands over his chest. His belly rumbled, the temptation to run round to Roy's Spar was strong. He had fifty pence, enough for two packs of space invaders and a couple of flumps. But instead, he thought about what was at risk. He reminded himself of all the times he'd gone a couple of days with an empty belly. He needed something to take his mind off it—a distraction to keep him busy.

Then he had a fantastic idea.

Bazz wet his hair in the kitchen sink, filled his palm with value washing up liquid, and rubbed it briskly over his scalp until suds began to develop. He ran through to the mirror in his bedroom. His head protruded forward like a pigeon in the park, trying to avoid the water running down his back.

A soapy drip invaded the corner of his right eye. The stinging was unbearable. He thrashed his head from side to side, fumbling on the floor for the towel. He was frantic; he opened the left eye a fraction to try to locate it. Now both eyes felt like riot police were tear-gassing him; the pain seared both lids shut. His blind search yielded nothing to dry his face, and he had only one option. He dived on the bed and burrowed his bubbly face and stinging eyes into the stale duvet. His eyes streamed, he thrashed around face down, he clawed at his eyes through the cotton for aeon's before the agony subsided. He lay traumatised and breathless, with a blotchy face and bloodshot eyes, terrified to move in case another toxic drip blinded him. He used the duvet to mop up any stray water and suds before getting to his feet and leaning towards the mirror. He looked like he'd been crying again.

He angled the cracked glass to get the best view of his profile. He'd never a parting. Just a generic, hair on top, kind of style, occasionally with short sides, when he had a fiver spare to visit the barbers a few times a year.

No one would expect him to have a parting. The perfect disguise. In his police photo, his hair was an unruly mess. That's who they'd be looking for. Not this new guy with a sharp side parting.

He used a bent black comb to create a line over his head above his right eyebrow. The remaining soap crackled as the comb reinvented Bazz from a dishevelled criminal, to a new clean-cut character. The residue would act as hair gel, keeping his perfect disguise neat. He combed and combed, then smoothed the lather down with his hands until every strand was glued down.

He barely even recognised himself! The police had no chance. He looked down at his hands to see them unrecognizable clean. Even his nails were white. He was like a new person.

Anna

She didn't know what number it was, but she would recognise the front door. Entering between the engravers and dry cleaners, she ran up the first flight of stairs.

It wasn't this floor. The smell of urine was almost drowned out with pine disinfectant. The first glossy black door had remnants of old graffiti. The original work had stated 'grass.' This was obvious due to the matt black paint used to cover each letter.

The second door on the first landing was looked after. Pink geraniums and ivy trailed from hanging baskets, and a welcome mat sat at perfect angles. The little card in the doorbell said Mrs. Henderson in a curly cursive that reminded Anna of primary school writing lessons.

Trust

Realising she was quite out of breath after the first flight, she decided to take the next slowly. She didn't want to turn up flustered. As she ascended, the scent of pine disinfectant turned to weed. That comforting smell that reminded her of home, her real home, from a long time ago. She didn't smoke it, but her parents had. She hadn't known what it was as a child; only later on did she realise what that familiar smell was. She kept it a secret though. She heard others telling their stories of home baking, fresh laundry, or steak pies being reminiscent of their wholesome childhoods. She was ashamed of the comfort she found in second-hand weed smoke.

The next door wasn't it either. The green gloss paint was scratched around the keyhole, and a wooden crucifix hung on a green tartan ribbon from the knocker.

The second door on this floor was his. A single spider plant hung in a macrame sling from the roof, and a plain hessian rug lay at her feet.

She took a deep breath and knocked. The door was thick and old; it hurt her knuckles and made very little sound. She flipped the letterbox instead. With each opening, she could hear the baseline of Funky Town from inside. He approached the door one foot heavy the other light. As the keys rattled she prepared a friendly greeting,

"Hey Shaun, how's it going?"

"Anna! What brings you here?" He looked delighted to see her.

She looked around and leaned in to whisper,

"Remember what we were talking about last week? That offer to help me out?"

"Of course, come in, come in." He stood to the side and tried to hold in his bloated stomach. She squeezed by, the bulging coats hanging along the wall forced more physical contact than she had planned. He ushered her to the living room, she took a seat on the cord sofa.

"You sit there and listen, put your feet up. Get comfortable." She nodded and smiled at his instructions. Shaun left the room, leaving Anna feeling nervous. She was wary of damaging his flimsy ego; she'd seen how easily he could turn. She knew this was going to get uncomfortable. Just nod and smile.

He returned with a well-stocked cheese

board, oatcakes, two knives, and two plates on a tray. He pulled the three-legged table around and placed it between them.

"Now, this is goats cheese," he stuck the sharp pronged end of the knife into the centre of the white velvety cylinder. "You've probably never had it before. It's really nice." She had tried it before and hated it, but now was not the time to go into that. She bit into the prepared oatcake and made the right noises. How much cheese would she have to eat before she could get out of there?

When only a couple of rinds remained, and he'd bored her almost to tears with his lecture on disco music, Shaun leaned back and brushed the crumbs from his hard gut. Anna watched the dark blue of his t-shirt become lined with remnants of cheese. The front was flecked with grease stains on close inspection. He caught her looking and coughed to distract her.

"So, tell me. You decided to take up my offer of a loan?"

"Yeah, if it's still available."

He nods, for far too long, and crosses his hands over his stomach.

"I knew you'd come round eventually.

You're too innocent to be dealing with the likes of Archie. You've no idea what sort of people you're mixed up with."

She looks at this sleazy creep sitting in a room decorated with his jail trophies, and nods again, like she's listening intently, to news she's never heard before.

"So you'll take my money, pay off Archie, and then you owe me."

Keep nodding.

"We don't need to concern ourselves with the repayment details right now, I trust you."

She kept nodding, trying not to think of the repayments he had in mind. She needed the cash, and to get out of there and be home for Archie's delivery at nine pm. The orange oval clock on the mantle said just after eight.

"Is that the right time?"

"It's still early. You'll be staying a while, won't you?" This didn't feel like a question.

"It's just, I'm pretty tired, I don't think I'm the best company tonight," she saddened her look to convince him.

"It's because of the stress, isn't it? All this worry about Archie, no wonder you're tired having that bad bastard on your case. Just as well I've stepped in eh?"

312

"Yeah, I really appreciate it. How about I come over at the weekend instead, you can give me an education on music?" She hated herself.

"Sure, I'd like that, and you'll be in a better mood once all that's behind you."

She arranged another smile and nod from her extra tired face. When he left the room, she wiped her lips with her sleeve, trying to clean away the words, and rid herself of how she'd acted to get what she wanted. He returned with four rolls, held with blue elastic bands.

"There's five hundred in each of these," he held them out, and as she reached for them, he predictably snatched them back.

"Ah-ha, not so fast. Tell me first, are you going to the club on Friday night?" His head tilts to the side as if he is expecting a kiss on the cheek.

"Oh, um, I hadn't planned it." She tried to gauge his reaction. What did he know? "Maybe, I think, but if I'm feeling better."

"I think I'll go, since you are." He smiled and let the rolls fall into her hands. "We can start really getting to know each other."

"Yeah, definitely." She planted them in her bag and began to edge away. "Cool, well, I'll see you there then."

Standing at the front door, his hand on the key, he stopped her from going any further.

"Is that it? You think you can just take the money and run?"

"I told you, I'm just exhausted."

He placed one hand on the wall above each of her shoulders, barricading her in fat, hard against the wall. His gut pressed against hers. With nowhere to go, she wanted to spit in his face, but she couldn't blow it now, inches from the door. His lips parted, and his breath deepened, he pushed himself into her a little more.

"OK, Friday. It's a date." Anna announced to his obvious pleasure. Then she had to do it, the final obstacle before leaving with the loot. The closer she got to his face, the stronger the smell of vinegar. She pursed her lips so tight they were bloodless and gave him the smallest, coldest kiss in the world. The sweaty gatekeeper seemed happy with it. He opened the door and guided her out with his other arm,

"Wear something special on Friday, a nice dress. Make an effort now. You owe me."

"Sure. Good night then, and thanks."
She gave a tired little wave and set off down
the stairs.

 "You be careful out there now!" He
shouted after her.

The Church clock was almost at eight-
thirty, she would have to run. Or not. She
peeled off a couple of notes and went into
the corner shop. She bought twenty Benson
and Hedges and splurged on a carton of
milk, a chicken and mushroom pot noodle, a
loaf of white bread and a pat of real butter.
After what she'd been through, she deserved
it. She got in the first taxi at the rank and sat
in the back, locking away her latest
experience and preparing for her next move.

It was almost nine. She ran up the stone
stairs, threw herself inside, and launched her
handbag into the bedroom. She stood
behind the front door breathing deeply,
trying to look composed. She was counting
on Archie's stupidity while gambling with
his violent side, and she knew she was on

very shaky ground.

As she heard his feet on the steps, she swallowed hard and squeezed her eyes shut tight for a second before turning the handle. Archie didn't wait. He forced himself inside, pushing her into the corner of the hallway. She stumbled backward and slid down the wall. He slammed the door behind him. Her arms instinctively wrapped around her head, and her knees drew up in front of her face.

"Get up. On your feet, fool." Archie ordered. She bit her lip so the pain and taste of blood would block out the other emotions threatening to explode. His hand gripped her hair at the roots. As he yanked, she cooperated and rose to her feet. He pushed his index finger into the middle of her forehead, forcing her head back into the corner. Prodding harder with each word, he shouted,

"This. Is. Your. LAST. Chance. You got that?"

He was so close Anna could see every hair in his eyebrows, the spattering of white hairs in his dark stubble, and the depth of the two horizontal lines across his forehead. She imagined sticking her thumbs into his eyes, waiting for the pop, but she just stood there, still, taking it all in.

"You made a big mistake putting my money in Davie's bank. It's me you answer to. Not him."

Deep inside, tears began to well, not from fear or sadness, but molten anger. She hadn't answered to anyone for a very long time. As the resentment boiled, her expression changed, and he saw it. Her eyes narrowed, her jaw tightened. He removed his finger from her head, hesitated, then grabbed her cheek between his thumb and forefinger, giving it a jovial squeeze as you might do to a toddler.

"All you need to do is make sure the cash is in my hand by the end of Friday night." He said.

Her teeth clenched so hard she couldn't release them, her eyes drilled into his. He broke away from her stare and pulled the pill bags from his pocket.

"I'll be at the club all night. I'll be watching you."

She could feel her hair sticking to the cold sweat on the side of her temple. She wanted to sweep it off her face, shove him hard in the chest, get him away, get air, and get out of this corner. But her fists were so tightly balled her nails felt like they were piercing the bones.

As he stepped out onto the stone stairway, he pointed once more,

"Last chance."

CHAPTER TWELVE
Thursday

Bazz

Thursday morning and Bazz was awake early, listening out for the crispy giro envelope to hit the floor. The day was finally here, and he felt as if his entire life had been leading up to this moment. All he had to do was cash that cheque, and go from overlooked loser to the man everyone wants to know.

Then it came. The snap of metal he'd been listening for, and the right envelope hitting the floor. He jumped out of bed with more vigour than he thought he was capable of. He was a different man now.

He slowly peeled the envelope open like

Charlie Grub, careful not to rip the golden ticket. There it was, in his very own hands. The most money he'd ever had in one go. Nine hundred and ninety-seven pounds.

He felt the joy rise in his belly. Today he was Charlie Grub, and the keys to the chocolate factory were as good as his. He punched the air, again and again. He squealed and punched his leg.

The excitement was too much for him; he lay down on the mattress and slowed his breathing. It was all coming together. He just had to make it in and out of the Post Office unseen. With his new hairstyle, that shouldn't be a problem.

He dressed with enthusiasm, so much that his hoodie ended up backwards. He spun it around his neck without taking it off his head. He felt his hair. It was hard and a bit dusty. He applied a couple of wet hands and brought it back to life, smooth, sleek, and unrecognisable.

His usual route avoided main roads and places where possible confrontation might be loitering. But today required an even sneakier path. Although in disguise, he still had to be careful to avoid drawing any attention. Then it came to him.

The river!

He could walk through the gardens behind the estate, up the riverbank, under the bridge, and come out at the Post Office. All without walking along the High Street. Why did he ever doubt himself? This was the perfect plan.

He looked at each house, assessing the likelihood anyone was at home, before deciding whose gate to use. With his hood up, he chose number six. With no cars parked and a very upmarket looking garden, he was sure they would be out at work. He slid through the side gate. At the far end of the garden, he could see the fence between him and the river. It was higher than he'd anticipated, but nothing he couldn't scale with a bit of a run-up.

He took a deep breath and took off towards the brown wooden slats. He grabbed the top; his feet slid frantically as he struggled to catch hold. The surface was sticky, his nose filled with overpowering creosote.

"Get oot ma garden ya junkie bastard!" a

shrill voice shouted from the back door, he
lost his grip, and his feet slid down. "I'm
phoning the polis!"

The adrenaline surge powered up his
legs and heart; he didn't need a run-up now.
He used his toes to find footholds in the thin
gaps between slats. With the grace of a
skilled rock climber, he pulled himself over
the fence. There was no time to catch his
breath on the other side - he could still hear
the furious woman shouting as he ran.

"You've ruined ma fence, you junkie
imbecile!"

He had a wee laugh to himself while
ripping through the ferns and sticky willies.
She's the imbecile, he thought. I'm not even
a junkie, shows what she knows!

He stopped a little further along,
crouching at the river's edge. He tried to
wash off the thick brown treacle from his
hands. It wouldn't budge. He looked at his
shoes and his jeans. Even his hoodie was
covered in the stuff. Great. The familiar
feeling of failure sunk through his belly. But
he reminded himself why he was there. He
had a mission today, and some sticky paint
wasn't going to ruin it.

He made his way further into this new

territory. It was fresh and unfamiliar. Things brushed against his face. His feet fumbled for firm stepping stones as the terrain got wilder. He knew he was only at the side of the park, but this felt like another world. The little stream had taken on the danger of Rocky Mountain rapids. The air felt fizzy as the water cascaded over rocks, creating foam and spray.

He forgot about the sticky hands as he gained confidence in exploring this new world. He was in a state of flow, his feet effortlessly finding the right stone to take his weight, using branches above to steady his transition up the river. He felt like Tarzan taking command of the jungle.

Right foot on the gravel at the water's edge... left hand on a tree trunk... left foot on a flat stone... right hand steadied with a branch... right foot on a mossy rock - the wettest, slipperiest rock in the entire river. He grips a branch, his foot slides off the front, with a splash, into the dark brown water. It's deeper and colder than he expected. His right leg is submerged halfway up his shin. He pulls, it resists, he pulls again. Panic starts to rise, and he increases the force. Then finally relief, it gives, and he pulls his foot out.

And it was just his foot. No shoe attached. He felt the swell of tears, but no, not today. He'd come this far. He'd do what needed to be done.

He prepared for impact, rolled his sleeves up, and plunged his dry foot into the darkness. His breath was short and fast as he steadied his body against the flow of the river. He leaned on the slipperiest rock with his left arm and began the underwater search with his right. He couldn't feel anything. He needed to go deeper. His cuff would have to get wet. As he felt the tide mark of water rise up past his knees, he conceded it didn't matter now anyway. He delved deeper, his hands feeling between stones, through the gravel bed, and under the ridge of the slippery rock. There was no sign of it, he stood defeated, half soaked, and half shoed. He was about to let the tears flow, then he saw it, a few meters further down, floating sole up, in a foamy dam of sticks and leaves. He had nothing to save now, so he splashed his way towards it. With the rescued shoe in his hand (he didn't want to risk losing it again), he waded and stumbled his way downstream.

The bridge turned out to be lower and darker than he'd imagined. Cartoons had inspired his concept of going under a bridge: a stone archway, well lit, with standing room underneath, and some stepping stones, or even a path. This bridge was dark, slimy, and scary. He thought about how far he'd come and reminded himself of the goal. He put the heavy, soaked shoe up inside his jumper. He got on all fours, facing the mossy dripping mouth of the bridge. He kept his eyes on the light ahead, and his head below the trailing green slime. The speed of his breathing was making him dizzy. Not far now, only a few more feet, almost there.

He made it! As soon as he was able, he stood up tall and threw himself onto the grassy embankment. He instantly recoiled, realising a little too late that the dominant plant was nettle. The right side of his neck and ear burned. He pulled his wringing sleeves over his hands and rubbed his unbearably stingy skin.

The Post Office was just meters away now. He scrambled through the vegetation, up and over the stone wall at the top of the slope. He was now in full sight with no tree coverage - one shoe, one filthy sock, his entire outfit smeared with brown and green, and completely saturated. He quickly put the other shoe on; he didn't want anyone to think he was daft. His stained and wrinkled hands smoothed over his side parting, he recoiled again, feeling something horrible, like a slug. Looking at his hands, he saw he hadn't avoided all the bridge goo, and was now wearing some as hair gel. He pulled up the soaking hood, and pulled the cords tight. He wasn't going about looking like he'd been attacked by Slimer.

He looked up and down the street, only an old lady dragging a shopping cart, and an IrnBru delivery lorry. He couldn't have timed it better. He skipped two doors up, and into the Post Office, he cringed at the bell above his head, ringing loud as he entered.

Only one person in front of him, perfect. He waited, trying to look inconspicuous, he casually put a hand in his sodden pocket.

The giro!

It wasn't so crispy now. It was soaked, and one corner had disintegrated. As the customer in front shuffled away, he was revealed to the cashier. Tears streamed down his dirty, nettle stung face. A puddle was collecting at his feet, and he smelled of creosote and stagnant bridge slime.

He handed his ruined future over to the stern-faced woman at the other side of the counter. He couldn't string the words together to explain. She was silent while she examined it, then him. His unstemmed tears flowed. She sucked air between her teeth and shook her head. His face began to contort, from silent weeping to brutal, ugly faced crying. The horrified woman looked around and put her hand up.

"Hey, come on now, pull yourself together! This isn't something I'd normally do. But you've clearly had a bit of a rough time of it. I'll tell you what I'll do."

Bazz rubbed his pained face with a wet sleeve. Maybe it wasn't over.

"I'll dry this out through the back, and I'll give it a little press later on. I'm sure it will be fine. Just, em, calm down. Then clean yourself up, please."

He nodded, open-mouthed, and watched

her counting out neat piles of notes with swift fingers. She folded them, added some coins, and slipped the bundle into a plastic bag. She slid it over the counter, into his shaking hands.

"Try and keep it dry. And I've kept a pound for the crisps and sweets you forgot to pay for the other day," she whispered through the gap.

Anna

She had a million acquaintances. On the weekends, they were friends. At midnight on a Saturday, they were family separated at birth. Weekdays were different though, and the only person she wanted to see was Claire. She wanted to wait outside her work, but she couldn't bear it if she rejected her. She wanted to knock on her door, but her heart would have broken on the spot if it was slammed it in her face. Instead, she went where she knew she was welcome.

"Fancy a night out, Christine?" A wizened face peered from above the chain. "Coming down to the club tomorrow? There's a decent line up of DJs. It's going to

328

be banging."

Christine opened the door and stood aside for Anna.

"No chance. Firstly I hate banging, and secondly, it will be full of untrustworthy cunts."

"Come on. It will be good. You've not had a proper night out for ages." Anna bounced past and found the biscuit barrel in the spotless kitchen.

"That reminds me. Talking of untrustworthy cunts; I saw you talking to that pikey, by the way." Christine stated as she followed her.

"Me? "When?" According to Christine, these were the worst breed of people. Anna held her eyes open, trying not to blink and reveal anything, taking a biscuit for each hand.

"Aye, I saw you. When I was leaving the pub."

"Oh that, eh, he was asking if I want to buy a dog."

"What the fuck would you want with a dog?" Christine dismissed every word with one raised eyebrow. Anna broke free from her inquisitive stare by looking deep inside the barrel and extracting another soft digestive. "You can't feed yourself, never mind a bloody dog."

"Yep, that's what I told him." Anna sprayed crumbs as she agreed.

"He'll be after something, they always are. Ocht, look at the mess you're making! Get a bloody plate! And go and sit down!"

A sprinkling of crumbs lay around where she stood, Christine skillfully collected the detritus with a dustpan and brush. While she finished the rest of the biscuits, Christine laughed at Anna's commentary of Supermarket Sweep. They always found great entertainment in the orange man, directing a bunch of slack-jawed contestants to fill their trolleys. Christine sat on the arm of the chair, waiting to start sweeping around Anna when the time was right.

"I'm getting the bus into town for some messages if you want to come?" Christine asked.

"Na, I'm just going back to the flat. I've no money anyway."

"You still skint? Thought you took that loan off Shaun?"

"What?" she couldn't hide anything this time, blinking and swallowing heavily.

"Saw him this morning. He told me you two are getting on very well."

"Aye, well, it's just to get Archie off my back. I'll pay him what's due first, then what I make on Friday goes straight back to Shaun."

"You're playing with fire there. He reckons you've got a date tomorrow."

"He does?" Anna tried to look confused. Christine's slow nod extracts more words than Anna wants to supply.

"I said I'd probably see him there. Not see him specifically. Just see him, in the same way I'd see anyone there. It's nothing like that, he just offered a hand, and I took it."

"He's got other ideas hen. You don't want to be leading him on."

"I'm not, anyway, he seems more reasonable than Archie. And it was your idea."

"Don't count on it. I got the two of you talking to get you out of trouble, not into it. I certainly didn't think you'd be getting cosy with him!"

Anna shuddered, the vinegary memory almost spilling out. Please don't ask any more questions. Get back to the shopping trip.

"What you getting from the shops anyway?"

"Biscuits, since the barrels empty." Christine snipped, then continued, "So, you took the loan, but you're are still dealing for Archie tomorrow? Do you want them both after you?" Christine tipped her head to the right.

"It's OK, I just took him up to make it easier, cover all bases." Anna knew Christine would extract more than she ever wanted to say. She sat there in silence, and eventually, the vacuum got filled.

"It's short term. A couple of days." No reaction. The space grew, and words brewed to fill it up.

"It'll be fine. By the end of this weekend, everyone will be paid, and I'll be out of here."

"Uh, hu. You've got it all under control then?" Christine asked, slow and sarcastic.

"Yeah, it's not a problem. Everything is working out just fine." Anna folded her arms and resolved to say no more.

Jackson

Operation Brown Owl. This was the biggest night of her career. The chance to prove her intuition was strong, and her methods got results. It wouldn't cost much. Enough officers would be on hand for the event anyway. That's how she sold it to the Chief Inspector. Her very own operation! He'd said, "Please your bloody self, but do not fill my cells with drunks." But, she could tell he was impressed.

By Saturday, the streets would be clean. Whoever these Scousers were, they'd be easy to spot. She'd lied a little, to make the operation more sellable. She'd assured her boss that she knew exactly who she was watching. She'd had descriptions and seen photos from a couple of anonymous tip-offs. She'd be sacked if he found out, but she wouldn't get caught. She knew from the pit of her stomach; once she got there, it would all fall into place.

She knew most people in this town, a gang of Scousers with too much money, and a herd of druggie youngsters trailing after them, would not be difficult to spot.

The officers drafted into her operation were a little more sceptical. As they took their chairs at the single exam-style desks, sighs filled the room. Jamie poured the warm, bitter coffee into polystyrene cups and handed them out. From the back row, an officer said,

"Do you remember the last time we did something like this with Walker? Jameson nearly had a heart attack from chasing a lassie through the park, and Anderson had gravel rash up his face from jumping that wall."

"It's pointless. The wee bastards will just swallow whatever they've got as soon as they see a uniform." Another replied.

Jackson stood, hands behind her back and began,

"We are not after the idiots taking the stuff. It's the evil people selling it. We are no longer dealing with the cardboard gangsters, the likes of Davie King or Archie. This is big time now."

More sighs, and a groan.

"You take your queue from me. I know who they are. When we get close enough, on my signal, we strike. They won't be expecting it. They don't know what kind of force we have up here."

"Who are we looking for exactly?" One asked.

Jamie stepped from behind Jackson, placing one hand on his hip,

"Liverpudlians. You know, Scousers. From Liverpool. That's in England."

"Very good, Jamie, sit down." Jackson hissed. "Look, don't any of you concern yourselves with that. I know, and I'll give the signal. OK?"

Two rows of half-hearted nods.

"I want half of you in plain clothes, half in uniform. We are going to take these guys out of the picture and send a clear message to anyone else that fancies their chances in my town."

"I just know you're going to get them! This is so exciting!" Jamie made his way around the tables collecting coffee cups. Jackson shook her head at his outburst.

"You are all excused, be back here on Friday at five pm for the operation briefing."

The unenthused group filtered out. Jackson took her black covered note pad and flipped to a fresh page. In her best handwriting, she titled the page "Operation Brown Owl". She tapped the end of her pen on the pad as she pondered what else to write. She thought back to the results of grilling Wendy.

Back in the interview room, pushed further, she had spilled plenty more information. Addicts were easy like that; she could always get them to sing. She'd pushed for a description of the Scousers. At first, she said she hadn't even seen any! But with a little of her unique Di Jackson brand of persuasion, she soon gave a full description. Two men, long mousy hair, one with a beard, around 6ft. One slightly taller than the other. Then, as she turned the screw a little tighter, she'd revealed a third accomplice, shorter in stance but with similar hair.

Thank you very much, Wendy.

At first, she'd been adamant she had no names to give, but by the end, she supplied three possibilities. Barry, Robin, and Morris. She noted these points down. They certainly didn't sound like anyone around here. They would be very easy to spot.

The details of the contraband were interesting. Through all her previous drug training, she'd never heard of the "squidgy, rubbery, coloured stuff" that Wendy described. Highly dangerous, she thought. The usual effects, dancing, chewing, delirium, were reported, but more potent, more powerful. Highly, highly dangerous, she confirmed.

She snapped the notebook shut and slotted it into its holder. She arranged the abandoned chairs at their desks, held her shoulders back, and straightened her spine. This operation was going to be the making of her.

Anna

Something about Christine knowing she'd visited Shaun, and seen her with the pikey really rattled Anna. As if someone else knowing made it all real. She'd gone straight back to the flat to avoid any more complications. It was grimmer inside than usual, but she only had to get through tonight, then tomorrow was the big day.

The big day.

She wasn't quite sure how this was all going to work. The possible scenarios were infinite; most of them bad. She wished someone would come and take the burden from her shoulders. It all felt unbearably heavy. Somewhere inside, was a far distant memory of not being responsible for anything, just tagging along with the grown-ups in charge. If something was too hard, her mum would have fixed it. If someone had threatened her, her dad would have sorted it all out. A million years ago, in a different life. Now, everything was up to her, and only her.

Should she back out of it all?

Cancel everything?

Was she way out of her depth?

Should she just stay put? Try and get a job; be normal.

She could give it all back. Call off everything, send Archie to Davie, and forget he ever existed. She felt sick.

The most important thing in her life was Claire, and she'd lost her now. There was no point even thinking about trying to make it work here. The closest thing she had to family was Christine, and she could feel her wearying of her too.

A good three inches of whiskey remained in the bottle, and now was the time to finish it. She held the open bottle under her nose; she didn't gag. She'd started to like the smell, and the knowledge it gave her that soon, she'd feel OK again.

She looked out over the rooftops from

the living room window, the alcohol and dusk combining to create a soft filter on everything. The streetlights came on, and the temperature dropped. There was an old blue blanket folded up on a shelf below the TV. As she pulled it out to wrap around her shoulders, a thin spiral-bound notebook fell from the shelf. In the drawer, she found a pen. Perhaps if she wrote her 'to do' list down, there might be a chance of actually ticking something off it.

She sat by the window, cross-legged and cosy, chewing the end of the pen in a trance, staring thoughtfully, thinking nothing at all.

A feeling was growing. Something was pushing the attic door in her mind. She took a swig from the bottle. It didn't help. She turned to a clean page and began.

Dear Mum,
How are you? I hope you are in heaven, or a similarly nice place.

She scribbled over the words and ripped the page out. She took another swig and started again.

Trust

Dear mum.

I miss you.

I am sorry I made you think I was running away from you.

It was never you.

I'm so scared of being stuck here. On boring days, I can feel roots growing down from me, getting wound up in the fabric of this town. Slowly, unstoppably growing down, through rock, sand, bones, and earth, fixing me to this place forever.

My body is torn between growing wings and keeping these roots. I want to kick them free and take off in any direction. North, south, the destination doesn't even matter. I just don't want to stay here waiting to die.

This is the closest my wings have ever been to flying. I don't know what's out there for me, but it has to be more than this. More than you had. More than Dad left us with.

Is this the part of me that reminded you of Dad? The bit you shook your head at? The bit you tried to ground and lecture out of me?

I need to tell you a secret, Mum. I used to lie in bed, wanting to crawl in beside you to sleep before you died. I'm sorry, I couldn't. I was preparing myself, getting ready to be my own family, my own comfort and support. I'm sorry.

Soon, I'll disappear. I'll get far away from here, away from the old worn path to school, away from the memory of empty chairs at the table and the cupboards left with foods that only you liked.

I watched you disappear slowly, from your body, and from my life. You know what? It made Dad's click-of-the-fingers, disappearance trick seem kinder.

Tears were rolling down her face, a drop landed on the paper, and the ink spread within it. She dried her eyes with the blanket and ripped the sheet from the book. She folded it twice, took the silver zippo from her pocket, and lit the corner. White turned to orange, then black. Smoke swirled and caught in her throat as she dropped it in the ashtray and watched it turn to dust.

She opened the window, and threw Davie's special lighter as far as she could, over the shed roof, clattering into plant pots beyond.

No one was going to stand in her way. She was getting out of this place, and she knew exactly how she was going to do it.

CHAPTER THIRTEEN
Friday

Anna

Anna woke up, noticeably fresh, considering she'd finished the whiskey and got into bed with a plate of toast.

The rucksack was still in the corner by the window from her last attempt, it lay empty and discarded, like her and Davie's plan. Picking up denim items, she rolled them into balls and stuffed them in. Claire would definitely disapprove of her packing strategy. She checked her passport, laughed at the photo, then zipped in the front compartment. She checked the pocket of her jacket, feeling the thin gold St Christopher on a delicate chain. She popped open the paint-splattered stereo and pulled out her precious mixtape. She would find somewhere to play it soon.

As she packed, five hard, loud knocks on the door startled her. She stopped moving, stood still, waited. Who could it be? Plenty of people wanted things from her, but not yet, not till tonight. She leaned against the wall, and made a list of everyone possibly looking for her today;

1- Archie,

2- Shaun,

3- Ronin,

4- Bazz,

5- The police.

Her stomach flipped. She realised she had the pills inside the flat. After last weekend she'd avoided hiding them in the coal bunker, opting to keep them safe and dry in jumper pocket. It lay at the other side of the room, in the sight-line of the door. Just where she'd dropped it. Adrenaline pumped as she crept behind the bedroom door, knelt, and stretched across the floor to retrieve it. She planned to throw them out of the window as soon as she knew it was the police.

With the bags in hand, she crawled to the window and gripped the handle. Looking out from the first floor, it didn't seem too high. Maybe she could make it onto the shed roof a few feet below.

Then another noise, a rattle, a crunch, and a scrape. A second key in the lock.

Davie? Did he come back for her?

Anna was about to shout; then, a dull hard thud stopped her. A heavy shoulder shoved the door with the handle down. The landlord! The letterbox flipped angrily five times. On the sixth, it stayed open. The sound in the flat changed, the traffic was louder, and the air seemed fresher. Anna could feel his eyes on her things, scanning the floor, waiting for a noise. She opened her mouth wider to breathe deeper but stay silent. Finally, it flipped shut.

She ducked under the windowsill, listening, his footsteps stopped halfway along the path. She knew he was looking up at her window. She felt his eyes burning through the concrete, exposing her on all fours in her knickers, with a handful of drugs in a messy bedroom. She didn't have time to deal with this. The place should have been empty by now, and it would be soon enough, she'd post the keys through on her way out. He was right at the bottom of today's priorities.

The night's event was going to be the biggest of the year, and everyone would be there. All the under-agers, the new couples who hadn't been seen for ages, the settled married ones who'd scored a babysitter. The few magical old-timers who'd never grown out of it, even the junkies would have scraped enough together for a ticket. There would be plenty of stoners. Drinkers too, the ones who saved their tables, hung around the bar and ended up fighting outside at the end of the night.

They'd all be making an effort. You'd be guaranteed to see friends, enemies, exes, and future mistakes there. Ben Sherman shirts would be hanging on the back of doors, aftershave waiting to be splashed on liberally. Only a few more work hours to go. Clancy's hairdressers on the High Street would be running on a backlog of blow drys already.

What could she wear? The solitary dress hanging by one strap on a lopsided coat hanger? It was black Lycra, ankle-length, with slits on either side up to her hips, and a mesh panel around the midriff. It had been waiting for a special occasion, and this should be it.

She sighed and looked at her belongings on the bedside table, rolls of borrowed cash, bags of pills, and a pair of extra-long socks.

After removing the elastic bands, she flattened out the notes and moulded them around her ankles. Half on each side, with a twenty, put aside for tonight's expenses. She inserted the pills in her bra. The only things left were the socks. She had owned them since high school. Black 'over the knee', originally, they were to compliment a black and white tartan mini skirt, but she had been forced to opt for white slouch socks and tights instead. Being taller than average meant the over the knee style had been just out of reach. She pulled them over the crispy ankle bulges, to rest reassuringly tight in the knee crease.

She stepped back into yesterday's jeans and put on a worn-once-kind-of-clean black vest. The boot-cut denim hid the strange shapes of her legs beneath.

She yanked at the dress. She couldn't be bothered stepping up to reach the hanger, so she tugged harder till the plastic snapped. She balled the dress up and squeezed it in. One day soon she'd wear it.

Looking around the flat, she tried to conjure up some memories. She had an urge for sentimentality. She wanted a montage of their best moments together. She walked from room to room. There were no romantic laughs, cooking together in the kitchen. No cosy nights on the sofa. No candlelit shared baths, and no memorable nights of passion in the bedroom. Just cheap pizzas with boring soap operas. Clammy comedowns and tight muscled sleep, between third-hand bedsheets.

The remnants of her last supper lay by the sink, crumbs of toast in the bed, and a Garfield mug with multiple tea rings balanced on a narrow windowsill.

The rucksack holding her entire existence was heavy; she had to pull it onto both shoulders to balance. At the front door sat a pair of pristine denim wedges, no scuffs, no pulled threads on the buckle holes.

She sighed; tonight was not the time for breaking in new shoes. With more sadness than leaving a pair of heels merited, she reached for the door handle. She stopped silent again. Feet were bounding up the stone steps. She was frozen once more.

The letterbox opened. In slid a glossy sunset. The letterbox flipped shut, and the footsteps scuffed away. She peeled the old chewing gum off the peephole and saw the back of the post-woman.

It lay at her feet, shining up at her, a little snapshot of the future on a threadbare brown carpet, in a grim Scottish hallway. Anna bent at the knees to avoid toppling and picked up the postcard. On the reverse, in his recognisable childish writing,

'Apartment 24,

Carrier Santa Agnes,

San Antonio, Ibiza.

See you here soon??

Xx'

She folded it in two and slipped it into her back pocket. She left the flat and posted the key through the letterbox.

Bazz

He woke with a jump; this was it. Bazz's day was finally here. There were preparations to make. He'd need a decent meal, a wash, and clean clothes. He couldn't remember ever being so excited. His mind raced with all the things he needed to do. He still had one big decision to make- how would he act tonight?

He'd be cool, of course.

And mysterious. He wasn't going to give anything away. Mainly because he didn't want anyone to realise how stupid he could be. He knew his time was limited, so he only wanted to get this weekend out of the way. Maybe next weekend too. He had heard of people having warrants out for months before eventually getting caught. Imagine that, he thought, he could be the main man for months before going to jail. That would be enough time to build up a bit of a reputation.

If he went in there as plain old Bazz, he'd be eaten alive, this little bit of extra time had to be used wisely. He thought about what else he might need to do to build up respect out there. He wasn't into confrontation, and he definitely was not a fighter. His angle so far had been deflection; in times of trouble, he relied on the age-old method of 'be cheeky and run away.' That wasn't going to be suitable in this case.

Maybe he'd need to threaten someone. He hoped not. He was the new guy on the scene. He could do things differently. He could be a likeable, friendly dealer that everyone simply paid straight away because he was sound. He liked that idea.

His good clothes were soaking in the bath in the last of the washing up liquid. He needed to get more for himself. And he was hungry. He was sure Anna would be cool about him borrowing a few pounds, he could pay it back later. He smoothed the crispy side parting to make sure he was disguised. Outside, he looked up and down the road, and ran to Roy's Spar in the next street.

Trust

With the thick wad of notes in his pocket, he felt like a king. He picked up a tuna sandwich and a bottle genuine Fairy Liquid instead of the Happy Shopper cheap stuff. He swaggered up to the till. After waiting his turn, he asked, loud and clear,

"Twenty Regal Filter mate, and a lighter. Not one of the cheap ones, either." He made sure everyone in the queue saw him peeling the note off the big bundle before he slapped it down on the counter.

He could definitely get used to this, no one in the shop had said a word, but he felt it. They'd changed how they looked at him.

Bazz washed his best t-shirt with the quality washing up liquid. He looked forward to his turn in the bath as he liked the smell of this new stuff. His knuckles whitened with wringing and twisting as hard as he could, but it was still wet. It wouldn't dry outside in time, and he had no gas to put the heating on. Just before he started to panic, the spore of a brilliant idea began to grow.

The microwave. He flapped the wrinkles

out and folded the t-shirt in four. The inside plate was small, so he folded it again. Five minutes on full power. As he watched the steam rise from the rotating cloth he studied the inner walls of the appliance. Brown speckles and orange drips coated the roof, the smell was filling the room. He made a mental note to add a washing machine and tumble dryer to the list of things to get once he was in business. The bell pinged, and the door opened. A cloud of noxious steam made his eyes water, he attempted to pick the t-shirt up, but quickly drew back and blew on his fingers. He grabbed a fork from the sink, wiped it on the thigh of his jeans, and it fished out.

The smell was new, not nice new, but a combination he'd never experienced before. He hoped it would go away before tonight. He put it back in for another five minutes and left it to cool before putting it on. It was still a little damp, but warm enough to feel nice. He couldn't see the brown singed streak up the back, and his senses were used to the terrible stench his genius idea had created.

He did a five minute work-out with his makeshift weights. After three reps with the double Argos catalogues he was exhausted, but he pushed through. He was proud. He lay on the mattress for a rest and felt his strained bicep. It was definitely bigger! He wondered if Wendy would notice.

He decided to treat himself to a little think about her. He crossed both fingers and tried to cross his gnarly toes, wishing she would turn up at night. He'd give her a freebie. Maybe two. Not to take advantage of her, just so she knew he was a generous guy. He hoped she'd wear that bright blue vest; it really brought out her eyes.

Archie

He poured himself a half pint of Southern Comfort, and topped it up with lemonade. Opening the wooden wardrobe door, he came face to face with Samantha Fox. Her poster had hung undisturbed since the '80s. He picked out a dark blue polo shirt. His favourite jeans were clean; he turned the pocket inside out to check the stain was still there. It disappeared a little more each time, but the light brown corner of fabric reminder him of what he was capable of.

That little bitch better make good

tonight, he thought. This was her last chance. Davie's bird or not, he was not getting mugged off by that silly wee cow.

But, there was something about her. The way she didn't flinch when he tried to crush her hand unsettled him. He'd used the strength of his grip to intimidate plenty of people, male and female, and they had all submitted. But not her.

Then later, at her flat, he'd been so desperate to assert his dominance, but the way she looked at him forced him back. He cringed at the thought of squeezing her cheek, forced to back off. She was a liability. Who knew what she could be capable of, luckily after this weekend, he'd be cutting ties with her for good.

A beige colour, radio alarm clock with a line of cigarette burns around the edge crackled in the background as he dressed. It was tuned to Atlantic 252. Sister Golden Hair began to play, and it reminded him of being little. Of his mum getting ready for work, breathing in clouds of her hair spray in the mornings. He turned it off.

The house was silent. His Dad's door was still closed, and it had been a few days since the nurse was last there. She'd be back tomorrow. Tonight he'd get most of the money he needed. There would be some corners to cut, but he could still give his Dad a decent send-off. When the time came.

On his way out, he picked up the burgundy topped pot-pouri air freshener and sprayed it every few steps as he backed towards the front door.

Ronin

His skin was tight and dry. He'd gone to the swimming pool the night before, to relax, and pick the black from under his fingernails. He could have used the tin bath in front of his mum's log burner, but he was getting too old for that. Plus, he didn't want to arouse any questions. He wore his funeral shirt and replaced his elastic snake belt with a real leather one.

He had until tomorrow evening to buy the horse. Everything was ready, he had the key for the spare horse-box, and he'd been hiding food all week. Every available space in his caravan was packed with stolen hay.

The freezer bag full of cash fit perfectly into his front pocket. He was ready to make his mark.

Leaning out of the caravan door, he whistled at Tina and Maria,

"You girls going out tonight?"

"Shhh, keep it down, we don't want the whole site to know!" Maria hissed.

"Let us in for a fag," Tina said, pushing him inside, "It's like a fucking chicken coop in here, what's all this straw?"

"Never you mind. Listen. I've got some news for you. I'm going there tonight, to the club. I'm going to take over the show. You girls watch me."

The girls look at each other, then back at him. He can't tell if they're impressed, or if he's made more trouble for himself.

"What do you mean?" Tina asked.

"The drugs. The drugs you all buy. You'll be buying them from me."

"Does Robert or Stephen know about this?" Maria asked.

"This is my business," Ronin replied.

"What about Big Stewart, or Wee Robert? Do they know?" Tina added.

"Wait till your Da finds out!" Maria whispered.

"Never mind any them. I'm my own man. Wait and see."

Tina nudges Maria, and he sees that look

between them that he knows means trouble.

"Will you give us some free then, since we're family?" Maria asked in her sweetest voice.

"I'll give you nothing since you're family. I'm not being responsible for that."

"Though you were your own man?" Tina asked, looking smug.

Caught again. These two played him every time.

"Listen, if you girls help me out, I'll see you right. You just let all your little friends know, I've got what they need."

Shaun

With Brylcreem warmed between his palms, he slicked one hand, then the other through his thinning crop. His prominent cows-lick meant this was really the only style he'd ever had. He looked in the mirror and liked what he saw. Pretty good. He could probably get away with saying he was ten years younger than he was.

He lined up the needle on the Boney M album. It crackled into life, he limped to the sofa and began preparing what he'd say to Anna when he got her back there.

He hadn't been out to a club for a long time. He was looking forward to it, but not into hanging around there all night. He would do whatever was necessary; once she'd had a few drinks, she'd be more suggestible, then he'd start work getting her back to his place as early as possible.

She was around twenty, but he wasn't exactly sure. Roughly the same ages as junior Shaun or Shaunette would be. Having her there would be good practice for if, when, they showed up. He'd get a decent idea of what young ones were all about, so he could be a cool dad. Not an out of touch embarrassment like his parents were.

There was wine and of plenty of cheese in the fridge. New soap and a fresh towel by the bath, and the outfit was ready for her to slip into.

CHAPTER FOURTEEN
Friday Night

Anna

By early evening Anna sat on the low graveyard wall waiting for Bazz. Her rucksack was hidden behind the white angel beyond the gate. She leaned back under the dappled shade of the big tree, hoping to merge into the background. Soon, Bazz came bouncing up the path towards her.

His usual smile concealed his teeth, but he couldn't contain his emotions as he got closer. Long dimples gave his face an unusual dimension. It was contagious, and she caught it, her own mouth spread wide, they met each other with glee.

"Well, well, this is it. The big night then,

eh?" Bazz rummages in his front pocket and produces a bundle of notes and coins. "Er, I had to spend a couple of quid, you know, fags and that. Can I give you the extra tenner later?"

"That's a good start," she laughed "It's OK, I'm just kidding, keep the coins, and this, get yourself a drink." She handed twenty pounds back to him. "I've got some stuff to sort out, but I'll meet you in there, by bar just after nine."

"No problem, I'll be there."

"One thing though."

"Yeah, anything." He stood wide-eyed, waiting for instructions.

"You have to be careful, discreet, you know? I feel guilty putting this on you. I don't want you to get in bother."

"Discreet is my middle name. Seriously though, don't feel guilty, this is the best thing that could ever happen to me."

She took both his hands in hers and squeezed. "Promise me, you won't mention my name, or let anyone take them off you. OK? You keep them in your pocket, don't let any big bullies try and con you out of them."

"You can trust me. You're the only

person that's ever given me a chance. I can do it."

"I know." She squeezed a little harder.

He took off back in the direction he came from, shoulders back and head high. Once he was out of sight, Anna folded the new pile of notes around her ankle, and wondered what on earth that horrible smell was.

Ronin

By nine pm, the queue outside the club had grown down the steps and slinked around the corner. Ronin had been standing at the entrance since seven, guaranteeing his place at the front of the line.

The doors opened, and two shiny headed bouncers allowed the crowd to filter in, two at a time. He marched through the dusty plume of the smoke machine, straight to the last table on the left. He didn't buy a drink. Didn't talk to anyone. He just waited, with his eyes fixed on the entrance.

Anna

As she approached the building, her stomach clenched at the prospect of waiting in line. The smell of a hundred different perfumes mixed with smoke turned her already churning stomach. She needed to get in there, as soon as possible, away from eyes and questions.

She recognised most people, and given the circumstances, any one of them would have welcomed her in front of them. Whether they liked her or not, she was the one that would make their night. She spotted a couple of guys from the Viper Room, a few places from the front. She walked straight up and was greeted warmly. It dawned on her that one of them could have taken her money. She chose not to mention it, show no weakness. They offered her a cigarette and asked how Davie was as she nudged in the line beside them.

From behind, she heard a mumbled comment,

"Nice choice in footwear," followed by giggling from three perfectly groomed popular girls she hadn't seen since high school. She looked down at the tattered denim trainers and felt very out of place.

She should be standing with Claire, immune to the sneers of other girls. She felt her heart beat faster. She wished to get in out of the light and away from their judgment. As much as she longed to get into the darkness, she was dreading passing the bouncers. This part of the night was always the worst, knowing they could refuse her entry, or sweep her into a side room and call the police. She didn't look their way, just laughed and pretended she was engrossed in a perfectly natural conversation, but all she could hear was her own blood pumping. Her mouth tasted strange, her body's instincts preparing her to run away.

Her turn came, then after the longest five seconds of her life, the bald head nodded his approval, and she entered.

Her ankles felt like she was dragging a ball and chain around. She wanted to be invisible, but with most of the venue looking for her, that was impossible. Hands reached out to her, overwhelmed her; her name was playing on repeat.

"Ten minutes. Give me a sec. I'll see you in a bit." She assured everyone as she passed through the cloakroom and made her way into the main hall. Through the strobe-lit fog, she could see the solitary figure at the last table on the left. She took the seat next to him, he pulled her head close and shouted in her ear, "You got the goods?"

Anna pulled the corner of the bag from her bra, high enough for him to see the contents, he nodded.

"Cash first." She pulled the drawstring bag open between her knees, pointed inside, and mouthed "Money." He reclined on the chair, attempting to look casual while sliding out the plastic-wrapped bundle. He slithered forward and deposited it where she directed. She drew the strings shut and shouted, "Wait here," in his ear. He nodded and tapped a non-existent watch on his wrist.

She headed towards the bar; she only needed to find Bazz now. She kept moving while searching for his face, she scanned the crowd, trying not to make contact with all the eyes on her, like hungry toddlers waiting for biscuits.

The cloakroom lit up the entrance, creating silhouettes of everyone walking through the door. She tried to stay in the darkest corner by the bar to assess the outlines entering. While she was looking for

364

tall, skinny Bazz, she missed a short, fat someone.

It was getting too much, her heartbeat, the adrenaline, the watching, and the weight of thousands of pounds of other people's money. She gave up her post, leaned on the bar, and ordered a double vodka and coke. She lit a cigarette and relished the cold stingy gulps.

Her breathing slowed as the alcohol did its work, she continued scanning ahead, through the crowd, trying to pick out Bazz's familiar shape.

As she squashed her cigarette into the ashtray, a heavy hand fell on her shoulder from behind. A body pressed against hers, and a finger tickled her earlobe. The vodka threatened to come straight back up as she realised it was Shaun. He pulled her close, and the hair on the back of her neck stood on end as his lips made contact with her ear.

"All alone? Lucky I came. Buy me a drink then!"

She managed a wide fake smile, but she couldn't talk. She pulled away from his grip as she leaned over to get the barmaid's attention. She ordered herself another double and him a pint of lager. While she waited, on her tiptoes, drumming her fingers on the bar, still searching the crowd beyond, she became aware of someone shaking hands with Shaun behind her.

Archie. She felt her legs disappear, the vodka burned up inside her throat, she swallowed it back down. One man stood at either side of her, holding her inside a blockade of trouble. Backed up against the bar, her instinct was to lash out and run. But her brain overruled, she didn't rush, just witnessed their pseudo-friendly small talk, and smiled at them as if waiting obediently to be acknowledged.

"How's it going, Archie?" Anna shocked him with a long, tight hug. It was the last thing she wanted to do, but a distraction was required immediately. "It's so good to see you!" She spun him round in an awkward, disorientating dance move. She grabbed his elbow and waist, in some over-enthusiastic waltz, pushing and sliding, till he faced the other way. Archie looked annoyed, but the obstruction was breached. She had created the escape route, and now she was taking it.

"Shaun, if you'll excuse me, I need to use the bathroom." She rubbed the side of his arm. "I'll be back in a second." With an overzealous gentlemanly gesture, Shaun cleared the way with his arm, and she headed for the toilets. Aware of both their eyes on her back, she took her time.

"She's something else her, isn't she?" Shaun grinned.

"You're not wrong pal. She's a nightmare." Archie replied.

"Well, since I sorted out your little problem, you don't need to worry about her. She's my problem now." Shaun winked.

"Anna? She's with you?" Archie laughed.

"It's not that hard to believe. Look, you've got your money back, so it's time to stay away."

"Once she pays up, I will happily wash my hands of her. She's nothing but trouble."

"She's got the money. I gave her two grand to get you off her back. Believe me, I'm going to make her work to pay that back." He winked at Archie again. The lines across Archie's head deepened, and his eyes narrowed, something was dawning on him.

"You gave that wee cow two fucking grand cash, to pay me?"

Shaun nods, Archie's face reddens, he shakes his head as his lips tighten.

"When did you give her that?"

"A few days ago, when we were arranging this date for tonight."

"You mug. You absolute idiot. That will get her ticket to Ibiza alright, the little fucking cow." Archie wheezed and thumped his chest to catch a breath as his head spun in the direction of the toilets.

"Ibiza? What are you talking about?" Shaun's nostrils flare, and his temperature rises along with the pain in his swollen toes.

"Her man, Davie King, he fucked off to Ibiza a couple of weeks ago. She's heading out there to meet him."

"Her man? She's not single?" His blood pressure pushes his eyeballs, and his toes throb. "She's got some explaining to do."

They both head towards the toilets, one wheezing, one limping, both furious. A new song fades in, the DJ plays Sandstorm, and the whole place erupts. Their pathway's blocked. They race each other, elbowing and battling through the moving crowd. Topless sweaty bodies in jogging bottoms, first pumping with bottles of water hanging out of back pockets. Girls dragging their boyfriends up. Friends holding hands in the air. Archie pushes through with his gritted

teeth bared, leaving a wake of shocked
dancers.

Inside the toilets, Anna locks the door of
the disabled cubicle. She pulls up the socks
higher and tighter to secure her stash. She
wipes the sweat from her forehead and bites
the skin on the side of her thumb. This was
not part of her plan.

Someone knocked on the door.

The only way out of there was a long
thin window five feet up. She hoisted herself
up on the sill, balancing one toe on the
slidey toilet rim. The sole of her trainer
slipped, she steadied herself with the
handle. To her surprise, it opened easily.

Knock, knock, knock.

Using the undignified leg swing she'd
perfected at high school swimming, she got
half her body on to the window ledge. She
lay along the ridge, one leg either side,
hanging in the balance.

Knock, knock. Harder this time. Faster,
urgent.

She tipped towards the darkening night, the ground outside was much lower. This would hurt, she took a deep breath and prepared to jump. Blue flashing lights emanated from the corner of the building.

KNOCK KNOCK KNOCK. Ferocious now, the door rattled. Time was up. Her leg swung down; she hung by the crook the other knee. She positioned her elbows, preparing to jump. Someone was approaching from outside, footsteps running towards her. Getting closer, rounding the corner, it was too late to climb back in. The footsteps stopped, and their eyes met.

The knocking stopped.

Her breath stopped.

DI Jackson. Tawny Owl. Standing ten feet away.

The chaos of the night continued around them, but there, time changed, seconds passed like minutes.

"The Scousers. They're in there." Anna's voice was a tense, loud whisper, theatrical and desperate. She let go with one hand, the remaining left shaking under the tension. She held her hand up, crossing her thumb over the pinkie, her middle three fingers stood straight in the middle. The traditional Brownie salute. It was all she had, a grasp at some common ground, a shared moment. She mouthed the word "Please? They just came in." The torchlight was highlighting her welling eyes.

More rushing footsteps, more police approached, Anna could see their uniforms as they passed the corner.

DI Jackson lowered her torch. She walked backwards, two slow steps at first, still looking the rebellious wee Brownie in the eye. Then she turned and quickened her step, shouting towards the oncoming feet -

"No one round this way, back up towards the main door, it's time to go in!"

The landing was sharp like she'd been shot in the heels. She tried to walk away, not so fast as to draw attention, but fast enough that no one stopped her. She aimed her heavy ankles towards the graveyard and fixed her eyes straight ahead. The sound of the bass and excited crowds began to fade away. A car horn spikes her anxiety. She didn't look, she continued, faster and faster. The horn blew, three more times. She knew that sound. At the furthest point of the car park, familiar lights flash from a red Astra in the corner. Claire. She changed direction and ran towards her friend, praying for no interception. Anna got in the back door and clambered in to lie on the seat.

"What the hell are you doing?" Claire peered into the darkness behind her.

"Please, just drive, I'll explain once we get away from here. Don't stop for anyone. Please, let's go."

Claire knew that desperation in Anna's voice. With no more questions or fuss, she drove between the cars towards the exit. They edged out of the junction, past eager pedestrians toppling off pavements and tripping over kerbs. When they were all out of sight, Claire glanced in the rearview mirror,

"I decided to come tonight because we need to talk. I need to tell you something. I've been sitting out here for ages, thinking of what to say."

"I'm not going to change my mind. I'm still going. There's no way I can stay here."

"I know, I'm not trying to change your mind anymore, but I need to tell you something." Claire tilted the mirror to gauge Anna's expression. Finding no reflection, she looked back to see Anna's slipped down into the foot-well.

"What's going on? You are acting mental, even by your standards. Is Archie after you? What's happened?"

"Look, I need to get out of here. I need to leave this place right now. Things have got pretty messed up."

"Come on, let's go to mine. No one knows where I live. We'll figure it out."

Inside Clarie's little bungalow, at the far corner of Spey Court, they keep the lights off. The vertical blinds drawn, and the snib is on the door. By the glow of the two bar fire, they lie belly down on the swirly patterned carpet. They light cigarettes by poking them through the bars, the dots of a thousand fags line the neon rods.

Anna sat, rolled up her jeans, and took down each sock in turn. Clarie's eyes widened in the darkness as the notes unravelled. She emptied her pockets and bag, and fished around inside her bra to lay out her findings in the fire's glow.

"There should be about six grand there, and two hundred pills."

"Jesus Christ. Six fucking grand! Who's is it? Who's looking for you?"

"About two hundred hungry ravers, I've ruined everyone's night." Anna laughed.

"Seriously, who should we be worrying about right now?"

"Archie mostly. And Shaun. Wee Bazz will be looking for his pills too."

"Give it all back, go down there and hand it all over, the cash, the pills, everything."

"Someone else too. I got myself into something. I didn't mean to, it was kind of forced on me."

Clarie's head shakes slowly from side to side, "Who?"

"Ronin, he gave me three grand, I owe him five hundred pills that don't actually exist," Anna whispered.

"Are you fucking kidding me? You idiot! What the hell are you thinking? Claire hissed.

"OK, calm down. Keep your voice down." Anna resumed her position on the carpet.

"Call it all off, cancel all deals, this cannot happen!"

"Ssshhh, please be quiet, it already has

happened, and I don't need you having a
go."

"Me? Me having a go is…" A long
shadow passed the window behind the sofa.
Faces turning to each other, they lie,
breathing shallow, listening hard. Claire
stretched an arm out to flick the fire off, the
bars fade to black.

"None of them know where I live. It'll be
one of my neighbours or something." A gate
groaned through the darkness. They waited
till the stillness returned.

"Look," Claire said, "I need to tell you
something. I couldn't let you go without
telling you. That's why I came tonight."

"I'm not going to change my mind..."

"Listen for god's sake!"

Anna stops, surprised by Clarie's tone.

"It was me. I took Davies's money the
night before he left."

"What-" Anna can't comprehend, "what
do you mean?"

"I just wanted you to stay."

"No, you wouldn't fuck me over like
that… my life depended on that money."
Anna's voice wobbles.

"I don't want you to go to Ibiza with
him." They sit in silence, then Claire

continued, "You know the money that went missing at the Viper Room?"

Anna nodded slowly, dreading the next revelation.

"That was me too. You were sleeping, and...."

Anna moved into a kneeling position, Claire remained still, facing the darkened fireplace.

"I'm not having that. You're lying."

"The first time, I took a grand and a bag of pills from your pocket in the toilets when you were throwing up. Remember when we were saying goodbye at your leaving night?"

It was blurry, like the night had happened to someone else, but she remembered the time in the toilets. Claire had wiped the mascara from under her eyes and rubbed her back while she was sick. And, as it turned out, also emptied her pockets.

"How could you do that? How could you help me to fix the pills last week knowing it was all your fault? Then you took that fucking money too? Who even are you?"

"I don't know, it got out of hand, I only

want the best for you, and running away
with him is not it!"

"So getting me into debt and having to
sell more drugs is, is it?"

"I didn't know that would happen. I just
wanted you out of that situation. I'm sorry I
made it worse."

"I can't believe this. I should be in
bloody Ibiza right now. Instead, I'm hiding
in the dark with half the town after my
blood."

"I had to try something, you wouldn't
listen, it wasn't…"

"Shhh…" Anna put her hand up and
breathed, "Someone's at the door."

They were both frozen in fear. Neither
moved as the door handle turned down,
rattled, and pinged back up.

"The snib's on. It's OK. Stay down."
Claire whispered. Anna brought her hand to
cover her mouth.

Faint footsteps moved away from the
door.

Then, bang!

The wood around the lock splintered.
The door swung so violently, it bounced
back, to meet the heavy hand of the figure
filling the doorway. Shaun.

"You are a lying little bitch, I know you're here, I saw you jumping into that car that's sat outside." He hit the light switch, illuminating the two, staggering to their feet. Anna in front, protecting Claire.

"Look, calm down. I don't know what your problem is. You lent me the money! I gave it to Archie, like we said."

"Don't you give me any of that. I'm not one of your daft wee druggie pals. They might fall for your nonsense, but not me. Hand it over..."

Claire picked up piles of cash and held them towards him. Stray notes fluttered to the ground like Autumn leaves signalling the end of the fruitful season and the start of the barren winter.

"Fucking take it, and get out of my house."

Anna's legs shook as her last hope was handed over and stuffed into Shaun's coat pockets. He snarled at Anna.

"You didn't think to mention the fact that you've got a boyfriend? That you're moving abroad?"

"Well, I didn't, I didn't really..." Anna stammered.

"Thought you could take me for a mug,

did you?" He lunged forward, wrapping both hands around her throat.

"I didn't mean, I just, it... Ah..." Her face was reddening, swelling as she struggled for breath. Both of her hands pulled at him forearms.

"You are a twisted wee cock tease. I thought we had something." He squeezed harder, his fingers whitening, her eyes streaming. She swung her feet, attempting to kick him.

"I thought you had potential, but you're just another little skank."

She couldn't find his shin with her kick; then she remembered his feet, the obvious pain they caused him. White fuzzy dots of light swarmed before her eyes. Her tongue filled her mouth, lips tingling, almost bursting. With her last spark, she stamped towards where his feet should have been. But his body was far from hers; he predicted her every move, she was slow and confused.

"Settle down, sweetheart, or I will break your jaw."

She swung and stamped, useless. Until one connected. Only a tap, but his face reacted as if his toes had been smashed with a mallet. He leaned back with pure rage on his face, and he swung his right arm back to attack with his fist, her captive head his target.

But he stopped, his face became blank. The rage subsided as his grip loosened around her throat. He was becoming shorter, dropping down, his eyes unfocused. As he slumped toward the carpet, he revealed Claire. She stood behind him with her blood-smeared iron held in both hands.

Anna slid down the wall into a crumpled pile of snot and tears. Some clarity came as she swallowed down air and felt the blood drain from her ears. Her temples throbbed, and her throat rasped with each ragged breath, like something inside was broken. With her head on the carpet, and a metallic taste in her mouth, she lay making sense of the sideways scene before her.

This lump of anger, lay now, subdued like a tranquillized rhino. Claire crouched by his side. A liver coloured stain was growing around his head. She tentatively placed two fingers on his stubbly neck. No words came, they were not needed.

As his blood seeped into the carpet, the pair acted in silence, on shocked autopilot. Anna forced the door closed, and Claire turned off the lights. The purple of the early summer evening diffused through the blinds, giving them just enough light to see.

"Am I going to jail?" Claire broke the spell with her trembling voice. Anna didn't answer; she was holding her breath to hear a new sound outside. Someone else was there.

A gentle tap on the door.

Fuck.

"Anna, it's Bazz. Are ya in there?"

"I'll get rid of him. He's just drawing attention!" Claire whispered. Anna opened the door a couple of inches. It was difficult to move, the angle was wrong, and it dragged on the floor.

"Eyah, what's all this? I've been waiting for you at the bar for ages. The police came in. I didn't know if they got you."

"I was just coming, just had a lot on my plate tonight."

He ran his bony finger down the splintered door frame, his neck stretched from side to side, trying to see inside.

"Everyone's desperate down there. I've been looking all over, I couldn't run coz I'd sweat me stamp off me hand. But I guessed you two would be together somewhere."

"You'll need to wait. We have to sort…"

He wasn't waiting any longer; he put a foot over the threshold,

"I can't wait, I'm sick of waiting!" He levered himself to see over Anna's head and into the room.

"You can't come in, get out," Claire shouted. He pushed a few more inches and surveyed the whole scene. He gasped.

"Just get in and shut the door," Anna snapped. With the door closed as firmly as possible, all three of them circled the giant corpse.

"What happened? Did you's kill him?" Bazz looked in awe at them in turn. Neither answered. Clarie's eyes were streaming. Tears rolled, into her open mouth, down her neck, soaking her top. Anna reached out and squeezed her shoulder.

"It was an accident, well, self-defense."

Clarie's body shook as she sobbed, "I'm going to jail. My life is over. What have I done?"

Bazz looked deep into Anna's eyes, straightened his back, pulled down his hem, and expanded his chest and said,

"That's not going to happen. It was me. I killed this bastard."

"What the hell are you talking about?

Stop acting the fool this isn't funny. It's serious!" More tears streamed as Claire spoke.

"I am serious. I'll take it. I want it. What else have I got?"

"What do you mean? You can't take the blame. You'll go to jail!"

"I'm going to jail anyway. And, maybe it was self-defense? Look at the door, it's been kicked in, he forced his way in and attacked me."

"You can't do this," Anna replied.

"You's don't understand. My life is shit. But this? This would make me someone else. I'll have a pocket full of pills, and I've knocked off this old gangster. That's the best thing that could ever happen to me."

"But you're just young, and its nothing to do with you. It's my mess. I'll be taking the blame." Anna looked at Claire to see if her words were comforting her. More tears streamed, and her face twisted with anguish.

"Girls. Ladies, I've never been so serious about anything. I'll go to jail. I'll be out by the time I'm thirty. Three meals a day, I'll get into the gym, no one will fuck with me. Please?"

"Bazz, Barry, you can't. It wouldn't be

fair. I'm going to sort it out, neither of you is getting punished for this." Anna rubbed Clarie's shoulder as she spoke.

"Listen," Bazz continued, "what's not fair is this bastard here turned me auntie against us. He made her chuck me out. She was the only person I had back then, and now she hates me, because of him."

"You know him?" Anna asked, shocked.

"Of course I do. He moved up here and started going with me auntie Kay. He ruined my life. Remember when I did that thing at the bridge? Well, it was his fault. This could not have happened to a better person. I hate this bastard."

Anna smiled and nodded, then reached out to Claire,

"Come with me?" One hand gently squeezes her shoulder.

"You're nuts, I'm not going to Ibiza," she sobbed, Anna laughed and held both her shoulders,

"Neither am I! I haven't been for a long time."

"Why did you get yourself in all this debt? Why didn't you tell me? I would never have stolen the rest of the money to try and stop you!"

"That's when I decided, on Sunday. I'm leaving here, this place, this life, but not to make one with Davie bloody King. He doesn't mean anything to me now. I don't think he ever did."

"It's my fault, all of it. I took the money, now I've done this. I've ruined all our lives." Claire lowered her head and sobbed.

"Eyah, not mine, you haven't." Bazz said, "Wait till that Wendy hears about this! She will be well impressed!"

"Or mine." Anna added, "Look, you mean more to me than Davie ever did." She shook Claire's shoulders gently, coaxing her to look up. "Come on, how many times have I tried to get you to leave this place with me? This is it; we can do it now."

"But I can't, my work, my house, everything I've saved for, I couldn't just leave it all."

"You can, and you can have it all again somewhere new."

"But the police! This is my house, it's a murder scene!"

"You weren't here," Anna replied, "you were away, Bazz was looking after your house. Bazz?"

"Aye, I was looking after Clarie's house

because she was away somewhere. Got it."
He gave a thumbs up.

"But, what about the rest? The pikeys?
Archie? They will want their money, we can
just give it back, and you can stay here with
me, and..."

"You owe money to the pikeys?" Bazz
interrupted, "From the camp down by the
river?"

"Ronin gave me three grand, I owe him
a lot of drugs, but I don't have them."

"I do you mean." Bazz's long dimples
appeared. "I've got his money, and I've got
his pills. I'll be in a cell before that hillbilly
bastard can catch up with me. And, I
fooking hate pikeys." His face was glowing
with something Anna had never seen in her
hopeless friend before. He'd struck gold.
Revenge on his two worst enemies, and a
new reputation for violence, and drugs.
He'd hit the big time. He lit a cigarette and
reclined on the armchair, using the width of
Shaun's shoulders as a footstool.

Anna handed him the iron,
"You hit him with this, on the back of the
head. He came at you first, but you
managed to get away and protect yourself,
he was going to kill you. OK? You ran here

because you were looking after Claire's house, and you thought it would be safe."

"Got it." Bazz beamed. "Ere, maybe I'll get a new name! Like... The Iron Man."

Anna wiped Clarie's tears away with her sleeve,

"Come on, pack a bag, and bring all that extra money you've got hidden." Anna laughed, "And get your passport. Let's drive far away from here. We can leave your aunties car at a train station where she can get it later. With all the money we've got, we can start a new life, a proper one, somewhere nice."

Claire's eyes were still flowing, but there was a subtle nod, Anna continued,

"You'll easily get a job, and I'll do something. A job, maybe college. Whatever, I'll pull my weight." Another nod, a little more convinced. "We can eat nice food, wear nice clothes, go to coffee shops, walk around art galleries." Claire smiled a little and began to dry her own face between sobs. "We can get a flat and decorate it with nice stuff, buy recipe books, and fancy pans. We'll get a proper set of plates instead of mismatched hand-me-downs. But we need to move now. Come on."

Soon Claire was at her side with two holdalls weighing down her small shoulders. She stuffed bundles of twenty-pound notes into her big black handbag. Anna handed Bazz all the pills she had, and a few notes.

"Thank you. You're a real hero." She hugged him.

"A hero AND a gangster," he announced as Claire buried her face in his t-shirt, her body still trembling. He patted her back as she dry sobbed and whispered into the top of her head, "Get going you, and don't worry, I've got it all under control."

Once they were in the car, Claire was about to turn the key, but she reached for the door handle instead,

"I need to get a couple of things."

"We can buy more things, let's just go. We've caused enough noise in the street. We can't afford for any curtain twitchers to see us."

"I know, it's just stuff, but it's easy for you, you haven't got anything." Claire hesitated, then let go.

"I've got clean knickers, loads of cash, and I've got you. That's all I need." Anna took Clarie's hand from the gear stick and squeezed it,

"Please, let's leave now." she pleaded.

They drove to the graveyard, Anna picked up her bag from behind the big white angel, then made the phone call from the red glazed box.

"Police, please. I just saw Shaun McAllister assaulting Barry Smith. He chased him into 14 Spey Court ... Yes... Shaun said he was going to kill him." She hung up before she was asked for any other details.

"What about Scott? Are you going to tell him you're leaving?" Anna asked as they drove.

"Scott? He's history. He said he thought you were trouble, and that I shouldn't spend so much time with you."

Anna put a hand on her chest. "Me? Trouble?"

"As if eh?" Claire laughed, "My mum always warned me about that kind of thing. If a guy tries to change you, leave before you get in too deep."

Keeping to the speed limit felt like crawling, like running in a nightmare, the car wheels stuck in treacle.

As they got closer to the edge of town, the orange petrol light flashed on.

"Shit, we won't get far on that. Goddammit." Claire hit the steering wheel. "There's only one garage open at this time of night."

"Just turn round, it will be fine."

After u-turning, Claire was visibly more anxious heading back towards the scene. Anna spoke to take her mind off it.

"Remember back in high school? When we used to make up plans and talk about all the amazing things we wanted to do when we grew up?"

"Of course I do, I never forgot."

"We wanted to get away from where we came, to be more than we were supposed to be."

"No one had any hope for us, you know." Claire's eyes move quickly between the road and mirrors.

"Crap jobs, bad men, bad choices, and drowning our sorrows in horrible pubs, I reckon that's what most folk would have predicted for us." Anna laughed, watching Claire tapping the wheel and sucking her bottom lip. "I know this isn't the ideal scenario, but we aren't exactly the ideal people, but we can make the most of this."

Claire nodded, concentrating on the road, Anna continued,

"You want to hear something funny? Every single one of them, you know what they said? All of them said the same thing, Archie, Shaun and Ronin, they all called me a silly wee girl."

Claire shook her head and laughed, "Well, they seriously underestimated you, didn't they?"

"Every time I heard it, it made me hate them, it made me want to take their money." After a pause, "When did you decide to take my money?"

Claire tensed, as if she'd almost forgotten the confession.

"This entire mess is my fault, isn't it?"

Her eyes filled and reflected the streetlights, as she blinked a fat tear made a path towards her chin.

"Mess? Come on, don't start crying again. Somehow this has turned into the best thing you could have done. Look at us now, like Thelma and Louise."

"I am sorry though. I just didn't want to lose you. I grabbed the chance that you would have to stay, and everything would go back to how it was before Davie came along."

"David King. You know I don't miss him? Not a bit. There was nothing to miss."

"I thought you were upset he'd gone. I thought you'd be devastated." The car slowed as they reached the bright forecourt of the petrol station.

"Na, I'm not sad now. He's just another one that underestimated me. But he'll figure out he made a big mistake soon enough."

"Sit back, try and stay in the shadow, I'll be as quick as I can," Claire said as they stopped.

Sitting in the motionless car, alone and waiting, Anna felt vulnerable. She pulled her top up over her chin and crossed her arms tight over her chest. She watched as Claire wrestled with the nozzle, and willed the petrol counter to move faster.

She watched her browse the snacks inside, guessing she was trying to act normal and not raise concerns. Anna's concerns however, were very high indeed. Headlights from behind caught her eye in the side mirror. She shrunk down between her shoulders, trying to become as small as she could. The lights were bright, higher than a car, she couldn't tell the colour, but it wasn't white. She was confident it wasn't the police. She shook away the feeling, remembering that the world was still going on around her, and people still needed petrol. Normal people, doing normal things, oblivious to the drama unfolding for the occupants of this little car.

Now Claire was looking her way; Anna could see her face and the expression change. She froze, unable to turn and look, she eyed each side mirror without moving a muscle. The cashier was making her way to the counter; Claire threw the notes towards her. Anna heard a heavy metal door slam. Claire was running through the shop now.

Slow, heavy steps approached from behind. She couldn't move. She could only see trousers, and a big hand reaching for the handle right next to her. The lock! She pressed it down, just as he pulled the handle.

"Well, well. Exactly who I've been looking for." Ronin crouched and pressed his square forehead against the glass. His breath steamed up the window as he rattled the handle again.

Claire jumped in her side and pressed down her lock. She couldn't get the key in the ignition, she peered into the darkness below the steering wheel, juggling with the keys. Ronin stood in front of the car, and he slammed both hands on the bonnet.

"You silly wee girls are going nowhere. Do you think you can take me for a mug? Open the fucking doors right now, and give me my money." His fists were balled, and his teeth bared. He was like an animal, a tiger that had been poked with a stick.

"Shit. Shit. Shit. Come on!" Clarie's terror was numbing her fingers to the simple job of getting the keys in the barrel. He stalked around the car, and he picked up a fire extinguisher. The key was in; she turned them - nothing.

"Shit, come on, come on!" She turned them harder; the engine started. Anna wrung her hands together and bit her lip. Claire tried to move, but the car stalled. He raised the red metal above his head. The engine spluttered back into action again. As he aimed at the windscreen, the car hopped forward, hitting his shins. It stalled once more. He recoiled, letting out a painful roar, he staggered towards the passenger door. He hit the window, and it shattered, Claire screamed, a million sharp cubes of glass showered Anna. He reached in and grabbed her hair, his other hand grabbed her glass-covered top. He jerked her head out of the window. Scarlet blood streaked his arms. She dug her nails into his wrists, trying to rip herself free. The car jerked forward, and he lost his footing. Still holding her hair, his hand grabbed the frame to steady himself. Claire swung the steering wheel to the right and accelerated. Anna screamed. He lost his grip on her hair, and he rolled to the ground. They wheel spun onto the road, leaving him on his knees, clutching an arm dripping with blood. They heard his roar fade away as they gained some distance.

Anna looked at her blood-covered hands and clothes. Her hair was full of glass, and her scalp ached. Her hands grew sticky as the blood dried. In the sun-visor mirror, she inspected her face, scared to find out how much of the blood was hers.

"Just keep driving, we can sort out this mess when we get out of this hell hole."

CHAPTER FIFTEEN
Saturday

Archie

He couldn't bear the smell in his house. He unlocked the back door and sat on the step, looking over his Mum's garden. It was out of control. The stinging nettles that would never have been allowed had taken over the borders. The only colour was the yellow heads of unruly dandelions. Once proud roses hung in sodden brown clumps.

He picked a dandelion clock from a crack in the concrete by his foot. 'Wishes' his Mum had called them. Twirling it between thumb and forefinger, he studied the soft downy ends on their thin stalks. So fragile, ready to be displaced by a breath.

What was left for him to wish for?

As the first rays of orange broke over the rooftops, he blew every seed off and watched them float away as he gasped to get his breath back. He zipped his jacket against the chill and put his hands in his pockets. He felt something new, cold, and unfamiliar. Something he hadn't put in there. He pulled out that glossy sunset on a folded postcard. He turned it over and smiled.

Davie's address. The same Davie King that started all this. The friend he'd trusted. The one who'd left him dealing with Anna, and the very person who had his money.

He looked up to see the last dandelion seed caught on a draft, rising up, floating over the fence and out of sight.

The strange way Anna had tried to dance with him before running off. Now it made sense.

He took a deep breath, put his sleeve over his nose and mouth, and returned inside to his room. He pulled a fake leather suitcase from under the bed and tipped the old football strips out. He threw in polo-shirts, y-fronts, the two pairs of shorts he bought to go to France for the world cup, and a short-sleeved beige shirt that he'd worn once to a wedding. He didn't have time to find out if they'd still fit, but he could pick up something later. Hair gel, deodorant, soap, and his toothbrush were placed on-top. He folded the postcard inside his almost expired passport and zipped them both in the front pocket.

He had nearly two hundred pounds, including his carer's allowance, a decent haul of coins from the kitchen drawer, and the forgotten tenner from his old jacket. But it wasn't enough. He didn't want to disturb his Dad, but he knew the Christmas club money was on the top shelf of the airing cupboard.

The door handle squeaked as he turned it, but no sound came from inside. His mouth watered at the smell. He slipped in, eyes to the wall, and retrieved the sixty pounds. He spoke into the cupboard,

"I'll be back soon, Dad. I'll sort everything out, don't you worry."

Nothing stirred as he closed the door behind him.

Christine

She hadn't hung around to see Anna, or the repercussions of her disappearance last night. The rising tempers of men had been her queue to leave.

As she made her bed, there was a knock on the front door. Her first guess was Anna; hungry, and in need of sympathy or money. Between the carefully tilted blinds, she could see a blue transit van parked at her gate. Her second guess was someone looking for Anna, angry, and in need of revenge or money.

She got halfway down the stairs before the second louder knock. She opened the door on the chain, to see a few inches blood-soaked pikey on her doorstep.

"Your young pall in there?" The chain pulled tight as he slammed the door with his palm.

"Anna? No, sorry, bud. Can't help you." Christine moved her head back from the gap.

"Don't you give me that. I see you with the wee reprobate all the time. She's got three grand of mine, and I'm taking it back. Today." He bounced on the step, still pressing his hand on the door.

"Wait, you gave Anna McVay a big wad

of cash, and you seriously expect something in return?" Christine let out a chuckle then balled a first over her mouth to stifle the rest. Her cheeks tingled as her face heated up.

"We shook on it. She owes me."

"Good luck with that, bud."

"What the fuck are you laughing at?" He slammed his bandaged hand against the door, hard enough to dig the chain into the wood.

"I'm just saying, you should know better. Like I always say, trust no cunt." A little more chuckle escapes from her rosy face.

"But she's your fucking sidekick, what are you playing at?" His lips curl back over his teeth in rage.

"You've been had, pal." She let out the last of her amusement in a hearty laugh as the pikey slams her gate and gets into his van. She watches him skid out of her street and adds his name to the list of bad guys now after her young friend. She closed the door and bit her lip, she laughed again, shaking her head.

Just like her Dad, she thought.

After checking all the locks three times, and then three more, she brewed a cup of

tea and turned on the TV. Sitting on the arm
of the chair, she watched DI Jackson
announce her success during the night. Her
tea goes cold as she listens out for footsteps
approaching. She stares at the muted TV,
waiting for the next news broadcast, trying
to piece together the fractured snippets.

Ronin

He drove to the west end of town, up the
wide green street, towards Hillary's place.
He couldn't bring himself to go to her, or
tell her his plan had failed, that his dreams
were broken and he'd let her down. He
parked a few drives down, where he could
see the curve of privet that led to her house.

He'd waited at the table for hours. Every
minute getting angrier, but refusing to leave
his position. He hadn't left the table to get a
drink or even to use the toilet; he was not
going to miss her. He could have made the
money, Tina and Maria had put the word
out. He'd spent the night turning people
away as he had nothing to sell.

There had been a few commotions, folk
getting rowdy, the police showing up,
nothing he'd got involved in. He'd

eventually given up, and started driving the streets searching instead. Slowing down for groups of people on their way to parties, waiting at crossroads, letting drunks stagger across, desperately looking for the girl with his future in her hands. He'd stopped for petrol, and who did he find? Just sitting there, quite the thing, as if she hadn't told him to wait at that table hours before. He gritted his teeth, embarrassed of being left on his knees on the forecourt as she disappeared with his money.

He turned the radio on low and reclined his seat; makeshift bloody bandages wrapped his shredded arm, which rested on his chest. Closing his eyes to the anger and frustration, he struggled to think of how to explain it to Hillary. He'd find Anna and get the money back... somehow. He drifted off just before the news coverage of last night's drug seizure and murder.

He awoke a couple of hours later to the clatter of a horse-box bumping onto the road. He wiped the dried saliva from the corners of his mouth and sat up. The horse was gone, and with it, his chance to save Hillary and himself.

But he'd get the money back. He could still save the day. He walked up the drive like he was battling against the wind, he found her still in her riding gear, sobbing.

"He's gone, it's too late."

He crouched down beside her, put a hand on her blotchy wet face.

"The bank is coming for the house keys on Monday. It's all over." Her face twisted with sorrow and pain, tears rolled down. He supported her weight and pulled her floppy body to her feet.

"Come with me. I will look after you."

Gemma

She dusted the upside-down bottles in the optics, getting ready for the Sunday session. All the beer mats were replaced, and the drip cloths freshly laundered. She sprayed some polish on her yellow duster and began buffing her way along the wooden bar. She polished the charity box, the long glass 'yard of ale' ornament, and then the phone. The little red light of the answering machine flashed; she pressed play.

"Can someone please pass on this

message to Anna, the apartment is ready, it's even got a balcony, I started the bar job, and there's a waitressing one for you. I sent you the address, and I've left a message every day with the bar phone number, please write or call…"

Beep.

Gemma pressed delete and dusted the receiver.

Anna & Claire

By late afternoon Anna and Claire sipped coffee on a leather sofa in an Edinburgh hotel lounge. They'd cleaned up on the train and got a couple of hours sleep. Now their bags were stowed safely between their legs as they waited to be shown to their double room.

Anna split the newspaper between them, she circled the flats to rent, while Claire smiled at the long list of office job vacancies.

Up on the wall, a large TV plays the Scottish news. Claire's puffy eyes look in horror at her own front door; police tape zigzagged across the garden fence.

"Won't they be looking for me?" her voice sounds like it could break into a scream.

"Shh, that's why I booked us in here as the Thompson sisters. Bazz knows what to say, and we just need to stay away. The police will be happy to have a confession. They won't be looking for us. Look!" Anna pointed to the TV. On the screen stood a woman, looking like she had exited the womb in police uniform. A banner of text scrolled below her.

Operation Brown Owl hailed a success after disrupting the flow of illegal drugs to the area.

Large cameras and long fluffy microphones jostled for position as DI Jackson began her statement.

"Our enquiries are ongoing, but I am pleased to announce that our operation has disrupted the supply of dangerous drugs to the North East of Scotland. We have a key suspect in custody in connection with a major organised crime ring, now also being questioned in connection with a murder."

The camera angle changes to focus on the car behind her, they see his familiar face pressed up to the window, a gummy smile beaming at the gathered press's flashing cameras.

Bazz

Inside the back of the police car, Bazz admires the weight of the handcuffs around his skinny wrists. The officer in the front seat lowers the windows a few inches to let out the heat from Bazz's over-excited body. He looks out at each camera in turn. Over the crowd and snapping cameras, he heard Jackson's statement. His cheeks dimple with delight. That is really him they are talking about.

Truth

The sequel to Trust, coming soon.

Six months into their new city life, Anna and Claire are thriving. They drink cocktails in nice dresses and eat interesting food from recipe books.

Then one phone call changes everything Anna thought she knew.

When they're forced to revisit the past, more is waiting for them than they could ever have imagined.

Visit www.aphrawilson.com and sign up for the release date.